A private yacht,
a crew of hot guys—
a shipwreck—
what more could
a girl ask for?

D1418447

Winnie clung to the wheel in terror.

Liza, Courtney, and Mookie emerged behind Patrick, screaming at the tops of their lungs and diving for the life jackets under the cockpit seats. But another jerk of the boat sent them sprawling to the wooden grate on the floor.

"There's water in the cabin!" Courtney yelled. "Oh, my God!"

"Jack!" Winnie shouted, watching Patrick tumble back belowdeck. *"We've got to radio for help!"*

Letting go of the wheel, she crawled toward the hatch cover, yanked it open, then stumbled inside and desperately groped for the radio's coiled wire hanging from the wall. Quickly she grabbed it and clicked the receiver.

"HELLO? HELLO?" Winnie shouted. Then her photographic memory clicked in. Girl Scouts. Seven years ago. Seamanship badge. There was something about sending distress signals at sea. *"Mayday. Mayday. Mayday. This is the* Bluebeard. *This is the* Bluebeard. *We have struck a reef about thirty miles southeast of Sucia Island. We're going down. Please—send—HELP."*

Don't miss these books
in the exciting FRESHMAN DORM series

FRESHMAN FREEDOM

LINDA A. COONEY

HarperPaperbacks
A Division of HarperCollins*Publishers*

This is a work of fiction. The characters, incidents, and dialogues are products of the author's imagination and are not to be construed as real. Any resemblance to actual events or persons, living or dead, is entirely coincidental.

HarperPaperbacks *A Division of* HarperCollins*Publishers*
10 East 53rd Street, New York, N.Y. 10022

Copyright © 1993 by Linda Alper and Kevin Cooney
Cover art copyright © 1993 Daniel Weiss Associates, Inc.

All rights reserved. No part of this book may be used or reproduced in any manner whatsoever without written permission of the publisher, except in the case of brief quotations embodied in critical articles and reviews. For information address HarperCollins*Publishers*,
10 East 53rd Street, New York, New York 10011.

Produced by Daniel Weiss Associates, Inc.,
33 West 17th Street, New York, New York 10011.

Cover illustration by Tony Greco

First printing: August, 1993

Printed in the United States of America

HarperPaperbacks and colophon are trademarks of
HarperCollins*Publishers*

❖ 10 9 8 7 6 5 4 3 2 1

One

Courtney Conner bit her bottom lip and stared out the tiny hydroplane's window to the turquoise water below. The left wing dipped, sending the craft swooping down past a chain of bushy green islands, ringed by white beaches and swaying palm trees.

"The Caribbean," her good friend, KC Angeletti, shouted over the roar of the plane's engines. She leaned over Courtney's lap to get a better view, her stray dark curls tumbling over her cheek. "I'm going to pinch myself. I can't believe this is really happening."

"Believe it," Courtney shouted back. Though the passengers were crammed shoulder to shoulder in the ancient ten-seater island-hopper, it was still practically impossible to hear over the engines. "And don't fool yourself, KC. You deserve it."

KC rolled her eyes and grinned.

Courtney gave KC a serene look, then glanced across the tiny aisle to their other friends from the University of Springfield, Winnie Gottlieb and Liza Ruff. Winnie was slumped in the aisle seat, snapping a large wad of lime-green gum and staring into space. Jammed next to her, Liza was smiling ecstatically while she bounced in her seat and drummed the overhead storage shelf with her blood-red nails. Up ahead, two honeymooners kissed in their seats. A bunch of tanned guys who'd lugged diving equipment on board were staring at KC's long legs, which were sprawled in the aisle.

Courtney fell against the rubbery seat back and smoothed the loose hairs from her tight French braid. It seemed impossible that yesterday they had been packing their bags back at the University of Springfield, bleary-eyed from a week's worth of exams. Now they were on break, and Courtney was treating three of her friends to a fantasy vacation.

Two weeks ago, Courtney's parents had sold their fifty-foot luxury yacht, the *Bluebeard*, moored on the small American island of St. Ramos. The sales contract called for the yacht to be delivered by its captain and two-man crew to its new owners on the larger British island of Gregory Cays. Knowing that Courtney would be free on break, her parents had wanted her and a few chosen friends to enjoy the idyllic journey.

"Look at that, Courtney," KC yelled, her eager smile still floating over the view. "Look at that huge yacht moored off that empty beach. It looks like it's stuck on a reef!"

Courtney cupped her hands over her mouth and shouted back. "That's just the clear water. The reef is actually way below the surface."

KC flopped back into her seat and stuffed her hands into the pockets of her crisp khaki shorts. She grinned and turned to shout into Courtney's ear again. "It's almost like a movie set or a touched-up photo. I bet this is the kind of place where nothing's what it seems. It's all just a wonderful dream." The hydroplane dipped down through a low cloud, sending a violent shudder through the passenger area. Courtney's stomach lurched, and she braced her sneakers against the steel supports under the seat in front of her. The cobalt water seemed to be only a few feet under the pontoons now. Looking over, she could see that KC, Winnie, and Liza had stiffened their backs against their seats, wide-eyed.

It's okay, it's okay, Courtney wanted to shout over the deafening noise. She had a sudden urge to wrap her arms around everyone and tell them their troubles would soon be over. In a few minutes, they'd feel the sun, they'd see the water, they'd smell the wild hibiscus and taste the mangoes. They didn't know it yet, but their week in the Caribbean was going to be the best seven days of their lives. And nothing would be the same afterward.

Courtney gave herself a secret smile. After all, she knew. She'd spent the happiest days of her life sailing in the Caribbean with her parents. And now her friends were going to have the same memories. It was almost too good to be true.

"I don't know how I'm ever going to thank you, Courtney," KC shouted, shaking her head in disbelief at the jewellike islands rushing by below.

"Thank my mom and dad," Courtney yelled back, giving KC a quick, one-armed hug. "My parents gave us the perfect opportunity to escape our lives as ambitious study grinds."

KC's eyes sparkled.

Courtney grinned back. Of all her friends, she knew KC was the one who would have the most fun. KC always loved the good things in life, but could never afford them. She had to scrape by just to pay her tuition bills. Not to mention her membership dues in the prestigious Tri Beta sorority, where Courtney was president. At least for this week, Courtney thought, smiling, KC wouldn't have to worry about money.

EERRRAAAWWW, the hydroplane screamed, taking a sharp turn to the left. Another round of vibrations shuddered through its rickety metal frame. Courtney tried to open the porthole window to let some of the stuffy air out, but it was stuck.

"I can still see my Intro to Business study notes when I sleep," KC shouted in her ear, apparently getting used to the motion and nerve-racking roars. "Do you think I'll still want to be the CEO of a giant corporation after experiencing paradise?"

"Yoo-hoo!" Liza Ruff cupped her hands around her mouth, pretending to yell something down at a sailing yacht through her window on the other side of the aisle. Her flame-red hair flounced. Her flamboyant pineapple-print halter dress blazed. Next to Liza, Winnie was staring dully at the plane's water-stained ceiling. A huge green bubble rose from her mouth. She blew it out, held it for a moment, then sucked it in and snapped it. Then she frowned and slumped farther down in her seat.

Courtney gave Winnie a sympathetic look. Winnie was a high-school buddy of KC's, and Courtney had heard all about Winnie's miscarriage several weeks before. Shortly after that, Winnie had broken off her marriage to computer whiz Josh Gaffey. Things had been rough for her, but Courtney knew a trip to the Caribbean was exactly what she needed. She looked affectionately at Winnie's small, muscular body and her brown hair that grew in funky spikes all over her head. As usual, Winnie was wearing a stack of jangly bracelets and a barely-there tank top. Winnie needed time, Courtney thought. But Winnie would be okay. There wasn't any problem these islands couldn't cure.

Suddenly Courtney felt her heart pounding in her chest. All she wanted was for the plane to land and the adventure to begin. She hadn't been to the islands in more than ten years, but her happy childhood memories were now all coming back in a rush. Snorkeling through pink reefs and letting the striped angelfish flutter against her bare skin. Taking the helm of the *Bluebeard* while her father untangled the sheets. Watching her mother scuba dive for exotic sea treasures. Eating fresh coconut, papayas, and sweet potatoes. Back then, she hadn't had a care in the world.

Courtney blinked back a tear and felt the plane beginning to descend sharply. The wind whistled outside her window. Now she was twenty years old. She was the president of a large university sorority. She was a straight-A student studying international politics.

Would her life ever be as simple and carefree again?

Courtney's thoughts were broken by a familiar shriek. Liza was bouncing up and down again at the window and waving. Winnie was leaning over the aisle, saying something to KC.

"She's waving at a bunch of guys crewing a sailboat," KC turned to drawl into Courtney's ear. "Can you believe how tacky she can be?"

"Whoo! Yahoo!" The tanned divers sitting in front of Liza joined in. They got up onto their knees and stared over the tops of their seats at the four friends.

"Hi, honey," Liza yelled over the engine, lowering her rhinestone-studded sunglasses and giving one of the guys a wink. "Are you ready to *par*-ty in paradise?"

Courtney watched in amazement as Liza raised her snow-white arms over her head and began making cha-cha movements with her shoulders.

Winnie was covering her face with her hands while the guys began laughing and cha-cha-ing with Liza.

Courtney and KC looked at each other and began giggling. The plane bumped through another low cloud, sending the guys crashing back in their seats.

"AAAHHHH!" Liza screamed, then unbuckled her seat belt and lunged over the top of the guys' seats to see if they were okay. "Hey," she shouted at them. "I'm ready for one of those big, fruity drinks with the umbrellas in them. Aren't you? Let's all get together when we land in St. Ramos. A round of umbrella drinks on me."

KC leaned over to Courtney. "What's the deal with Liza?" she shouted into her ear. Liza had dropped back down into her seat and had pulled out a large cosmetic bag. She zipped it open and began rummaging through it, trying on various shades of lipstick and vigorously powdering her nose. "Why did you invite her? What could you possibly have in common with Liza Ruff?"

"She asked me," Courtney shouted back. "I didn't have the heart to turn her down."

KC gasped. "Liza actually invited herself?" she cried, her eyebrows arched in amazement.

"She wanted to help cheer up Winnie," Courtney shouted.

KC rolled her eyes and collapsed back in her seat, shaking her head.

Courtney knew KC thought she had been nuts to invite Liza. An entire week with someone who had a boy-crazy Brooklyn joke for every hour of the day? Maybe she *was* nuts. But she couldn't help admiring Liza's guts. Liza had what it took to make it in show business. And with her lush looks, offbeat singing style, and incredible sense for comedy, she had the talent to back it up.

Courtney lifted her chin defiantly. So what if Liza was different? She had a responsibility to expose herself to people outside her social circle. Whether it was Liza, or the people down at Springfield's homeless shelter, or the patients at the AIDS Hospice, Courtney was determined not to live her life surrounded only by the wealthy, privileged, Tri Beta sorority types. Her life was going to be richer and better than that.

Plus, Courtney thought, Liza had a heart of gold beneath her brassy exterior. All she needed was a little refining. Just enough so that she didn't completely blow it when she had to start dealing with agents and producers.

KC punched Courtney's arm. "You have your work cut out for you, Courtney."

The plane suddenly took a sickening dive. Courtney's heart stopped. She reached over and tried again to yank open the window. She was desperate for air. There seemed to be something wrong with the plane. Landings weren't supposed to be this way. They always kept them smooth for tourists. Didn't they?

The wing below Courtney and KC's window dipped sharply. The aircraft banked to the left through a pure-white cloud. Everyone felt a sudden stomach-pulling drop.

Courtney and KC gripped their armrests.

"Is it always like this?" KC shouted at her, her face contorted in horror. The plane was tilted down at a crazy angle, and the wing tips were swaying up and down as if something had sent them spinning out of control.

Courtney was shaking her head back and forth, but her eyes were squeezed shut. Sweat broke out all over her body. Something was wrong. Something was definitely wrong with the plane. There was no way a pilot would subject paying passengers to this kind of death-defying travel.

KC's face was white. "What? Wha . . ."

The plane began nodding even more sharply to the right. All the baggage stowed above their seats began sliding, and Liza's cosmetic bag fell to the ground, sending lipstick tubes and mascara wands tumbling toward the cockpit. Courtney had a sudden terrifying image of Liza's lipstick getting caught in the pilot's controls.

KC leaned over, listening to one of the guys in front of them. Then she shouted into Courtney's ear. "Some kind of ongoing problem with northerly winds."

Courtney nodded, but an abrupt, midair roller-coaster dip sent her tray table slamming down into her lap.

Winnie was covering her deathly-gray face with her hands.

Liza was silent for the first time in twelve hours.

Oh please, God. Don't let us crash. Liza, Winnie, and KC are my responsibility. Courtney murmured a silent prayer into her balled-up fists. *Please let everything be okay. I'll make sure they have a wonderful time. I'll take care of it. Really, I will.*

Courtney peered out the window. Her eyes widened as a peninsula of bushy green land swept up underneath the plane. There was the sound of whistling wind, and as the plane dipped back and forth, the view from the window switched crazily between blue sky and green land.

"Oh, my . . ." KC yelled, digging her nails into Courtney's arm.

"The pilots have been through this hundreds of times," Courtney yelled back, desperately trying to calm KC.

There was a sudden drop in the engine noise, then a hard jerk as the plane's pontoons finally hit the blue water. Courtney felt her heart start up again. Tears of relief sprang into her eyes. She could feel the blood flowing back into her head and her toes and fingers. They were going to be okay.

"We've landed," KC yelled joyfully as the engines began to scream through the high-speed water-ski landing.

Courtney let out a spontaneous whoop. Every nerve end in her body was tingling. She thought of the sand, the water, the wind in the sails. She wanted to leap out of the plane that second and see it all.

"Yahoo!" Liza screamed, followed by whistles and whoops in the front. Applause broke out, and Courtney relaxed against her seat back. Through the window, she caught her first glimpse of St. Ramos, a quaint port tucked inside two green arms of land that formed a U-shaped harbor. Crystal-clear blue water lapped up against the harbor's sugar-white beaches. Palm trees waved gently on the hilltops.

"Look at all those fantastic YACHTS!" Liza screamed above the roar of the taxiing plane. "I bet they're filled with high-rolling TV producers."

Courtney's heart was pounding. She stared at the clusters of white sailboats moored in the St. Ramos Harbor, their matching sky-blue sail bags rocking in a gentle wake. The water was so clear, they seemed to be floating on air. As the hydroplane puttered toward the dock, they could see the small town itself, a group of pink, turquoise, and white stucco buildings gathered at the waterfront, then climbing the gentle hills and perching there like tropical birds overlooking the beautiful, azure sea.

"KC, look out the window," Courtney urged, flattening herself back. "Look at the water. Look at the beach. You're not going to believe how wonderful it is."

KC's eyes were gleaming. Across the aisle, Winnie was staring ahead quietly, her spiky bangs hanging over her brown eyes. Liza was already slathering her bare arms with suntan lotion.

Finally the pilot shut off the engine. Courtney's ears were flooded with blissful silence. There was a comforting sensation of lapping water rocking beneath the pontoons. The pilot got up and shoved open the door, sending a wave of warm, sweet-smelling air into the plane. Courtney breathed it in as the pilot threw out a line to a guy waiting on the dock.

"Ooh," Liza squealed happily, rubbing her arms. *"You've got your suntan OIL,"* she sang. *"You've got your hunky GUYS. You've got your MILLIONAIRES. And you shake it all about. You do the hokey-pokey and you turn yourself ABOUT. THAT'S WHAT IT'S ALL A-BOUT!"*

"YEEAAAHHH," the guys in front yelled in approval.

Courtney laughed out loud. "I'm really excited now, KC," she burst out suddenly. "I can't wait. I just can't wait for it all to begin."

"Are we really here?" KC pinched herself on the arm.

Liza hooted.

Winnie stared.

"We're really here, KC," Courtney cried, clapping her hands together victoriously. "And everything is going to be perfect. Just the way it was for me."

Two

"I could learn to live here," KC murmured, stepping cautiously down into the gleaming, palm-studded lobby of the Windjammer Hotel.

"Of course you could, silly." Courtney nudged her playfully in the side, skipping ahead of her. She looked back over her shoulder and slipped her hands into the pockets of her white shorts. "*Especially* you."

KC smiled and felt her pulse rise. By the time they'd reached the hotel, eaten, and unpacked the night before, it had been too late to explore St. Ramos. This morning they'd all risen early and had just finished a light breakfast of soft-boiled eggs, muffins, and papaya in the hotel's dining room. At last it was time to head for the *Bluebeard*.

But KC couldn't help pausing at the edge of the red-carpeted steps leading from the restaurant. She drew in her breath and took in the elegant scene. Huge crystal chandeliers dangled from the wooden ceiling. The polished oak floors contrasted with the whitewashed, paneled walls. Large ceiling fans stirred the air. Charming wicker furniture was scattered about the lobby. Couples in polo shirts and windbreakers strolled through.

"Come on, KC!" Courtney was calling, waving to her. "We're supposed to meet the *Bluebeard*'s captain at nine A.M. sharp." In her shorts and striped polo shirt, she looked as if she were right at home.

KC grinned back, hoping she looked as if she belonged too. She hopped down the steps and strolled through the lobby. Then she pushed open the huge wood-and-glass front door that led onto the old hotel's enormous wraparound porch. Outside, pink and red bougainvillea blossoms climbed the porch columns, framing a spectacular view of the St. Ramos scene.

Her gaze roamed eagerly over the manicured lawns that led down from the hotel to a narrow street. A wide promenade ran along the town's seawall, and beyond it, a blazing-white beach met the lapping blue water of the harbor. KC breathed in the scent of flowers, salt air, and distant spices. Native St. Ramosans on bicycles passed by. Others sped by on motor scooters. In the distance, she could see the vast yacht harbor, packed with pristine racing sloops, vast wood-trimmed cruisers, and tall-masted luxury yachts.

KC raked her hair back with her fingers and let the

cool morning breeze fan her face. She wanted to take in every detail, but it was almost too much beauty to absorb at once. So much sky, so much water, so much sun, so much money. So much of everything. "Over here, KC," she heard Courtney call from beneath a wooden archway across the street from the hotel. St. Ramos Yacht Club. PRIVATE, the sign on the arch read.

KC headed eagerly down the wooden front steps of the Windjammer and looked both ways before scurrying across the busy street toward the seawall. She squinted and pulled her sunglasses out of her bag.

Up ahead, Liza was waving at her gaily. Her skintight leggings and floppy captain's hat were attracting the attention of several passersby. Next to her, Winnie stood quietly, teetering on a pair of skimpy high-heeled leather sandals, gazing through a pair of small binoculars. In her red leather miniskirt and purple tank top, she didn't exactly look prepared for sailing. But that was just Winnie, KC thought cheerfully.

"Courtney's just checking in with security," Liza said, drawing near. "And lookee what we have here," she added in a sultry voice as a tall, blond windsurfer strolled past her toward the docks. She lowered her rhinestone-studded glasses and checked him out. "My kind of place," she murmured. "Hi, sweetie!" she said loudly, wiggling her fingers in greeting as he turned around.

Courtney emerged from a small wooden office, cheerfully waving a key. "All set."

KC joined her. "What's the captain like?"

Courtney smiled. "I've never met him. But he's English. His name is Alistair Hark. My parents say he knows everything there is to know about sailing in these islands. They were really sorry they had to let him go when the boat was sold."

KC nodded and followed her three friends down an unsteady gangway to the dock. She clutched the railing excitedly and stared out across the pleasant tangle of masts and bobbing pleasure boats. There were sailboats and cruisers of all sizes, from tiny dinghies to sleek racing sloops, to ocean-liner-sized cruisers. T-shaped masts nudged each other in the blue sky, fluttering with tiny, triangular flags.

KC stepped down onto the floating dock and felt the movement of the water under her feet. Up ahead, Courtney was walking quickly, examining a few of the large cruisers and stopping to chat with a middle-aged couple moving a cooler down to a small sailboat. Each side of the dock seemed to be alive with activity. Shirtless guys with deep tans and dark sunglasses were checking sails and coiling lines. An older man on a shiny wooden cruiser was giving his boat's bow a coat of shellac. On a sturdy-looking white cruising vessel, a white-haired woman wearing a swimsuit was wringing out a rag into the water.

KC moved ahead, feeling more comfortable by the moment. It wasn't at all the way she thought the pampered rich spent their leisure time. She'd imagined diamond-studded matrons lolling on the decks. But the people down here seemed more like an off-beat collection of adventurers. There was laughter, shouting, the sound of cranking winches and buoy bells clanging lazily in the distance.

KC breathed in the smell of brine, paint, and cooking food as she strode farther down the dock, temporarily losing sight of the others. Up above, sea gulls hovered and screamed.

Squinting, KC headed down past a bank of hoses and outdoor showers. Then she saw that the dock branched off to the right, where the larger sailboats were moored.

KC blinked. At the end of the dock she could see Courtney, Liza, and Winnie climbing a ladder to the deck of a magnificent white yacht. Its huge aluminum masts soared against the blue sky, and it was rimmed all around with a shiny railing hung with tightly wound nylon lines. Sleek portholes circled the low-slung cabin. It was trimmed with a top railing of glossy wood.

"KC!" Liza waved at her over the railing. "Can you believe it? *Heaven, I'm in heaven*," she began singing, spreading her arms out.

KC clenched her fists together with excitement, then skipped ahead. When she reached *Bluebeard* she grabbed a rung of the aluminum ladder and climbed up the side of the gleaming white hull. At the top, she peeked over the railing and took a deep breath.

Her eyes widened as she took in the boat's deep, luxurious cockpit, rimmed with a U-shaped bench that was covered with blue cushions. Liza and Winnie were sitting in the cockpit, getting their balance, while Courtney was already heading up toward the bow. KC sucked in her breath. The boat gave off a fresh, clean smell. Everything looked expensive, shiny, and well-kept. Her eyes swept over to the right, toward the back of the boat.

The stern, she reminded herself, trying to remember her sailing facts from the book she'd checked out of the university library the week before.

The helm, she thought, grabbing on to the shiny railing and lifting her tennis shoe over onto the deck. Then she sat down with her legs dangling into the cockpit. The helm consisted of a huge, stainless-steel wheel positioned on a wooden stand, which also held a throttle and a few small gauges.

She looked over to the left, toward the bow. "The foredeck," KC whispered, checking out the front two-thirds of the boat, a snow-white expanse, dotted with several skylights and crowned with a magnificent mast. Along the boom, KC could see that the sails were neatly tucked away in yacht-club-blue canvas covers.

"How do you like it?" Courtney called from the shiny outcropping that hung in front of the bow. A stainless-steel railing ran around it.

KC stood and grabbed a long wire that ran down from the mast. *A shroud,* she thought. She grinned and looked at Courtney's perch. "The pulpit's bow. Right?" she shouted.

"Right!" Courtney shouted back. "You've been doing your homework."

"Cabin boy, oh, cabin boy." Liza plunged her head jokingly into the hatchway that led belowdeck into the cabin. KC looked down and watched Liza yank off her captain's hat, then fan her face in mock irritation. "Would someone *please* fetch my bags and get me something tall and cool to drink?"

"Dream on, Liza," Courtney called with a mischievous smile. She'd come back from the bow and was dropping down so she could lie on her stomach over the cabin's hatchway. "No one's going to wait on us hand and foot on this journey. In fact, the captain will probably make us help sail the boat."

"Really?" KC's eyes widened with excitement. "Well, where *is* the captain?"

Liza shook her pudgy finger and lounged back into a stack of pillows on the cockpit seat. "Naughty, naughty. Captain Hark's tardy on his first day of actual work."

Winnie looked nervous. Her single sailboat earring dangled against her cheek as the wake from a passing boat rocked them a little. "I don't know anything about sailing."

"But what a great way to learn, Win," KC said, sitting down on the deck and rubbing her hands together.

"It's okay." Courtney swung her legs around and slipped off the foredeck. Then she jumped expertly into the cockpit and began heading down the hatchway, followed by Winnie and Liza. "We'll just be the worker ants. Wait till you see our quarters."

KC watched Courtney with envy. Courtney was so nimble and confident on the boat. She seemed to know exactly what to do. KC slid awkwardly into the cockpit. She stared at the maze of lines, pulleys, winches, and knots covering the boat. They were starting to make her a little nervous. Would she ever know what they were all for?

Courtney stuck her head up the hatch and waved KC down. "You've *got* to see this, KC. Come on down."

"Okay." KC saluted, stepping down from the seat cushions to the cockpit's polished wood-grate floor. The boat rocked gently and she grabbed a cleat near the hatchway for balance. Then she put a cautious foot on the first rung of the steep ladder leading belowdeck.

"Careful," Courtney said. "Turn around and climb down backward. There are just five more steps. You'll get used to it."

KC squinted until her eyes adjusted to the inside light. She was looking ahead into an elegant, teak-paneled room that stretched about fifteen feet toward the bow from the bottom of the hatchway. Though it was cramped, she could see that pains had been taken to make use of every inch of space. At the opposite end of the room was a cabin door, which KC assumed led to sleeping quarters. Another, smaller door was tucked into the left end of the wall.

Left, port. Right, starboard, KC mentally recited. Winnie stood uncomfortably at the bottom of the hatchway, while Liza pranced about, flailing her hat and saluting Courtney.

"This is what we call the main cabin area, or the saloon," Courtney explained. She pointed toward a long, highly polished teak dining table flanking one side of the room. Banked up against it was a long upholstered bench tossed with linen pillows. On the opposite wall was a matching bench. Courtney flipped up a leaf in the table, which took up most of the floor space but created an eating area for at least eight people. Fine prints and antique nautical maps lit by carefully recessed lights lined the room.

Courtney snapped the table back down, then turned and pointed to an efficient-looking kitchen area running along the boat's port side, to the left of and in back of the hatchway. "Here's the galley," she said gaily, turning the water off and on. "Fridge, freezer, water, lights—everything we'll need."

KC's eyes snapped open. There was a stainless-steel double oven, a good-sized refrigerator, plenty of counter space, and dozens of beautifully polished teak cupboards, fastened securely with brass latches. Tiny windows cut into the side of the hull let in the bright sunshine.

"Ooh, I can't wait," Liza said, hopping up and down. "It's like a little dollhouse, and I want to start *playing*. Hey, got anything in there to eat yet?"

Winnie sat down on the bottom step and frowned at Liza.

KC stared at the stove. "How can you cook when you're at sea? Doesn't hot food spill all over the cook?"

"No," Courtney explained with a laugh. She knelt down and pointed to a device under the stove. "It's on gimbals, like the dining table. See? It's a little device that keeps it balanced, so it stays steady even in rough weather, or when the boat's heeled over."

"What *will* they think of next?" Liza called in her foghorn voice, throwing her hat like a Frisbee across the room onto one of the cushioned benches.

KC just nodded. It was amazing how ingenious wealthy people could be when it came to having a good time. No-spill yacht vacations. Why not?

"Mom used to serve meals on her best dishes in

here. Come on, I'll show you our cabin," Courtney said, edging around the counter that separated the galley from the main cabin area. "Okay, now, watch me. I'm walking toward the *forward* cabin."

"Because you're walking toward the front of the boat, toward the bow," KC said. "The cabins in the back are called the—"

"Aft cabins," Courtney finished, slapping KC's outstretched hand. "All right. Now, we're getting the deluxe forward double-berth. So look out."

"Forward, behind—it's all the same to me," Liza quipped. "All I know is that it spells R-I-C-H."

KC wanted to crawl into a storage compartment.

Winnie rolled her eyes.

Liza planted a hand on her hip and bit her lip. "Okay. Sorry, Courtney. You'll have to remind me when I max out in the tackiness category."

Winnie stirred from her perch on the step. "We'll be sure to do that, Liza," she said tartly.

Courtney gave her a patient smile and opened the tiny cabin door.

"It's lovely," KC gasped as the group moved ahead into a small but elegant sunny cabin, with two built-in bunk beds crafted of polished wood. Gorgeous chintz fabric covered the beds, and there were lace curtains over the portholes. There was practically no room to move between the two bunks, but KC thought it looked comfy enough.

"Where are we going to put all of our stuff?" Liza said, flopping down on one of the lower bunks.

Courtney gave a proud smile and reached for a shiny

brass fixture. Then she swung out a small door under the lower bunk that revealed enough space to stow even Liza's overstuffed suitcase. "This room has three other compartments just like it. And two closets at the end of the room for hanging clothes. Next door, there's another forward storage area for oversize belongings.

"The head," Courtney continued, opening a tiny door off their double berth. "Complete with sink, shower, and lovely toilet. The crew has a separate facility."

"Oh, darn!" Liza teased.

"Don't bump your head as you go through the door," Courtney warned, turning back into the main cabin. With a mysterious look, she opened a narrow door in the wall. "Check this out." She giggled, pulling out the black sleeve of a wet suit. "Four of them. I called ahead and rented equipment for all of us. The air compressors and tanks are stowed in another forward compartment. The other compartments hold games galore, fishing gear, snorkeling equipment, extra clothes, and even little floatable lounge chairs you blow up and toss in the water."

"I'll take one of those," Liza announced.

KC felt the boat rocking again. She braced herself with her hand against the wall and watched with growing excitement as Courtney continued the tour. Living on a yacht would be cramped, but it looked as though the *Bluebeard* was equipped to meet their slightest whims.

"I'll show you the other staterooms," Courtney chattered, turning and leading them down an aft passageway on the other side of the boat from the galley, where there were two smaller berths, each equipped with two comfortable bunks. A second, smaller head was located off the passageway. "The captain, first mate, and cook sleep in this area."

"Would you take a look at this," Liza boomed. "Hey, Courtney, if astronauts used teak, this could be the space shuttle."

Courtney laughed, backing up into a small space under the hatchway's steps in the middle of the boat. "Isn't it amazing? This is what we call the navigator's niche."

KC squeezed ahead and looked over Courtney's shoulder at the high-tech nook, filled with monitors, receivers, gauges, and displays. A small standing table was covered with charts.

"It makes it pretty simple to navigate," Courtney explained, switching on the black and green radar screen, and pulling the black ship-to-shore radio off its hook. "We'll always know where we are on this boat."

There was a quick step in the hatchway, and everyone backed into the tiny galley. A tall, gray-haired man with a deeply tanned, lined face appeared. His navy blazer was studded with brass buttons, and his wiry eyebrows were knitted over his steely gray eyes. KC smiled at his nautical clothing, wondering briefly if she'd stumbled onto the set of Masterpiece Theater.

"Why, Miss Conner," he said, ducking down to keep his head from bumping into the top of the hatch. He turned toward them with a polite smile and a tip of his cap. "I recognize you from photos your parents have shown me. Welcome to St. Ramos."

Courtney extended her hand. "You must be Captain Hark."

The man shook it and gave a courtly bow. "Alistair Hark. Please call me Alistair."

"These are my friends, KC Angeletti, Winnie Gottlieb, and Liza Ruff," Courtney said politely, gesturing. "They'll be joining us for the sail, and will be happy to help in any way they can."

"Yes, yes," Alistair said with a brisk nod. His terrier eyebrows lifted, and he looked at the group with polite concern. Then he braced his arm with authority on the galley's counter. "Welcome to the *Bluebeard*, ladies."

"Thank you," everyone chorused back.

KC noticed a flicker of sadness pass through his eyes. "For the past eight years, it's been my home, as you know," he said.

Courtney made a sympathetic face, then winced as Liza murmured, "Lucky you."

Alistair gave everyone a stiff-upper-lip smile. "But of course when I received the news that the *Bluebeard* had been sold, I realized at once that—after all—it's only a boat."

KC shifted on her feet.

Alistair coughed and clasped his hands together with vigor. "Would you ladies care for a short tour?" he inquired. "Perhaps we could review our safety procedures. I suspect," he added, giving Winnie's wild outfit a brief once-over, "that we are not all experienced sailors?"

"KC, Winnie, and Liza are all very eager to learn," Courtney said, folding her hands behind her back and giving him an imperceptible I'm-the-boss-here look.

"Good," Alistair concluded, motioning for the group to join him on the deck. KC and the others jammed into the main cabin area and headed back up the hatchway. Once in the brilliant sunshine, they obediently took their seats in the cockpit. KC's pulse speeded up as she gazed up at the tall mast rocking against the sky. She didn't want to miss one detail. After one week at sea, she wanted to know everything there was to know about sailing.

"As Courtney is aware," Alistair began, "the *Bluebeard* is a fifty-foot deluxe fiberglass yawl with state-of-the-art rigging and navigational equipment. Our mainmast is ninety feet." Alistair pointed back to the tallest mast, located in the center of the boat. "And the mizzenmast stands at sixty feet." KC followed his gaze to a smaller mast near the stern.

"Gee, you need two sails to get this thing going, huh?" Liza piped up.

"Three, actually, Miss Ruff." Alistair gave her a short glance. "The jib sail extends over the bow. Now—by sail alone, the *Bluebeard* is capable of approximately fifteen knots with the wind and about eight knots against."

Liza stuck her forefinger into her mouth and raised it up into the air. "There's no wind today, Al," she cracked. "What are we going to do for power?"

Alistair formed his weathered lips into a tight smile. "We are equipped with a one-hundred-and-fifty-horsepower diesel engine for that purpose, Miss Ruff. We also have on board a convenient dinghy, equipped with an outboard motor. Life jackets are stowed beneath the cockpit seats."

KC felt her eyes shining. An outboard, too? She fantasized about anchoring in a deserted blue harbor and taking the dinghy out to lie on the unspoiled sand. Maybe even in the buff.

"Our crew currently consists of myself, our cook, Mack Retta, and Jake Nalley, our first mate," Alistair went on. "Please come this way."

Everyone followed him up onto the starboard deck as he gave a brief tour, pointing out the mainsail, mizzen, and jib sail winches.

"Main-sull?" KC asked, grabbing on to the boat railing for balance. "What's that?"

"The main*sail*." Alistair arched his eyebrows slightly. "The largest sail attached to the mainmast and furled onto the boom."

"See, KC?" Courtney pointed to the side. "The boom is the bottom of the mainsail's triangle. The sail is stored under that blue sailcloth covering. It's *furled*. When you raise it, it's *hoisted*. When you lower it a little in high winds, you *reef* it."

KC nodded excitedly. "Right, I remember. And the rope that controls the angle of the sail against the wind is called the *sheet*."

Courtney shook her head with admiration. "When did you have time to read up on all this, KC?"

"Take note of these shrouds and stanchions on the deck," Alistair ordered, pointing to several wrapped wires extending down from the masts to the deck. "In rough weather, you're going to need to know where they are at a moment's notice."

"Is there really a chance we could be thrown from the boat?" KC asked.

"Well, yes," Alistair replied, stepping up to the mast and holding it lightly while he looked down on the group. "Never walk freely on the deck when there is the least spot of weather. Needless to say, ladies," he continued crisply, "look aloft when you are on deck. Be prepared for a quick jibe."

"That's when the boom swings across the deck when we're tacking against the wind, KC," Courtney called over her shoulder.

"Excuse me, miss." Alistair suddenly seemed to notice Winnie, who had dropped down onto the narrow starboard deck and was hanging over the railing, staring into the water. "Gauging from your attire, I assume you have not spent much time at sea."

Winnie looked down guiltily at her impractical miniskirt and slippery sandals.

"That's why I need you to pay particular attention now, Miss Gottlieb," he reminded her stiffly. "Proper footwear and sailing attire is of extreme importance."

Courtney stepped forward. "I'll make sure Winnie has the right gear before we anchor off, Captain Hark," she said evenly.

KC tried to ignore Winnie, who obviously wasn't enjoying Alistair's crusty seaworthiness as much as she was.

"You ladies will be expected to help with a variety of duties. There are ongoing cleanup chores, of course. But we may also need help securing lines, furling sails, and even taking the helm for short periods."

"I'd love to help," KC couldn't help saying. "Really—anything."

"Thank you, Captain Hark," Courtney said with brisk efficiency when he was finished with a few extra safety tips. "I think we'll need a supply run. Is the St. Ramos Mercantile still in business?"

Alistair nodded.

"Good." Courtney dug a notepad out of her purse and jotted down a list. "KC and I will make the run. Liza and Winnie can stay here and get acquainted with the *Bluebeard*."

KC gripped the deck railing and looked out at the water. In the distance, she could see a long-winged white bird skimming the surface of the glassy harbor. KC felt a sudden pang. Two days ago, she was just another freshman, cramming for midterms in her dank dorm room.

But this. KC's eyes swept up to the tall mast and the tiny flag that fluttered at the top. A cool breeze fanned her face and lifted the dark curls off her forehead.

This is what she worked for. This is what she wanted. This was where she belonged. This could be the best thing that ever happened to her in her life.

Three

"**H**ey, Winnie," Liza shouted, sticking a cloud of flame-red hair out of the hatchway. "Check it out. Mister Reggae's Caribbean-Style Potato Chips."

Winnie closed her eyes in frustration. Since Courtney and KC had left to go grocery shopping, she'd been out on the deck, flipping through a yachting magazine and wondering why she'd come. But Liza was on top of the world, rummaging through the *Bluebeard* as if she owned the place.

Liza heaved herself into the sunny cockpit, holding the shiny bag of chips. Then she stood up and adjusted the straps on her tomato-red halter top. She took a few mincing steps toward Winnie and flopped down next to her. "They've got lime juice and little flecks of red pepper in them. Want one? Say please!" She waved a chip in the air, trying to tempt Winnie.

"No, thanks." Winnie felt for the rim of the boat's cockpit in back of her and pulled herself up on the ledge above Liza. Why *had* she come? What made her think she'd want to spend an entire week in cramped quarters with Liza Ruff—one of the biggest nutcases on the U of S campus? Not to mention Courtney and KC, whose cheerful banter and silly sorority stories were getting worse by the moment. It was almost like watching an old beach-party movie from the sixties, Winnie thought miserably. Except that she couldn't get up and walk out of the theater.

Winnie chewed the side of her thumb, feeling her eyes fill with tears. Coming to St. Ramos had been a big mistake. Snobby yacht captains, luxury hotels, and exclusive clubbiness might be fine for Liza, Courtney, and KC, but she was suffocating. When Courtney had invited her to the Caribbean, she'd imagined colorful steel-drum bands, friendly natives, and carefree sailing types. She thought it would make her feel alive and adventurous again.

But it didn't. Courtney's Caribbean made her feel lonely. It made her feel like a prisoner in someone else's world. Winnie stiffened inside, wondering if she'd ever have a life worth living again.

Why had she let Courtney talk her into it? Sure, she'd had a miscarriage. And, of course, she was separated from Josh. But this claustrophobic Love Boat was exactly what she *didn't* need. She had to get away.

Off the boat. Back on the plane. Anywhere but here. Or she knew she'd lose her mind.

Liza clambered up next to her, the boat rocking slightly as she did. "Hey," she whispered loudly into Winnie's ear. "Where's our crusty old captain?"

Winnie pointed toward the mast with her head. "He's doing something with the sails."

"He gives me the creeps," Liza muttered, stuffing a large chip into her mouth and glaring up at Alistair. The next moment Winnie saw that the captain was looking down at them with an expression of impatience. "Hi," Liza called to him, waving. "Want a chip? They're great!" She leaned toward Winnie. "Of course, they're probably *his* chips. Uh-oh. Here he comes. I'm gonna get it."

"Aha," Alistair called, placing one white shoe down on the deck. He grabbed a shroud for balance and stepped effortlessly down into the cockpit. "I see you ladies have settled in."

Winnie stared at Alistair's steely gray eyes and lanky, sunburned arms, deciding at that very moment to detest him. She hated the condescending way he'd criticized her clothes. And now she didn't like the superior way he was looking at them.

Slowly he drew a pipe case out of his jacket and tamped down a clump of tobacco in a stubby-looking pipe. "Two crew members. Ready and willing to learn."

"Right," Liza snapped back, stuffing another chip into her mouth. "I'm happy to help out, as long as I don't have to break any nails in the process."

Winnie slowly clenched her fists.

Captain Hark's face hardened. Then he lit his pipe and puffed it thoughtfully, his gray eyes glinting.

Liza slapped her thigh. "Hey, Cap. Just kidding. Just trying to liven things up around here. We're all out here to have a good time, aren't we?"

Alistair didn't take his steely gaze off Liza. "Miss Ruff, I myself am here because I'm being paid. However, I'm not being paid enough to baby-sit a spoiled teenager. You'll help out and you'll like it. Is that clear?"

Winnie's eyes widened. Mr. Refined Yacht Captain was turning into an Academy Award–winning Captain Hook. She had a sudden urge to find a ticking clock so that she could scare him away. This was the guy who was going to take them safely through the treacherous Caribbean?

Liza pursed her lips and put her hand on her hip, momentarily at a loss for words.

Alistair blew a puff of smoke in Liza's direction. "As a matter of fact, I've already secured another position. So if you don't mind, I'd like to get to Gregory Cays as quickly as possible. Without any trouble."

"You're the troublemaker," Liza snapped back.

"Very well," Alistair replied, puffing. "I accept that role. You girls are assigned to cleaning the brass in the aft cabins. Terribly tarnished, you see."

Liza gasped.

"You'll find the cleaning supplies under the galley sink." Alistair stood up and turned to climb off the boat. But a moment later he twisted around and looked back down at them. "A warning, ladies."

Winnie shaded her eyes and looked up at his tanned face.

"It is bad luck to cross a captain on your first day at sea," Alistair said, his expression eerily distant. "The natives here believe it, you know."

"Right," Liza came back with a sarcastic toss of her head. "They wouldn't dare, huh?"

Winnie shivered.

"Destiny." Alistair's eyes remained coldly fixed on them. "It's not a matter of chance, you know. It's a matter of choice. And the choice is yours. Good day."

Winnie shifted. A small cloud drifted over the sun, blotting the warmth for a moment before it reappeared. Suddenly she realized that her heart was racing and her hands had turned to ice.

"Some luxury cruise," Liza complained when he was gone. "Here I am in the Caribbean, stuck cleaning toilets with . . . with . . ."

"Captain Hook," Winnie whispered.

Liza's eyes were blazing. "Yeah! With Captain Hook breathing down my back."

Winnie wanted to shove a cleaning rag down Liza's throat. Why did she have to complicate things by ticking off the captain? Suddenly everything felt off-kilter and wrong. It was as if her mind had lost its balance and needed a moment on dry land. Abruptly Winnie grabbed her purse and climbed up to the deck. Then she slipped over the side to the top rung of the ladder and made it down to the dock, where she began to hurry back toward civilization.

"WINNIE!" she could hear Liza wailing in the distance.

Winnie ignored her and headed back down the lively dock, hoping she wouldn't run into Alistair. Once she reached the top of the yacht-club gangway, she stopped and looked up and down St. Ramos's main street, trying to catch her breath.

Instinctively Winnie headed toward the busy section of town, away from the Windjammer Hotel. The wide promenade that ran along the seawall seemed like a good enough route to follow. Her leather sandals slapped against the hot concrete. Motor scooters and Jeeps whizzed by.

She paused and felt herself relax as she lost herself in the view of the mottled blue harbor, studded with anchored boats and the occasional windsurfer. A soft breeze gently lifted her bangs and she instinctively reached her hand out for Josh's.

Then Winnie froze. Josh was gone. She'd left him, and now he was thousands of miles away.

"KC's right," Winnie whispered to herself. "St. Ramos *is* a paradise. That's what's so awful. Why should everything be so beautiful when everything inside of me is as black and cold as the inside of an old coal mine?"

She started walking again, running her hand along the rough seawall, half closing her eyes and letting the sun warm her face. The smell of sizzling meats mixed with the scent of the hot asphalt and the far-off aroma of honeysuckle and hibiscus. A few hundred yards ahead, the seawall ended, and it was replaced with a long row of waterfront shops and restaurants. Winnie moved casually ahead, swinging her oversize bag from her shoulder and staring up at the large, colonial homes poised on the hill above the town.

Gradually the sidewalk became more crowded, and Winnie thought she could smell candy popcorn and french fries coming from the little tourist spots along the street. Large groups of senior citizens in white shoes and muumuus were posing for group pictures. Rows of gift shops sold silly straw hats, and sleek restaurants extended into the harbor on pilings.

Strolling quietly past Curio's Yacht Charter and the Blue Water Diving Company, Winnie stared at the healthy-looking guys in cutoffs bustling in and out of the swinging glass doors. Music throbbed through the doors of the dockside bars. Brightly lit duty-free shops were packed with tourists stocking up on cheap booze and jewelry. She gazed absently at the antiseptic-looking golf stores and dime-a-dozen craft boutiques hung with sad-eyed straw puppies and driftwood paintings.

Everything was as typical and familiar as a trip to Los Angeles, Winnie thought dejectedly.

After ten more minutes of walking, the busy section of town gave way to a rustic stone wall fronting the water. Winnie drew in her breath and looked at the sparkling harbor. She walked on, trying to clear her mixed-up thoughts. Had she gotten too far away from the old Winnie? The Winnie who took crazy chances and lived on the razor's edge? The Winnie who knew how to have fun?

Winnie wiped a stray tear off her face with the back

of her hand. In less than a year, she'd married Josh Gaffey, become pregnant, and had settled down into a comfortable routine of studying, Crisis Hotline volunteering, and hanging out with her friends.

Whatever happened to the old Winnie? She used to dye her hair purple and live on Cap'n Crunch cereal. She used to ride motorcycles with the wind in her hair. Her life had been one constant stream of loud music, corny TV shows, and all-nighters. Her life was an everything-on-it pizza. A giant hang glide. A candy store.

Where had it all gone?

Winnie moved slowly ahead, staring at the tips of her painted toenails peeking out of the ends of her sandals. She stopped when she realized that the street had actually ended. She looked up. The main sidewalk curved away from the water, around an historic bronze statue that had been placed in the middle of a circular plaza. A paved street headed up into the bushy hillside, and another cobblestone street pushed farther along the waterfront.

Beep, beep. A guy on a tiny scooter honked as she stepped toward the grassy plaza. Her skin began to prickle all over. The statue was of a barrel-chested man wearing a baggy captain's coat and cap. His craggy face stared out over the water, and his stubby pipe was clamped sternly between his lips.

Winnie tiptoed around the front of the huge figure. Beneath his feet lay a plaque.

"Placed in memory of St. Ramosan sailors lost at sea. May they rest in peace. There is a destiny that makes us brothers—none goes his way alone."

Winnie stepped back. She felt a shiver run through her body. "Destiny?" she muttered to herself, trying to remember what Alistair had just said to them about it. "What was he saying? What is the statue saying?" she whispered, turning away quickly and heading nervously back across the street.

Too tired to climb the hill, Winnie wandered down the older cobblestone street that continued along the waterfront. She shook her head, trying to forget Alistair. The far-off sound of steel drums teased her ears, and the warm cobblestones felt good beneath her feet. Bougainvillea and honeysuckle climbed the stone wall on the side of the street opposite the water. A couple of blocks ahead, there was a row of rickety, two-story buildings with second-story porches overlooking the water.

Winnie's heart pumped. Five minutes down the narrow waterfront lane, it looked as if she'd reached the real St. Ramos—a noisy, busy section of town, filled with exotic people actually going about the business of everyday life. She moved eagerly forward, pushing her pink sunglasses up on her nose and beginning to smile. The steel drums got louder. Up ahead, the street fanned out into a large town square, dominated by an open-air market. Women wearing brightly colored scarves carried baskets of fruit and vegetables. Small children played ball in the street. It was as if she'd walked through a curtain into another, richer world. The air smelled of spices and frying sweet potatoes and plantains. There were shouts of laughter.

"Hey, you," a dark-skinned woman seated behind a large fruit stand was yelling at a shopper, "don't squeeze dat mango too hard." Winnie wanted to hug her.

She headed into the market, her eyes drifting eagerly over the displays of plantains, papayas, spices, rice, and cooking oil. Homestyle cafés dotted the inside of the square, and had tables and chairs placed casually outside their doors, advertising curried chicken, pumpkin fritters, peanut ice cream, and tea made from fresh basil.

Winnie strode through the lively, dusty scene, feeling completely at home. The steel-drum music's source was a boom box positioned outside of a seamstress's shop, where a few men and women stopped spontaneously to move to the rhythm of the reggae music. No one seemed to notice Winnie's strange hair or out-of-place clothing. Everyone she passed seemed to take her as she was.

After walking for half an hour, she finally sat down at a tiny café table and took off her sandals.

"You want cold beer? You want cold tea?" a man with a friendly voice and a white shirt asked her.

"Tea," Winnie murmured, rubbing her feet. "And fruit—some kind of fresh fruit." She dropped her foot, wondering why Courtney hadn't mentioned this part of town. Maybe her parents had never taken her here when she was little.

A moment later the man returned with her tea and an earthen dish filled with a huge papaya salad. Winnie eagerly ate the cool, rich slices of fruit. She drank the strong tea and stared at passersby, relishing the easy, loose-limbed feel of the place. Time had stopped. She had nowhere to go, and all the time in the world.

When she was done, the midday sun was burning down on her head, and the gritty street dust was mixing with the sweat on her neck. She stood up and left her money on the table. Then she noticed a shaded back alley that appeared to be a shortcut back to the touristy section of town. Winnie headed into it.

The alley was cool and quiet. Halfway down, a stack of crates and boxes leaned against a brick wall. At the end, she could see the cobblestone lane and the turquoise sea beyond. Then her view was suddenly blocked by the narrow figure of a guy ducking into the alley. She couldn't see his face against the blinding background, but he was running from something.

Winnie suddenly froze. She heard the sound of loud voices. All she could do was stand in the alley, her feet braced and her hands held out on each side, wondering which way to duck. The guy was running straight toward her as hard as he could. Suddenly he looked up. His dark eyes locked on to hers. A split second later he looked over his shoulder, just as the outline of two policemen appeared in the alley's entrance.

Winnie gasped. But before she could make a move, she felt his strong arm grab her around the waist. He dragged her swiftly behind the pile of crates and banana boxes, his warm palm clamped firmly over her mouth.

"Mmmggghhh." Winnie struggled to cry out. She wrestled with all her might to get away, but it was no use. Her body was pinned sideways to the clammy cobblestones, pulled up next to the strange guy's chest.

Winnie continued to struggle against him. She could hear his heart pounding with adrenaline, but she couldn't loosen his muscled arms. Her cheek was pressed against his torn sweatshirt, smelling faintly of grass and salt. She twisted her body around, straining to push his elbow off her collarbone and his hand off her jaw. Desperately she looked up into his flashing brown eyes. He wasn't a native, but his deeply tanned face made him look as if he'd been in the tropics for some time. She felt him grip her harder, and she slumped in defeat. The sound of slow footsteps began to click down the alley toward them.

"Don't make a move," the guy whispered in her ear, clasping her even more tightly around the waist. His hand smelled like rope and seawater.

Winnie's heart was in her throat. She didn't know if he had a gun or a knife. She didn't know if he was a crazed, escaped murderer or a ruthless drug dealer. All she knew was that he could kill her any second.

"You see him?" Winnie could hear one of the policemen mumble on the other side of the crates. Desperately she tried to stretch her leg out, to tip over a box and get their attention. But the guy's viselike grip tightened painfully around her ribs.

"No, sir," the other policeman came back. Winnie could hear the tap of his nightstick against the damp cobblestones. She could barely breathe. She could feel the sweat beginning to soak through the front of the guy's sweatshirt, mingling with her own.

"He's hiding in the market," the other answered. "Let's check it out."

Winnie shut her eyes tightly, wondering if the guy would kill her and leave her in the alley to die. She wondered how much it would hurt. She wondered how they would find her.

After a moment Winnie heard the footsteps fade and felt the stranger's grip relax. Winnie shoved his arm away and scrambled to her feet.

"What the hell do you think you're doing?" Winnie screamed at him, ripping a wooden plank from one of the crates and holding it up in front of her. By this time, her heart was beating in her throat and her mouth was dry with fear. She tightened the grip on her stick.

The guy sagged back against the crates, panting, but she could tell that every muscle in his body was on red alert. He was handsome, and his straight brown hair flopped down over his forehead as if it had once been well-cut. Dressed in dirty hiking shorts, a sloppy, torn sweatshirt, and sneakers without socks, he looked familiar enough to blend into an American college campus. Except that his eyes were filled with fear.

"Why were you running?" Winnie demanded, spotting a long silver chain looped around his neck. She recognized the St. Christopher medal that hung on it.

The guy looked up at her, and Winnie suddenly felt a little confused, though she held her stick up even higher. After all, a moment before she had been convinced he was a ruthless killer. "What happened back there?" Winnie shouted angrily. "I want to know why you were running from the police."

Narrowing his eyes, the guy looked at her as if

she'd lost her mind. "Everyone on this island is running away from something," he spat back, fingering his St. Christopher medal, then letting it drop. "Why else would someone come all the way out here?"

Winnie opened her mouth to say something, but he stood up abruptly. "Why are *you* here?" he challenged her. "Or are you from one of those fancy cruise boats that crash here for a few hours to make everyone feel as if they've actually seen something different? Something exotic and *dangerous*."

"NO!" Winnie heard herself shout. She flung the stick across the alley, where it hit the wall and tumbled to the ground. Angry tears mounted in her eyes. "No, I'm *not* like that. I'm *not*."

"What are *you* running away from, then?" he shouted at her, his dark eyes narrowing. "What the hell are *you* doing here?"

"I . . . I . . ." Winnie cried, unable to answer. Her eyes met his briefly before he brushed back a wedge of hair and tucked in his sweatshirt. Then without a word he turned and began to run back down the alley.

"Wait!" Winnie heard herself shout, watching his dark silhouette disappear into a blinding block of light at the entrance. Hot tears were streaming down her face, and her heart felt as though it had swelled to the bursting point. "Okay," she sobbed into the alley's dark shadows. "I *am* running away!"

Winnie sank back down onto a crate and drooped her spiky head into her hands. "And if you'd just give me a minute," she whispered through her tears, "I might be able to figure out just what it is I'm running from."

Four

....

*L*iza finished rubbing the last of the brass railings in the aft passageway. Spotting a tiny dark smudge, she knelt and grabbed her metal can of brass cleaner. Then she dunked it upside down into her grubby white cloth.

"Dab, dab, dab," Liza muttered. "And rub-a-dub-dub."

She grasped the railing and heaved herself up in the tiny space. An hour before, Alistair had ordered her to polish the brass and clean the head in the aft cabins. And had she blown it off as Winnie had? No way. She had stuck around in a highly cooperative manner. She had done the dirty work.

Remember this, Courtney, the next time you and KC

feel like turning your noses up at me, she thought. *Remember who the good sport is around here.*

Liza planted her bare feet on the floor, trying to steady herself as the boat began to rock in its mooring. The fumes from the brass cleaner were starting to make her woozy. She glanced down at her blackened nails.

"Ugh," she groaned. "Alistaaaiiirr!" she yelled up to the ceiling through her cupped hands. "Where are you? I'm all done. Your cute little slave girl chamber-maid has everything all shiny."

Liza slapped her polishing rag against the wall, then sat down hard on the floor. The knees on her new white leggings were grubby. Her body was covered with sweat. And she was starving to death.

She clenched her fists. Maybe she was going about this the wrong way. "I'm sitting here like a poor dumb sucker, just trying to get along. And what do I get? Humiliation," she told herself, bitterly examining two broken nails. "I've traveled all the way to paradise, and already they're treating me like a poor kid from Brooklyn—which I am. But is it that obvious?"

Liza's eyes misted over. A couple of times she'd tried to escape into the sunshine. But Alistair had been on deck, giving her threatening stares and puffing grimly on his stupid pipe. It was horrible. Here she was—a guest of the super-rich Conner family, and within one hour on the boat she'd been turned into slave labor. She bit her lip and pulled herself up again, adjusting the straps on her halter top. Maybe if she stopped acting like a maid, people would stop treating her like one. She stepped into the tiny galley and put away her cleaning supplies. Then she jammed on her purple plastic sandals and headed up the hatch to pop her head abovedeck.

"Finished already?" a dry voice greeted her from behind.

Liza twisted around and looked up. Alistair was squatting at the base of the mainsail mast, clenching his pipe in his teeth. "Oh, uh—ahoy there," she called out lamely.

Alistair gave a slight chuckle, then looked away.

"I'm done," Liza called sweetly, resting her chin lightly on her folded hands. "Didn't think I could finish, did you? Well, I did. So there. Look at me, I'm a sport after all."

"Pardon me, Miss Ruff." Alistair drew himself up and returned her look. "But where in the world did Miss Conner make your acquaintance? I can't imagine that you have much in common."

Liza gulped. Alistair's rudeness was enough to take her breath away. It was obvious now how much contempt he felt for anyone without Courtney's breeding and wealth. And he clearly took her for a lowlife.

"Oh, Courtney and I are best friends on campus," Liza lied, slipping on her red, rhinestoned sunglasses. She hoisted herself up and stepped with great dignity over to the cockpit bench, then settled herself comfortably on the cushions. "We go way back. So many memories. The Denver Ladies Cotillion. St. Mary's School for Girls. Skiing in St. Moritz."

Alistair glared at her.

"Do you realize," Liza rambled on, leaning across the navy cushions in the yacht's cockpit, "that Courtney and I can actually trace our ancestry back to the *Mayflower*?"

Alistair was practically snarling at her. He whipped a line around a cleat and gave her a stony look as he swung down the ladder, disappearing down the dock.

"Good-bye!" Liza shouted after him cheerily. She crossed her slightly pudgy legs and patted the oversize white bow at the back of her head. She knew that harassing Alistair wasn't a smart idea, but she couldn't help it. She hated people who worked for the rich and pretended to be better than she was.

Stroking a fat coil of wound line, Liza stared up at the mast and tried to relax. She smoothed her hair back and listened to the sound of the large yachts rubbing against their moorings like huge, overfed whales waiting for their next adventure.

Sure, Courtney's aristocratic serenity was irritating. Alistair was a crank. And Winnie was a basket case. But since when did she get to fly to a tropical paradise so she could loll around on a million-dollar yacht for a week? After all, the sky was blue, and the sun felt like gold on her face.

"I'm feeling mag-iiiiiiic," Liza began singing in her throaty voice. *"I'm feeling won-der-ful,"* she blared, rising up on her knees and raising her arms into the air. She slid one hip out a little, feeling sexy and free. *"Because of yoooou. My heart rises toward the suuuuun,"* she sang, struggling to hold the note.

Liza shrugged and put her hand down to balance

herself as a wake rippled beneath the boat. She looked across the glassy water. The *Bluebeard* was moored at the end of the dock. From this position she could look straight out into the harbor and the white sand of the beach. Carefully she rolled herself over on her stomach and crawled to the very back of the stern. She stared dreamily into the crystal waters. The sun was working its warmth into her back and she could see schools of iridescent angelfish swimming in the waters below.

She sighed. A small sailboat sped past the dock out into the harbor. On a nearby yacht, she could hear tinkling laughter, and on the island's crest, she could see a row of palm trees swaying softly in the Caribbean breeze. There was a distant splash.

"My heeeaaarrrrt—it rises," Liza improvised, jazzing up the Broadway tune. Blissfully she sang to the warm, rippling water. *"Oh yes—it riiises. Yeah. You bet, it riiiises. And you're mine. Oh yes, you're mine."*

"Yeah. You're *mine*," the water sang back to her.

Liza frowned. She looked down at its shimmering surface. Was she hearing things? Slowly she lifted her head. *"I'm feeling maaaaagic,"* she sang again, tentatively.

"Oh yeah," the water answered. *"Black magic, baby. Working that magic on meeee."*

"You're off-key!" Liza called.

"Not!" someone shot back with a laugh.

Liza raised her head and looked out. Two guys wearing black wet suits and diving masks were swimming away from the beach toward the yacht-club docks. Liza's eyes opened wide. They seemed to be struggling to hold their heads above water as they sang at the top of their lungs.

"*I hear muuuusic,*" one of the guys crooned off-key before sinking underwater, flapping his arms awkwardly. Then he rose up to the surface again. He caught her eye and continued to swim straight out from the beach until he was only about ten feet away from the end of the *Bluebeard*'s dock.

"*Par-ty muuuuusic,*" the second guy echoed him, then coughed.

Liza giggled and cupped her hands around her mouth. "Cut out that racket down there."

"Tennis, anyone?" the first guy cracked, swimming toward the dock's ladder, which was located right next to the Bluebeard's stern. Liza stared at his bronzed face and shock of dark hair plastered to his forehead. Then he sank under the blue water, leaving a lather of bubbles on the water's surface. Emerging again, he shook his head. "Man. These weight belts are bad news. They were meant for Tinkerbell, not a big hunk like me."

Liza smiled. She looked over at the second guy, whose scraggly blond hair dripped down over his sweet, round eyes. A moment later the two of them were splashing awkwardly toward the ladder. But their oversize fins made it practically impossible for them to climb the slippery rungs. It looked as if they were beginners from the nearby diving school.

"Whoa!" the second guy yelled, falling back into the water.

"Pay no attention to the man behind that curtain,"

the dark-haired guy yelled, yanking off his fins and throwing them up on the dock. His muscular arms grabbed the rungs, and he scrambled up the ladder. A moment later he stood dripping on the dock next to the *Bluebeard*, his eyes glued to Liza.

"*Wizard of Oz*," Liza replied with a sultry stare. She rolled over on her stomach and crossed her ankles neatly in the air.

The guy laughed. Water streamed off his body and made little pools on the boards of the dock. His quick eyes seemed to be taking in every detail of the *Bluebeard*. "Hey, you're good. I'm Tony Bele," he introduced himself with a quick laugh, almost as if his name were meant to be a joke. He fell briefly into a bodybuilder's pose, then threw his head back and laughed. "I go to school in the U.S., but as you can tell from my fiery Filipino name, I'm no ordinary Joe College."

"I'll be the judge of that," Liza said, resting her chin on the boat's railing and coiling a line around one finger. "College student, hmm? Right." The yacht was rocking gently, and the soft breeze blowing through her hair was making her feel sexy and confident.

Tony posed again. "You bet. USC. Full scholarship with everything on it. Hey—this here is my pal, Mookie Moscowitz." Tony grabbed the hand of his lanky friend as he neared the top of the ladder. Then he pulled him up and smashed him into a powerful side hug. "Mookie didn't get a scholarship, but he's okay. He's from Chicago. And he cracks me up."

Mookie gave Liza a quick, scared look, then stared

down at his feet and smiled goofily. When he yanked his scuba mask off his head, she saw that he had scraggly, shoulder-length hair and big ears.

"So," Tony began quickly, his dark, almond-shaped eyes flashing up at her. "*Wizard of Oz*. We *thought* you knew something about the movie business. Right, Mookie?"

Mookie nodded vigorously.

Liza felt a thrill. She thought for a moment, then propped her chin up and batted her eyes at them. "You know what?"

Tony smiled, and his white teeth shone against the nut-brown color of his skin. "What?"

"I like you guys. How did you know I was in the movies?"

"Hey," Tony said, his quick eyes taking her in. "You some kind of rich Hollywood type or something? I thought I recognized you. Let me think."

Liza watched as the two dripping-wet guys shook out their masks and noisily dumped their heavy oxygen tanks and weight belts on the dock.

"You do that," Liza egged him on, going along with the lie. She couldn't help it. Letting him think she owned the yacht was irresistible. She'd had enough of playing Cinderella for one day. Plus, she kind of liked his cocky, handsome face.

Tony hesitated, then shook his head. "Nope. You're gonna have to tell us. Come on. Confession time."

"Liza Ruff," Liza replied.

"Oh, yeah!" Tony came back, nudging Mookie in the ribs.

Liza spread a wicked grin across her face. She was eager for some down-to-earth company. "Why don't you come on up and join me for a while?" she suggested.

"*Par*-ty-*par*-ty," Mookie began chanting, his humorous blue eyes lit up with excitement. Tony eagerly grabbed the *Bluebeard*'s ladder and scrambled up, followed by his friend. Once they were on board, they stopped and stood awestruck, dripping salt water all over Alistair's pristine deck.

"Hey, this is the life," Tony yelled, taking a flying leap into the cockpit of the yacht and landing with his legs crossed and one arm outstretched, as if he were waiting for someone to slide a martini between his thumb and his forefinger.

Liza giggled. Why couldn't she meet guys like this more often? They were more fun than Courtney, KC, and Winnie put together.

"Awesome rig," Mookie slowly agreed with a grin, still standing motionless on the port deck, as if he were waiting for someone to kick him off. He grabbed a shroud and sat down gingerly on the edge of the foredeck.

"What do they get for a boat like this?" Tony asked cheerfully.

"A million," Liza blurted. Actually, it was true. She had overheard Courtney telling KC on the plane.

Mookie clamped his dripping hand to his forehead. "Wow."

"Bucks," Tony agreed, nodding and looking pleased. He did a sudden, spontaneous riff on an imaginary guitar.

"It's only money," Liza said casually, sitting up and sliding over so that her legs were dangling down into the cockpit.

Tony was shaking his head. "Money. I wish it were that easy."

Liza slid down nearer to him and delivered a megawatt smile. "Whatsamatter? We're in paradise. Who needs money?"

Tony and Mookie looked at each other with bug-eyes. *"We do,"* they yelled in unison.

Liza jumped, then laughed.

Tony shrugged. "Sorry about that. It's just we sorta blew it . . ."

Liza took in his intelligent, high-cheekboned face and flashing eyes. Tony didn't look like the type of guy who blew things. He looked like someone who made things happen.

Mookie rolled his eyes good-naturedly, then jumped down into the cockpit. He made his way to the helm and began playing with the wheel. "You mean, *you* blew it, Tony. I didn't talk to the lady at the Windjammer."

Tony looked sheepish. He crossed his wet legs on the cushions. "It was that bad phone connection from L.A. We heard about this cool hotel on St. Ramos, so I called long-distance from the dorm at USC to check out the rates. This place is primo for scuba diving, in case you didn't know."

"Oh, of course," Liza said, recrossing her legs and adjusting her rhinestone sunglasses.

"So, anyway," Tony continued, his voice dropping

into an embarrassed whisper, "I thought she said fifteen bucks a night."

Liza's mouth dropped open. "Are you crazy?"

"Yes," Tony muttered.

Mookie threw his head back and laughed. "Tony thought rooms in the Caribbean were *all* el-cheapos. So he booked us for two weeks. Then, after six days, we found out that the room was really—"

"One *hundred* and fifteen dollars a night," Tony said, hanging his shaggy head dejectedly.

Mookie laughed. "We had to sell our friggin' plane tickets just to pay the bill."

"And now we're camping out until we can dig up the bucks to get home," Tony said. "Some diving vacation."

Liza smoothed her hair. Sure, these guys were a couple of California party boys. But they cracked her up. And that's exactly what her Caribbean vacation needed—a little cracking up. She stood up. "Come on, boys. How about a tour?"

"I'm stoked," Mookie said, eagerly getting to his feet.

"Connect me to this dream machine," Tony agreed.

Liza rose to her feet and went to the hatchway. Pretending she was rich was almost as good as being rich. She turned around, faced them, and drew her bare arms up above her head, Vanna White style. "*This* is the outside of the yacht."

Mookie and Tony nodded and looked around, as if Liza had just said something important.

"That," Liza lowered her voice and turned around,

pointing down the dim hatchway, "is the inside of the yacht."

"Primo," Tony breathed.

"Come on," Liza said, turning around and searching with her foot for the top rung of the hatch steps.

"Hey," Mookie called, "what's it like to be knee-deep in bucks?"

Liza stopped and looked back up. They were staring down at her as if they couldn't breathe until she answered their question. Then she braced herself, one hand on each side of the hatch, and took a deep breath. "I have absolutely no idea."

Tony's and Mookie's mouths dropped open. "You don't?"

"No," Liza admitted with a quick laugh. She didn't feel like lying anymore. She liked them too much. "It's not my yacht. I'm just a poor kid from Brooklyn who invited herself on a cruise with some sorority girls from the University of Springfield."

"Yawn," Tony and Mookie said in unison, turning to face each other and slapping high-fives.

"Hey, it's okay to be poor," Tony said with a twinkle in his eye, following Liza down the hatchway until they were in the main cabin area. "Look at us. We're getting by."

Liza watched the two guys descend. "Come on. Captain Hook's due back any minute."

"Captain who?" Tony began before he stopped, stunned in the middle of the main cabin area. "Awesome." He rubbed his eyes with his fists. "Am I dreaming? Get an eyeful of this stuff, Mook."

Mookie was fingering the little brass latches on the far wall, yanking them back and forth. The next moment, the cabinet door accidentally flew open, sending a stack of board games tumbling onto the floor. "Whoops," he said sheepishly.

"Mook!" Tony yelled, turning around suddenly, knocking one of the fine prints off the wall. It thumped to the ground, sending a large crack across the glass frame. "Oh, God—sorry."

"Never mind, never mind," Liza called, edging back into the narrow galley and waving them over. "This is where the rich people prepare their gourmet meals."

"Whoa," Tony and Mookie said together.

Liza slipped past them and pranced toward the forward double-berth cabin and opened the door as if she were announcing a new act. "And this is where the rich people lay their poor, tired heads at night after a hard day of being rich."

Tony and Mookie gawked at the teak woodwork, chintz bedding, and lace curtains. "This reminds me of the yacht on *Gilligan's Island*," Mookie remarked.

Tony slugged him in the side. "No, no no. The millionaire and his wife were shipwrecked on a little tourist tour boat. This is a *sailboat*."

Suddenly there was a loud, pounding noise in back of them, and all three turned to look. Liza felt her heart drop into her gut. It was Alistair.

"What is the meaning of this?" Alistair said angrily, pounding down the hatchway.

"Why, Captain Hark," Liza began, feeling the

sweat break out all over her body. She raked her hair back and tried to think.

But before Liza could say another word, Alistair had plunged into the cabin, grabbed Liza's arm, and was dragging her back into the galley. "Who are these people, and what do you think you're doing bringing them on board?" he demanded.

"It's Tony and Mookie," Liza answered sharply, pulling away from his painful grip. "Let me go!"

"*Never* let strangers on board, you silly girl," Alistair admonished her, dropping her arm with disgust. His tiny eyes were like ice beneath his thick eyebrows. "Do you have any idea—any . . ." he sputtered, casting a suspicious glance back toward Tony and Mookie, who were watching Captain Hark from the other end of the cabin. "The islands are full of types like this. And they're usually unscrupulous fellows." Alistair cast a scathing glance directly at Tony.

Liza's heart was beginning to pound with fear, but she willed herself to stay collected. "Oh, you can tell just by looking at them, huh?" she shot back. "What's the matter? Don't you like the one with the dark skin? Or maybe it's the blond. He looks like a Communist or a drug user, wouldn't you say?"

Mookie's mouth dropped open, and he looked slowly down at himself.

Tony flashed her an uncertain grin.

"You have no idea," Alistair ranted. "They could be drug runners or smugglers. Do you realize, young lady, that there are hundreds of people in St. Ramos who would be perfectly willing to steal this boat and throw you overboard to the sharks?"

"Well, thanks for the tour, Liza," Tony broke in nervously. Together he and Mookie began to pad past them toward the hatch.

"Yeah, we'll catch you later," Mookie said sadly. "Wouldn't want you to get eaten by a shark or anything." Liza giggled as Mookie quickly stuck his tongue out at Alistair, then lumbered up the steps after Tony.

Liza turned around slowly to face Alistair again. "How dare you," she said, feeling the anger turn in her stomach like boiling lava.

Alistair glared back at her. "You listen to me, young lady—"

"No, you listen to *me*," Liza growled back. "I'm a guest of the Conners, and I deserve to be treated with respect. So do *my* guests."

"Of all the nerve . . ." Alistair replied, giving her a horrified stare.

"You're the one with the nerve," Liza began to shout. "Imagine! Treating me like some kind of slave. Questioning my friendship with Courtney. How *dare* you."

Liza jammed on her sunglasses and began to head for the deck. In the blinding sunshine above, she heard light steps and laughter. Then Courtney and KC stuck their heads in the hatch and looked down.

"Ahoy there, Liza," Courtney called out. "We've brought back your runaway. We found Winnie in town! Here's our supper. KC and I thought we'd . . ." Courtney stopped when she saw Alistair staring furiously at Liza.

Liza winced. She looked up and watched KC's and Courtney's cheerful faces fall as their eyes adjusted to the dim light. Winnie followed, looking paler than ever.

"What's wrong, everyone?" Courtney asked quietly, slipping down the steps and setting down her bags on the galley counter. "Captain Hark?"

"I'll tell you what's wrong," Alistair sputtered, his face reddening and his British accent getting more clipped by the second. "You have a problem."

"Wh—what?" KC and Courtney exclaimed.

"A problem," Alistair repeated. "You young—ladies—are going to have to find a way to get to Gregory Cays without me. I will not spend another minute on this vessel with this . . ." He pointed dismissively at Liza. "With this . . . this . . . *person*."

Liza felt her heart sink into her plastic sandals.

"Oh no!" Courtney protested. "Please, Captain Hark. My parents are depending on you. We're all depending on you."

"Nevertheless," Alistair proclaimed, "my decision has been made." He gave Liza a cold stare. "The crew and myself have other arrangements now. More suitable. A much better *match*."

Five

"Kill, kill, kill, kill," KC was chanting to the rhythm of her footsteps as she and Courtney headed down the hall from their room at the Windjammer.

"Kill who?" Courtney laughed, calmly tucking the room key into the pocket of her white linen skirt. "Liza?"

KC stopped in her tracks, staring down at the forest-green carpeting beneath her feet, trying to calm herself. She couldn't believe how cool Courtney was being about losing Alistair yesterday. Here they were, two thousand miles away from home, just getting used to the sun and the fragrant air. Just settling into the luxurious yacht that was waiting to whisk them through the crystal waters and deserted beaches of the

Caribbean. *Only to have it ruined by Liza Ruff.*

KC sniffed and raised her head. They had no one to sail the boat, and it was all Liza's fault. KC should have said something to Courtney back in Springfield. If anyone could make an experienced yacht captain quit, it was Liza. But Courtney was too sheltered to understand the kind of trouble a brassy, insensitive person like Liza could stir up.

What were they supposed to do now? They certainly couldn't sail the huge boat all by themselves to Gregory Cays. Were they just going to fly back home after one day? Tell everyone that it was "just one of those things"?

KC fanned herself with her straw hat and followed Courtney down into the potted-palm-lined lobby.

A few minutes before, they'd had a huge brunch on the hotel's airy veranda. KC briefly considered poisoning Liza's passion-fruit juice. But luckily for Liza, she'd left after only a few quick bites of a large cinnamon bun, promising to solve all of their problems.

"Right. *You,* Liza Ruff, airhead extraordinaire, are capable of cleaning up this mess," KC muttered as she followed Courtney out the main entrance, trying to be as cool as her friend. "Where are we going, Courtney?" KC asked, heading past the hotel's fragrant frangipani bushes. They crossed the main street and headed toward the busy section of town past the yacht club.

Courtney tossed her head back and smiled mysteriously. "I have a few errands to do. Wish Winnie hadn't stayed in the room. The fresh air would do her good."

KC cleared her throat as they passed the postcard

stands and sandwich bars on the harbor. Between the waterfront buildings, KC could see the violet outlines of faraway islands against the blue of the sky. It made her want to cry. She wanted to see it all. And now everything was falling apart. "You're changing the subject, Courtney."

"Look." Courtney stopped. She sat down on the edge of a wooden planter filled with cascading bougainvillea blossoms. Her shoulder-length blond hair was pulled back into a French braid, revealing her delicate jawline and graceful neck. Her brown eyes glowed with determination. "I know you're mad at Liza. And I know you're worried about the trip. But everything's going to be all right. Okay? Trust me."

"God, you're so accepting," KC concluded with a sigh, ducking two brawny guys carrying a windsurfing board between them. "If Liza had messed up *my* parents' plans, I would have put her on the next plane to Springfield."

Courtney's face looked thoughtful for a moment. "Liza can be a pain, but at least she says what she thinks. I think we could all take a lesson from her in that area. As a matter of fact, I didn't really like Alistair either."

"Courtney!" KC burst out. "He was going to take us on a dream cruise! We were counting on it. And so were your parents. Now you've got a sales contract that says the *Bluebeard* has to be delivered by the end of next week. And you're stuck."

Courtney stood up and put her hand on KC's shoulder. "We'll work it out. I want everyone to have a trip they'll never forget. There's no way I'm going to let Liza—or a snotty captain with a worn-out British accent—ruin it. This is my vacation too."

KC nodded. She let Courtney link her arm through hers and drag her along the busy row of waterfront shops, each one looking more expensive than the last. "Okay, I've got it," KC said, stopping in front of a flower stand and facing Courtney with crossed arms. "You called your parents and they've worked something out for us. Right? Is that why you're not worried?"

Courtney squinted at KC, then shook her head and crossed the street. "I did not. My parents are on the first vacation they've had alone in twenty years. And I wouldn't disturb them—even if I could. They're in a safari camp somewhere in Kenya. No telephones. No mailboxes. No nothing. It's the only way my father can get away from his law office."

KC tensed. "Sorry," she murmured, tossing a strand of dark hair over her shoulder and glancing coolly at a group of tanned scuba-diving types gawking at them as they passed on the sidewalk.

"Everything's under control," Courtney tried to cheer her up, striding ahead confidently.

"But where are you taking me?" KC pressed. A few moments later, Courtney stopped in front of a wooden storefront. The sign hanging over the door read CURIO'S YACHT CHARTER.

"Here we are," Courtney announced. "I talked to our hotel manager this morning before you three woke up. He referred me to Thomas Curio, who owns this place. I guess he runs most of the yacht rentals in town and knows all the qualified skippers."

KC stared up at the huge carved head of a sailor that hung over the front entrance. "What? You mean you can just hire someone for a short trip?"

Courtney gave a secret smile as she pushed open the door and checked her watch. "When I talked to Mr. Curio this morning, he asked me to meet him at noon. Right on the dot."

A thrill of hope ran through KC. Their trip could be salvaged after all? It was almost too good to be true. "You mean, he's found a new captain for us? Just like that? Is that possible? How do you know if he's okay?"

Courtney motioned for her to be quiet, and KC's eyes opened wide as they entered the tiny shop. Photographs of racing sloops and men holding trophy fish lined the rough-panel walls, along with nautical maps, decorative rope, and faded prints of native St. Ramosans. A glass counter ran along one side of the store, containing tiny wooden models of racing sloops. Lush hanging plants hovered near the sunny window. Wet suits and diving gear hung neatly on the other side.

"Hello there, ladies," KC heard a friendly voice. A barrel-chested man wearing a small straw hat emerged from a back room door. Gray hair hung down his neck, and his fleshy face was pomegranate-red. But KC immediately liked his deep-blue eyes.

"Mr. Curio?" Courtney said politely, extending her hand. "I'm Courtney Conner."

"Miss Conner!" Mr. Curio boomed heartily in a lilting British accent. He shook her hand and began ushering them toward a back door. "Please come this way. We may be able to help you out of your little jam."

KC's heart jumped.

Courtney's face flushed a little. "Really?" She cleared her throat and recovered. "As I said over the phone, we lost our captain and crew yesterday, and we're due at Gregory Cays seven days from now. It's a fifty-foot yawl called the *Bluebeard*. We moor it down at the St. Ramos Yacht Club."

Mr. Curio's eyebrows lifted, then he nodded in recognition, rubbing his hands together over his loud, red-and-white print sports shirt. "Yes, yes. I know that one. A beautiful boat. You were right to contact me. There are plenty of would-be skippers in St. Ramos." His face fell a little. "But some of them are unscrupulous, I'm sorry to say. Terrible things can happen. Modern-day pirates. Drug smugglers. Why, I've heard of seamen taking stuff over the border in ice chests, air tanks—even the insides of their hats."

KC drew in her breath.

Mr. Curio took his hat off and crammed it back on again with a frown. Then his expression brightened, and he gestured for them to enter through the side door, where a few faded easy chairs were scattered around game tables in the pleasant back room. Shuttered doors opened onto a deck overlooking a lush yard. A green and red parrot was perched cheerfully on a wooden stand.

Squaaawwkk.

"Pipe down, Pepper," Mr. Curio ordered the parrot.

KC noticed a young man settled in one of the easy chairs, intently reading a yachting magazine. When he looked up, KC felt her pulse quicken. He had an intelligent, handsome face, framed by dark hair that fell casually around his neck. She gulped. His skin was a light maple-brown, and his eyes were a brilliant shade of green behind his wire-rimmed glasses. She watched for a moment as his gaze flickered over Mr. Curio and Courtney. Then his eyes fixed on KC.

KC stopped breathing.

"May I present Patrick Hanson?" Mr. Curio said in his courtly fashion, spreading his burly arms between the young man and the girls. "He's an excellent seaman. Known him for years, and I've highly recommended him many times before. He's your qualified skipper, Miss Conner."

Breaking his gaze, the young man stood up and walked around his chair toward the center of the room, giving everyone a friendly smile. Dressed in new-looking jeans, a pressed white shirt, and sandals, he looked like a typical islander, except that he didn't have the usual leathery skin of the sun worshipers KC had noticed around the St. Ramos docks.

"This is Miss Courtney Conner," Mr. Curio introduced him, as he shook Courtney's hand.

"And this is my friend, KC Angeletti," Courtney said, gesturing to KC.

Patrick took KC's hand wordlessly and shook it. KC stared at his old-fashioned watch and long fingers. His grip was warm, and his squarish jaw made his face look sensitive and kind.

"Hi," KC managed.

Patrick held her hand a split second longer. "Hi, KC."

KC felt her knees buckle. Spotting a small couch a few steps away, she quickly sat down. Mr. Curio motioned toward the seat next to her, and Courtney sat down too. Then he and Patrick took the two rattan chairs facing the couch.

"Sounds like you have a fine yawl in the harbor," Patrick opened the conversation. "Three sails?"

"Yes." Courtney smiled. "My parents have put her through the paces over the years."

"She's fifty foot with a long fin keel and a full skeg hull shape," Mr. Curio went on. "Forty-five percent ballast-to-displacement ratio."

Patrick nodded thoughtfully, and his glance caught KC's just as she looked up shyly into his face. "Nice," he murmured. "How many does she sleep?"

"Eight," Courtney replied, "with extra bunks in the main cabin area."

KC took a deep breath and gripped the armrest of the couch. Then she lifted her eyes once again as Patrick and Courtney began discussing the *Bluebeard*'s rigging. Her eyes boldly roamed over his body and took in his green eyes. Patrick was tall and muscular, but there was something thoughtful and refined about him. He looked more like a poet or a folksinger than a hardened skipper.

Courtney crossed her legs and rested her arm along the back of the couch in a take-charge pose. "We've told you about our situation, Patrick. Tell us about yours."

Patrick picked up a manila envelope from the table next to him and handed it to her. "My skipper's license, résumé, and references are enclosed here," he said quietly. Then he leaned forward and clasped his hands earnestly in front of him. "I'm twenty-one years old, and originally from Virginia." KC stirred. She had thought she detected a slight, refined southern accent. "I came to the islands right after high school and started working on boats to support myself," Patrick continued. "I'd planned to go to college, but I guess I was like a lot of people. I wanted to have a few adventures before I settled down to a profession."

Courtney opened the envelope and began sorting crisply through the paperwork. She cast a long sideways glance at KC, then dropped her eyes back down again.

"I guess you could say I caught the island bug, though," Patrick explained, giving Courtney a businesslike look, then letting his eyes drift back to KC, where they settled.

KC began wondering absently what Patrick looked like with his glasses off. Then it struck her: If Courtney hired Patrick, not only would they be able to sail through the Caribbean after all—they'd be living together for a whole week. They'd sail together. Maybe he'd even teach her how to dive.

She closed her eyes and prayed.

"After a while," Patrick went on, "I learned how to dive and fish, and got pretty good at it. Then eventually I got my skipper's license. I'd done a lot of sailing and I got to know these waters pretty well. In fact, I sailed a rental boat like the *Bluebeard* for several months."

Courtney was running her eyes up and down a piece of paper. "You haven't worked for about six months?" she remarked.

Patrick grinned sheepishly. "Hey, give me a break. Everyone who sails out here deserves a holiday once in a while. That's the trouble with living in paradise. You're surrounded by people taking vacations."

Courtney and KC laughed.

"But—no—seriously. After I saved enough money about six months ago, I stopped sailing so I could pursue my real passion full-time."

"Patrick's a painter," Mr. Curio broke in with a jolly laugh. "Spends all of his time in that little place of his, painting away, don't you, lad? Shame, too. Young Patrick here is probably the finest sailor in St. Ramos."

Patrick grinned and shrugged.

KC flushed. They'd not only found an experienced sailor, but he was the best-looking guy in the Caribbean. And he was also an artist, a thinker, a skin diver. . . . Was she dreaming?

Courtney's brown eyes narrowed. "But you're willing to give it up to sail again?"

"I'm broke," Patrick said straight out, leaning back and stuffing his hands into his jeans pockets. He shrugged as if he'd long ago given up trying to impress other people. "I've been painting like a madman for six months and I've pretty much drained my savings." He smiled again. "That's the bad news."

"What's the good news?" KC couldn't help leaning forward to ask. Her pulse was throbbing in her throat as she stared at his dimpled chin.

Patrick's eyes seemed to light up. His eyes fixed on her as if she were the only person in the world he wanted to talk to that moment. "The good news is that I've just talked an important art gallery in Gregory Cays into showing my two best oils."

"That's fantastic," KC burst out. Then she drew back and looked around, embarrassed.

"Great." Courtney smiled, looking sideways at KC.

Just then Patrick reached out and touched KC's knee, sending a bolt of electricity up her leg and into her chest. "No, it *is* exciting for me. Maybe the most exciting thing that's ever happened in my life."

KC's eyes widened. Their eyes locked, and she felt as if she were floating two feet above the couch cushion. "Of course, I don't get any money unless the paintings sell, but it's a big step for me," Patrick explained. "Anyway, I could use the salary from skippering the *Bluebeard*. And the job will also get me to Gregory Cays."

Courtney stood up, Patrick's papers in her hand. "I'll be right back. I need to make a few phone calls."

"I'll show you to the phone," Mr. Curio spoke up, rushing for the door. "I've got customers out there, anyway." He turned back. "Make yourself at home, KC."

KC smiled shyly at Patrick as Mr. Curio and Courtney left. A soft, lemony breeze blew in through the wooden shutters. Outside, she could hear the sound of flapping sails and sea gulls. Inside, all KC could hear was the thud of her heartbeat in her ears.

"So," Patrick began, "do you sail, KC?"

"No," KC said, struggling to remain calm. Her

heart was beating so loudly, she was sure he could hear it. "I grew up in the Rocky Mountains. But I've always wanted to learn."

"You're going to love it," Patrick said, leaning forward a little. "It makes you feel free."

"Free?" KC echoed, dazed. She looked away suddenly when she realized she'd been staring intently into his green eyes. Embarrassed, her mouth went dry, and she suddenly couldn't think of anything to say.

Finally the door flew open, and Courtney burst in. "I've talked briefly with two of your references," she announced. "And based on that, I'd like to hire you for the job of sailing the *Bluebeard* to Gregory Cays, Patrick. Starting tomorrow morning."

KC gasped.

Patrick's face flooded with relief. He looked at KC and gave her a huge smile. Then he stood up to shake Courtney's hand. "You won't regret this."

"Are you kidding?" Courtney flashed him a smile. "It sounds like you just saved our lives. And our vacation. *We're* the lucky ones."

KC tried to catch her breath. Minutes ago, her world was falling apart. Now it was as if a fairy godmother had floated down out of the blue Caribbean sky and waved her wand. It was magic.

"Well," Patrick said, putting his hand on his forehead, "you should think about hiring a crewman or two to help with the rigging. And a cook. You might as well treat yourself. Especially if it's your last sail on the *Bluebeard.*"

Courtney thought for a moment. "No, I'd like to

do the cooking myself. But we may need some help crewing."

Patrick crossed his arms and grinned mischievously. "I know some great seamen in St. Ramos. Strong, reliable—play a great game of poker."

"*C-O-U-R-T-N-E-Y,*" a blaring, foghorn voice suddenly pierced the calm of Mr. Curio's shop.

KC's heart stopped. She narrowed her eyes. *Liza?* She turned around and glared at the door as Liza sailed through, followed by two lumbering guys in wet suits. KC gritted her teeth. She recognized those guys. They were the ones they'd passed on the dock when she and Courtney had returned from grocery shopping yesterday. They were the ones Liza had foolishly invited onto the *Bluebeard,* enraging Alistair. KC crossed her arms over her chest and glared. The shorter guy was dark-haired, with a tanned face and a quick, handsome grin. Standing next to him was a tall, lanky goofball type with wet blond hair that fell down over his collar.

Mr. Curio followed closely behind Liza and her friends, waving his burly arms in protest. "Please, miss, miss . . ." he shouted. "This area is private."

Courtney raised her hand. "It's okay, Mr. Curio. This is my friend, Liza Ruff, and—"

"I've been looking all over this godforsaken town for you," Liza said in a loud rush, collapsing into one of the armchairs and fanning herself with her huge purple sun hat. She lifted her wildly patterned purple and yellow halter top out a little and blew into it. Then she raised her arms with exaggerated drama. "All of our problems are solved. This is Tony Bele and Mookie Moscowitz. I ran into them outside the hotel and told them about our *huge* problem," she chattered.

KC rolled her eyes.

"Anyway," Liza went on breathlessly, "we've been looking all over town for you and finally figured you'd be in one of these charter outfits."

KC wanted to kill her. Courtney wasn't going to take her seriously, was she? Just when everything was starting to come together?

"Listen," Liza continued, fanning herself, "Tony and Mookie here, they don't know much about sailing the seven seas, but for the price of two tickets back to L.A., they'll do all the gruntwork. Scout's honor. Right, guys?"

Tony and Mookie nodded, wide-eyed.

Liza was nodding vigorously and looking around the room for approval. Then her eyes fell on Patrick. Her red lips parted, and KC could practically see the wheels turning in her head.

"Hel-*lo*," Liza said softly, suddenly switching gears. It was obvious that Liza's theatrical instincts were on red alert, and that Patrick was her intended prey. "I'm Liza Ruff." She extended her hand and Patrick shook it warmly.

KC wanted to throw up. *Stop!* she thought desperately. *Go away. Disappear. Get out of my life!*

"I'm Patrick Hanson," he replied politely, staring at Liza.

"I attend the University of Springfield," Liza

breathed. "But I'm also in the entertainment business. Can you believe it? Only eighteen, and I've already been on national television—twice."

KC couldn't believe her. Desperately she threw a glance in Courtney's direction. But Courtney was already chatting with Mookie and Tony. All KC could do was stand there, helpless, while Patrick calmly listened to Liza.

Couldn't he see it? Didn't he realize that Liza was ready to pounce? KC could practically hear her sharpening her claws and getting ready for the kill.

They'd found the perfect captain, KC thought, a wave of fear rushing through her like a jumbo jet. Now if she could only stuff Liza's overripe body on the next plane out of St. Ramos.

Six

"**M**ookie and Tony are here!" Liza cried down the hatchway the next morning on the *Bluebeard*. Courtney could hear her bare feet thundering down the steps. "They're ecstatic about getting hired, Courtney."

"Liza!" Courtney called, pushing her cabin door open with her foot.

"Patrick needs his hat," Liza shouted. "He's gonna show me how to hoist the sail! Right back."

"Liza!" Courtney called again, before shrugging her shoulders and giving up. She squeezed herself down between the two bunks and carefully slipped a stack of shirts into a tiny compartment. Then she stood up again and zipped her empty suitcase shut. It had been only an hour since they'd finally checked out of the Windjammer. But now, just a short while before they were due to cast off, the yacht was literally rocking back and forth with activity.

Don't let me down, Tony and Mookie, Courtney thought. *It's true I was pretty desperate when I hired you yesterday. But I also thought you had some street smarts. And the kind of offbeat humor that makes for really good times at sea. So now, just do what Patrick asks. Please.*

Courtney felt a knot tightening in her stomach. Half of her wished she could telephone her parents in Africa. The other half was grateful she didn't have to. She clicked a compartment latch shut and backed up toward the door. Why *couldn't* she handle it on her own? She was as good a judge of character as her parents. Wasn't she?

Courtney bit her lip. She just hoped she hadn't taken on too much. The *Bluebeard* was her responsibility. At least she didn't have to worry about Patrick. He was definitely a find. She stepped up through the cabin door and edged past the table into the galley.

Patrick had arrived at sunrise, and had immediately begun checking the sails and navigational systems. Now he was testing the engine. Everything seemed to be under control.

But she was still feeling funny about Liza. Her silly pranks and continual singing were starting to seriously annoy the group. For the sake of the journey, Courtney hoped Liza would chill out once she began to relax. What Liza and Winnie both needed was a nice, relaxing trip. And some reassurance.

"Liza," Courtney yelled again.

"I heeaarr muuusiic," she could hear Liza blaring on deck.

Courtney shook her head and smiled. She pushed out one of the galley portholes and breathed in the salty, ropy smell of the moorings. Moments ago, the St. Ramos Mercantile had delivered the food she'd ordered into the galley. Boxes of fresh coconuts, papayas, sweet potatoes, and limes covered the counters. Fresh chicken and steaks in carefully wrapped white packages had been stowed in the refrigerator. Jars of gourmet capers and olive oil stood next to paper bags filled with fresh local herbs. Winnie was supposed to be unloading the groceries, but she'd slipped away long ago.

"Yeah, uh—okay," she could hear Patrick calling from the deck. "Just watch the hull, guys. The boat's in mint condition, okay?"

Courtney felt the boat rock and figured it must be Mookie and Tony climbing on board with their gear. She walked around the galley counter and craned her neck up into the hatchway. "Liza!" she called again.

"What?" Liza's head appeared, a cloud of red hair fastened back with a huge red blossom.

"I need you." Courtney waved her down. Why was Liza so afraid of her? Didn't Liza know that she was bending over backward so that she wouldn't feel too bad about Alistair? Even hiring Tony and Mookie had been partly because Liza liked them so much.

"Oh, no," she heard Liza whimper. Courtney watched Liza take careful steps down the steep hatchway until she was in the main cabin. When she reached the bottom, Liza clasped her hands over her ears with drama. Her blue eyes looked terrified. "Don't say it, Courtney. Please, please, please, *please,* don't kick me off. Don't send me back to Springfield. I couldn't take it. The cold weather would kill me. I'm allergic to the mountains. There's a chemical in the dorm carpeting that's slowly destroying my health. There's a zoology prof who wants to murder me in my sleep. I wouldn't last two days. Besides, I'm helping Patrick. I can learn. I'll be good."

Courtney laughed. Stepping forward, she unglued Liza's red nails from her scalp. "Relax. If Tony and Mookie are here, *they're* supposed to help him," Courtney said. She pointed to Liza's white suitcase, covered with happy-face stickers. "I just want you to choose your bunk and stow your things away."

Liza looked dumbfounded. "Then you're not mad?"

Courtney shrugged. "Sure I was mad. But I got over it."

"Oh, Courtney," Liza screamed, throwing her arms around Courtney's neck and squeezing her until Courtney nearly passed out. "Thank you. Thank you. Thank you."

"It's okay." Courtney pried herself away.

Liza clapped her hands. "I'll make it up to you. I'll do anything. I'll throw myself overboard. I'll . . ."

"Choose your bunk, Liza," Courtney ordered. She squeezed herself around the galley counter and began pushing Liza toward the forward cabin.

"Okay!" Liza ducked her head and stepped into the

tiny cabin. "I'll do it right now."

Courtney followed her to the cabin door, then planted her hands on her hips and watched Liza unpack. "Yeah, well, we're here to have fun, Liza. And you know how to have fun better than any of us. That's partly why I hired Mookie and Tony, you know. They're fun-loving types like yourself."

Liza bit her lip, stuffing an armful of clothes into a tiny door. "Gosh. I hope they work out. I mean, they seem pretty willing and all."

"Why not try them out? Life's too short," Courtney interrupted, only half believing her words. Actually, she wasn't as brave as she sounded. She'd checked Tony and Mookie thoroughly. Drivers' licenses. Student IDs. Everything. She had even run a background check on them through the St. Ramos police, just to be sure. But she didn't have to tell Liza that.

"All done. Gotta go," Liza broke in, sliding her suitcase against the wall and rubbing her hands together as she backed out the door. "Patrick had some chores for me."

"There's something else." Courtney pulled Liza back and half closed the cabin door. "Winnie."

Liza stepped back into the cramped space and ducked her head as she sat down on the bottom bunk. Then she shook her head. "Winnie? She's a walking, talking bad mood, and I don't blame her. But don't you think she'd be a little better by now? I mean, this is paradise."

Courtney leaned forward. "I think the trip will do

her a lot of good. Especially if she gets into sailing. She's so athletic and smart. I just know she'll have a feel for it."

"Yeah, well, speaking of sailing." Liza began to get up, obviously anxious to get back to Patrick's commands.

The sound of heavy thumping and crashing, however, made both of them stop. Suddenly their cabin door burst open, and Courtney stared at Tony and Mookie. They looked like escapees from Disneyland.

Courtney giggled. Mookie was wearing sunglasses with little pink antennae topped with orange foam-rubber balls that wiggled in the air. Tony had on a straw hat with a red, white, and blue band that read *Nixon's the One*. Both were wearing loud Hawaiian shirts. Stuffed in their arms were large duffels, boom boxes, and cardboard boxes filled with tapes and paraphernalia.

"Hey." Tony fell back a little, banging into the back of the dining-table bench. "Sorry. Wrong room."

"Hi, guys!" Liza squealed behind Courtney.

"He said aft," Mookie whispered loudly to Tony. "I guess that means the sleeping cabins in the back."

"Righto," Tony said with a good-natured grin.

"It's okay," Courtney said cautiously, pushing open the door and looking for a place to put her foot in the main cabin. She stared at the mounds of junk Mookie and Tony were slowly dropping to the floor. In addition to the diving equipment and boom boxes, the two had also brought two electric guitars, several harmonicas, a large Jamaican drum, and a portable mike.

Courtney narrowed her eyes. What did they need all this stuff for?

"We're part-time musicians," Tony explained with an awkward laugh. Behind him, Mookie had plastered a silly grin on his face. "I guess you could say we're men of many talents."

Courtney tried to look into some of the boxes. Were they carrying something she should know about?

Liza was eagerly pawing through their stuff, while Winnie wandered pale-faced down the hatchway.

"Okay, guys. Your cabin's over here," Courtney said patiently, stepping over the stuff and gesturing toward the aft cabins, formerly occupied by Alistair and his crew. She opened the narrow wooden door, then looked back at their acres of junk piled on the floor. "We didn't know you'd have this much stuff."

"No problemo," Tony said.

"It's cool," Mookie joined in. "Anywhere's okay."

"Yes, but in a rough sea, it's important to stow everything carefully," Courtney explained, placing a hand on her forehead and wondering if she was getting in too deep. "What could you possibly need all this stuff for?" she began, a little impatient. "It's just that I—uh—know Patrick is going to need his storage space for his valuable paintings."

"Don't worry about my paintings," Patrick's voice came from behind them. Everyone watched Patrick set down Tony and Mookie's huge saxophone and small Pignose amp. Then he moved toward them and braced his arm above the doorjamb. "There's no way I'm stowing those paintings in the crew cabins. Hey, my future depends on those two canvases. You can put the overflow in my berth."

Liza planted her hands on her hips. "Well, where in the heck are you going to keep the paintings, then?"

"I've stowed them in the port-side storage area, next to your cabin," Patrick explained, adjusting his glasses. His dark hair had been pulled back into a ponytail, and his green eyes were reassuring. He glanced at Courtney. "The boat I skippered six months ago had the same design. It's an especially secure compartment for valuables."

"Good," Courtney breathed. *Thank God for Patrick,* she thought to herself.

Patrick flashed her a good-natured grin and turned to go back on deck. "Leave your stuff for now, fellows. I need your help above."

Wide-eyed, Mookie and Tony dumped some of their stuff on their bunks and immediately rushed to follow him. Liza hurried after them, wiggling her fingers excitedly over her shoulder at Courtney.

Courtney took a deep breath and tried to relax as she headed back into the galley. It seemed as though every time she had things under control, another problem cropped up. And she was the one who had to solve it. Her eyes scanned the galley counters, and she swiftly began stowing her meats and vegetables in the galley's tiny fridge. But after only fifteen minutes, she heard shouting above. Scooting around the galley counter, she bent her head into the hatchway to listen.

"Cut it out, Mookie," Patrick was yelling from the

stern. "We're going to leave the dock under power."

Courtney scrambled up the hatchway and turned around so that she could look up toward the mast. Then she clamped her hand over her mouth in horror.

Mookie had apparently been fooling with the mainsail winch and had mistakenly begun to hoist it into the breeze, even though they were still docked and a strong breeze had come up. Halfway hoisted, the sail had begun to flap crazily in the wind. The *Bluebeard* began to rock and crash against the mooring.

"Let it down, Mookie!" Courtney yelled, grabbing a shroud and scrambling up toward the mast. She turned around just in time to notice Tony untying the mainsail sheet from its cleat near the helm.

"Stop, Tony," Courtney screamed. "You're making things worse!"

Suddenly confused, Tony let go of the loose sheet, sending the boom into a swing while the sail flapped down onto the deck and into the cockpit. Courtney looked on in frustration. Now the entire cockpit was filled with sail, and the boom was swinging wildly over the deck.

"Whoa," Tony cried out, his head making a ghost-like bump under the collapsed white sail.

"Uh-oh," Mookie called out worriedly, clinging to the mast, not knowing what to do.

"What the hell are you doing?" Patrick was shouting as he headed toward the mast, pulling the collapsed sail out of his path. With the sail flapping wildly, Patrick made a desperate effort to haphazardly furl it onto the boom. But a sudden gust blew the loose boom into his chest, nearly knocking him from the boat onto the dock.

Liza screamed from her spot near the bow. Tony and Mookie froze in terror.

Desperately Courtney tried to grab the boom, but it swung toward her and she was forced to duck. The sail was flapping crazily, making it hard for her and Patrick to get it under control. Crouched on her knees, Courtney felt hot tears behind her eyes. Mookie and Tony were complete and total clods on deck. What in the world had she done?

Just then, out of the corner of her eye, she saw a dark-eyed, intense young guy scramble up the side of the boat from the dock and swiftly grab the swinging boom. Before she realized what was happening, the stranger managed to single-handedly furl the sail back down on the boom, then leap to the helm and secure the mainsail sheet with swift, sure hands.

Patrick stood up, rubbing his head.

"Sorry about that," Mookie said sheepishly.

Patrick ignored him and headed toward the dark-eyed stranger, who was standing on the port-side deck, his hands shoved into the pockets of his grubby hiking shorts. Courtney watched as Patrick shook his hand. She stared at the guy's straight brown hair, flopped down over his forehead. He wore a tiny hoop earring in one ear, and slung around his neck was a thin silver chain with a small, blue-and-silver medal on it. Wearing a sloppy, torn sweatshirt and sneakers without socks, he didn't look like a typical seaman. But Courtney could tell that he'd been sailing for many years.

"Thanks," Patrick said, gratefully shaking the guy's hand. "I'm Patrick Hanson."

Courtney climbed over the foredeck and scrambled to her feet. She held on to a shroud and extended her hand, still breathing hard. "Thanks."

"I'm Jack Frederick Cruz," the guy said simply. He didn't smile, but there was a steadiness in his dark eyes that Courtney immediately liked. She glanced at his wiry, tanned, and muscled arms. "I'm looking for Courtney Conner," he added.

"I'm Courtney," she said cautiously. "Looks like you've spent some time sailing."

"That's right," Jack replied quickly. "Look. I overheard these two guys early this morning in the diving shop." Jack pointed his head in Mookie and Tony's direction. "From what I could tell, it sounded like you needed another experienced crewman for your trip."

Courtney's mouth dropped open. After watching Mookie and Tony's performance, she'd been thinking the very same thing. "Well, I . . ." she stammered.

Jack looked her in the eye. "If you need someone," he said simply, "I'm interested. I'm experienced. I'm reliable. And I need the job."

Courtney sank down weakly into the cockpit, staring at the laces on her deck shoes and wondering how much more she could take. Look how she'd managed to mess things up so far. Who did she think she was? An employment agency for every out-of-work guy she happened to run into in St. Ramos?

Everything was hopeless—the vacation, the boat, the crew, the delivery of the *Bluebeard*. Hire another stranger on instinct for an important trip like this? Should she, or shouldn't she? What made her think she could make a decent decision when everything around her was falling apart?

Falling apart and sinking into the deep blue St. Ramos waters.

Seven

What are you running away from? What are you running away from?

Winnie was slumped over the *Blue-beard*'s galley counter, her hands clamped over her ears. Over and over, the memory of the stranger in the alley thundered through her mind. She could still hear his question ringing in her ears. She could still feel his hand over her mouth. She could still feel the beating of his heart.

She shook her head as if she could shake out her tangled thoughts. Then she popped a minted mango chunk in her mouth, briefly wondering why Courtney had suddenly rushed back on deck.

What in the world was going on up there? Was it

possible for this trip to run into yet another disaster? Maybe it was destiny, just like Alistair said.

Grasping the side of the counter for balance, Winnie stepped around into the main cabin, where she flopped down on the cushioned bench next to the dining table. She looked up at the rocking ceiling. Sea gulls were screaming outside the galley portholes. The reflecting water was sending a weird, wavy light into the boat that made her feel as if she had dived into a deep swimming pool.

She'd barely slept the night before. Had she really been knocked down in an alley by a strange guy who'd asked her a haunting question? Or had it all been a dream?

"Am I running away?" Winnie asked herself again, giving in to the unsteady motion of the boat beneath her back. She lifted one arm up into the air and stared absently at the jangly bracelets slipping down her bare skin. After a day and a half of tropical luxury, she was more confused and homesick than ever. What she seemed to want now wasn't adventure at all. She wanted ordinariness.

"A bowl of Cheerios," Winnie whispered, her eyes misting over. "A walk across campus. Cheez Whiz on a Ritz. Rain."

Winnie looked up. On deck, it was obvious that people were scurrying about as if something had gone haywire with the boat. From the look of the two nutcases Courtney had hired to help crew, the cruise still could be in deep trouble. She clasped her hands together and hovered them above her chest, concentrating.

Do something crazy, you guys. Sink the boat. Ruin the sails, she thought. *Just do something so Courtney can call off the trip and I can go home and veg out.*

"Let it down, Mookie!" she could hear Courtney shouting on deck.

Winnie propped herself up on her elbows. The boat was beginning to rock, as if the breeze were blowing it. She supposed she should go up on deck and investigate. But she didn't want to talk to Courtney and she definitely didn't want to deal with Liza.

Winnie gritted her teeth. Earlier she'd been unloading groceries when she'd overheard Courtney and Liza talking about her. Maybe *Courtney* thought a sea voyage would make her happy. But Courtney had no idea. She was just another know-it-all pop psychologist who'd read something about depression in a magazine. As if Courtney could possibly understand what it was like to have a miscarriage. *Or have your marriage fall apart in your face,* Winnie thought bitterly.

The boat jerked again, and Winnie stood up. She put another mango chunk in her mouth. Then she dabbed her eyes with the bottom of her baggy tank top and climbed slowly up the steep hatchway.

Stumbling into the bright sunshine, Winnie pulled on her hot-pink sunglasses and stared ahead.

Then her heart stopped.

Sprawled casually on the deck, his hand lightly gripping the lifeline, was the guy who'd grabbed her in the alley. She instantly recognized his dark, intense face and flashing brown eyes. Wearing the same wrinkly khakis and torn-up sneakers, he didn't exactly look like the type of guy the yacht club allowed down on the docks. But there he was, talking and smiling to Courtney and Patrick as if it were the most ordinary thing in the world.

Oh, my God. He followed me, Winnie thought desperately. *He thinks I know something.*

Winnie sagged against the top of the hatchway. She drew her hand up to her mouth and blinked. He looked different. What was it? His smile? He had very white, straight teeth. The kind of teeth that matched a clean-shaven face, not a five-day stubble. He held himself like a graceful, trained athlete. So why was he dressed like a bum?

What was it about him that was so full of contradictions?

Then Winnie shook herself. It *was* him. It *hadn't* been a dream. The guy had brutally attacked her, and was obviously running from the law. She had a sudden impulse to start screaming for the police. Then she had a second, stronger urge to grab him and ask him what he'd meant. And what he was doing here on the *Bluebeard*.

"Hey, Win," KC murmured, messing up Winnie's stand-on-end hair. She'd crawled on her hands and knees down the foredeck and was hanging over into the cockpit where Winnie was standing. "Look who we just picked up. Cute, huh?"

Winnie felt her heart speed up. She hadn't told anyone about her alley experience. Now, as she looked at his handsome, lean face, she wondered if she should have.

"Mookie and Tony made a mess of the rigging," KC drawled. "You missed it. It was better than the

Three Stooges, except that it almost wrecked our trip."

"Too bad," Winnie mumbled, her eyes fixed on the stranger. His arms were crossed casually over his chest as he leaned against the boat's railing.

"Anyway," KC whispered, "this guy came leaping up from the dock and caught the sail. Everything's falling apart and he seems to know just what to do. He's incredible."

"Yeah," Winnie murmured. For a moment, KC and Winnie stared at him as he continued chatting with Patrick and Courtney. After a while, the three began laughing together, and the stranger looked over toward the cockpit where Winnie was still standing.

Winnie held her breath. For a split second, their eyes locked.

The guy looked away quickly, then gulped. She could see him freeze, as if he weren't paying attention to what Patrick and Courtney were saying. Then a moment later he turned his head slowly and looked at Winnie again.

Winnie just stood there, clutching the hatch cover and staring back, unable to move. She couldn't bring herself to say anything. There was something in his eyes, something she'd noticed the day before. Maybe it was fear. Maybe it was understanding.

But whatever it was, Winnie knew it was familiar.

"He likes you," KC whispered, just as Liza came lumbering down the starboard deck and sprawled next to KC on her stomach.

"Guys, guys, guys," Liza moaned, her hair a frizzy cloud of red against the sky. "I'm telling you, girls, I've never seen so many cute guys in my entire life. It must be the sea air. The water. The local eating habits . . ."

Just then Courtney broke away and headed down the port deck, slipping her legs down into the cockpit bench. Winnie saw that her face looked strangely confused. Courtney motioned for them to huddle.

"What's wrong?" KC asked, twisting a strand of dark hair and casting a glance up toward Patrick on the foredeck.

"Is this Love Boat-time or what?" Liza cracked, crossing her legs in front of her.

"This guy wants to help crew the boat to Gregory Cays," Courtney said quietly, looking a little desperate.

Winnie's eyes widened. Courtney Conner, Miss Sorority President and Psychological Know-it-All, actually looked a little *confused*. It was almost enough to make Winnie laugh out loud. Could this be Courtney's first experience with feeling totally *out of control*?

"But we don't know anything about him," KC said. Winnie was silent.

Courtney frowned and cast a glance at Liza. "I know, but we seem to be stuck with Mookie and Tony, and we need another experienced crewman—fast."

"Run a background check on him," KC whispered.

"We don't have time," Courtney said quickly, wrenching her fingers nervously back and forth. "The *Bluebeard* has to be at Gregory Cays in exactly seven days. That means we have to leave today—right now— or we'll miss the deadline. My parents are counting on it. The sale could fall through if we don't."

"A million bucks!" Liza blurted, before clamping her hand over her mouth.

Courtney gave her a stern look. Then she pulled her knees up to her chest and stared determinedly at the mast. "All we know about him is that his name is Jack Frederick Cruz and he's spent a lot of time around boats. I'm going to be democratic about this. Since we're all in this together, I want to know what all of you think."

Liza pressed her lips together and looked down, clearly too embarrassed and guilty to say anything.

"We *could* use more help," KC said slowly. "I mean, Patrick's a wonderful sailor and everything. But I'd feel a lot better if he had someone really good to help him."

Winnie crossed her arms over her chest and stared defiantly at a passing cruise yacht, gleaming under the fiery St. Ramos sun. Two ladies in white hats sat comfortably in deck chairs, their laughter tinkling out over the harbor. Beyond them, a hundred masts swayed peacefully against the blue sky as if they'd never passed through a storm.

Comfort and predictability, Winnie thought bitterly. *People like Courtney and the other yacht-club ladies think they've cornered the market on it. They think they can swing into a gritty place like the Caribbean and still have it all under control.*

Winnie looked up at Courtney's pretty face. Did she have any idea what life was really like? Or would she go through life thinking it was a pretty picnic? She could haul Courtney down to the Crisis Hotline when she got back to Springfield. Or she could start right now, and say nothing about the guy Courtney was about to hire.

The guy who was definitely trouble.

"You need the help, don't you?" Winnie said softly, digging her nails into the palm of her hand. "So take a chance and hire him."

"Okay," Courtney said nervously.

Winnie sat perfectly still as Courtney approached Jack Frederick Cruz, shook his hand, and offered him the job. After a moment, he swung himself back down to the dock, then returned a few minutes later, carrying a beat-up leather suitcase. Winnie bit the inside of her lip when she saw that it was secured with a heavy brass padlock.

With one quick movement, Jack jumped into the cockpit and stowed his suitcase in a secure area next to the cabin door. Then he turned around to look at Winnie.

For a moment Winnie bravely held his gaze. He nodded as if he understood she didn't plan to say anything. Then he leaped up to the port deck and clambered over to the mainsail, where Patrick was readjusting the rigging.

Okay, Mr. Outlaw. Mr. Dangerous, Winnie thought with a sigh. *Go ahead and mess things up. Take us prisoner. Ransom us. Sink the boat. Maybe that will bring everyone down to where I am.*

Maybe then someone might begin to understand.

Eight

"Jack and Courtney, take the bow and stern lines," Patrick called out two hours later, one arm confidently braced against the wheel. "We're ready to cast off."

"OOOHHH," Liza sang from the starboard deck, throwing her head back and clutching one of the stiff shrouds that ran down from the mast. "I FEEL GOOD. DA-DA-DA-DA-DA-DA-DA. LIKE I KNEW THAT I WO-OULD."

Courtney laughed at Liza while she scrambled down the ladder to the dock. With swift, sure hands, she untied the stern line from its cleat. Then, still holding the end of the line, she fixed her foot on a rung of the ladder and pushed off the dock.

KC reached eagerly for the line Courtney held up for her. The sparkling water splashed against the white hull, sending dancing light into her eyes.

"Way to go, KC," Courtney shouted, jumping on deck.

"Ready, Jack?" Patrick shouted.

"Watch this amazing trick," KC laughed, coiling the line expertly around her thumb and elbow, as Patrick had shown her. She tied it off, then hung it neatly on the port railing.

"Wow!" Patrick yelped behind her. "One minute at sea, and already you can see her astounding potential. No—really, I mean it."

KC took a bow in Patrick's direction, feeling the thrill of his stare. She looked blissfully up at the puffy clouds in the sapphire sky, wondering what she'd done to deserve such happiness. They were leaving port. They were on their way, at last.

"Ready to cast off," Jack called from the dock. Holding the bowline, he gave the dock a powerful shove with his leg before he nimbly hopped back on the *Bluebeard*.

"Way to go," KC couldn't help shouting, still crouched on the port deck, her fingers clasped to the railing. The sun was warm on her bare legs. The air smelled like salt water, coconut oil, and the hot wooden boards of the dock. There was the faint, biting scent of the diesel fuel they'd just loaded into their gas tanks. Everything looked and smelled like adventure to her. And inside, she was swooning with excitement.

"Yahoo!" Liza yelled, shaking her hair in the

breeze. "We're off!" KC answered, watching Patrick ease the throttle forward gently at the helm. She gripped the railing to keep from toppling back. She watched as Patrick carefully steered the boat past the other moored boats, until they finally passed the last piling and pulled out into the emerald and blue harbor.

"We'll stay under power until we're out of the harbor," Patrick shouted at Jack up at the mast. "Then we'll head up into the wind and hoist the mainsail and mizzen."

KC watched Jack give a silent nod. He stepped toward the sail covers on the boom and began checking the flat nylon ties holding the mainsail in place.

"KC, will you get me that chart book in the navigation niche, please?" Patrick asked.

Saluting, KC hopped down and swung her body into the narrow hatchway. By the time she'd grabbed the chart and got back on deck, the *Bluebeard* was swiftly humming its way past the clusters of other bobbing boats and masts. Soon they were out of the harbor, leaving a gentle white wake in the warm seawater. KC stared back at the receding view. A fringe of coconut palms on the southern arm of St. Ramos Harbor seemed to be waving them a peaceful good-bye. The pink, white, and blue houses of the town were slowly turning into blurry patches of color on the bushy slopes.

Twisting around, she spotted Winnie up at the bow, sitting with her knees drawn up to her chest, staring quietly out to sea. Meanwhile, down in the galley, Mookie and Tony had been on vegetable- and shrimp-peeling duty—Courtney's orders.

"I'm going to watch your every move," KC heard herself call boldly to Patrick, settling herself behind the helm. They were out on the open sea now, and she felt ready for adventure. "Maybe I'll come out of this knowing something about sailing."

Patrick turned around and flashed her an optimistic grin. "You should," he called back, his white shirt whipping against his wide shoulders. "I think you'll like it, once you get the hang of it."

"I'd say we'll get a nice little eight-knot wind out around this point," Jack called to Patrick from the mast, where he was readying the mainsail for hoisting. "It'll be an easy beam reach out to the Pitons."

KC sighed. Their destination for that evening was one of the tiny islands stretching to the south of St. Ramos. According to Patrick, they'd be sailing out of the lee side of St. Ramos's magnificent mountains, making for a smooth sail until they were farther out and subject to the eastern trade winds.

At least for now, KC thought peacefully, there'd be no need for Courtney's vast supply of seasickness pills and skin patches.

"Ready to haul the mainsail," Patrick called through the breeze. Then he pointed to a heavy white line wrapped around a winch near the helm. "KC—untie the mainsail sheet from the cleat, but don't let go."

KC scrambled over and followed Patrick's orders. Then she watched Jack powerfully hoist the *Bluebeard*'s magnificent mainsail up into the blue sky. She felt a pull as the wind poured into it. The boat heeled over slightly, and she turned to brace her sneakers against the lifeline in back of her.

"Hoist the jib," Patrick ordered, staring confidently ahead as he reached over and rapidly rotated the winch that controlled the boom and pulled in the sail. Meanwhile, Courtney was scrambling up to the bow, where she hoisted the smaller jib sail. KC felt another pull and looked behind at the line of white wake churning behind them.

"Take the jib sheet, Jack," Patrick shouted as the boat began to thunder over the swells just outside the harbor. "Then ease off a little."

KC stood up on her knees and smiled, grasping the railing to keep from falling overboard. The boat heeled over as it hit another series of bumps. She let out a tiny giggle at first, then an out-and-out laugh of pure joy. Suddenly the clear water was racing beneath them, and the sky above her was full of billowing sail. In the distance, she could see St. Ramos's green slopes slipping by. Salt water sprayed her face. The sun shone. Her wet shoelaces slapped against her ankles. She never wanted it to stop.

For the next several hours, KC learned to take the helm, read the Fathometer, and use the wind gauge. Patrick even gave her a lesson in watching the movement of the wind on the surface of the water. She was beginning to understand how the sails connected to the sheets that controlled them.

Between her sailing duties, KC also had time to lean back and enjoy the amazing views. The flat blue stretch of water seemed to go on forever, though if she squinted, she could see the promise of other islands dotted here and there on the horizon. She felt free, strong, and sure of herself. After all, in less than one year of college, she'd managed to travel all the way from small-town Jacksonville to the exotic Caribbean.

If she could do that, she could do anything: run a large corporation, run for president. The possibilities were limitless.

Later that day, while Patrick busily charted their course and Courtney chatted with Jack about sailing, KC climbed up to the starboard deck with a towel so that she could lie on her stomach and stare down into the deep coral reefs slipping below in the cobalt-blue water. On her right, deserted sugar-white sand beaches passed by, each one looking more perfect than the last. Above, she could see the occasional white pelican, winging its way casually along the coastline. Tiny white terns dipped and screamed above the masts.

Around two o'clock, after a lunch of cool mangoes, banana bread, and Courtney's marinated shrimp salad, KC could see the fringy outline of a perfectly circular island about a mile away. Rubbing the sea spray off her sunglasses, KC sprang up to the bow and settled in for a better view. All around them, the sea lay flat and clear as bathtub water.

"Anchoring in the Pitons is tricky," Jack called back to Patrick from the bow. "The land drops off sharply only a few hundred feet offshore."

"Right." Patrick nodded, steering straight ahead. "Let the mainsail out about ten feet and ease off on the jib. We'll make a short stop here for a few hours."

The *Bluebeard*'s bow cut neatly through the glassy water.

"We'll drop anchor off the stern a couple of hundred feet out," Patrick ordered. "Jack, you take the bowline in the skiff and tie it down to one of those overhanging palms. Courtney and KC, you'll furl the jib and mainsail."

KC jumped up, then watched as Courtney's privileged yachting background sprang into action. On Patrick's command, she calmly let down the jib sail and piled it neatly on the bow. Then she unhooked the line securing the mainsail winch and slowly let the huge sail down.

Courtney pointed to the boom. "Right over here, KC, we're going to gather the sail back down onto the boom and tie it with these little ties. The wind's died down, so we shouldn't have any problem."

KC nodded, aware that Patrick was watching her every move. She, in turn, watched Courtney, determined to learn everything she could while she was on the *Bluebeard*. Struggling to control the flapping sail, she clung to the boom and scrunched it down into place. Courtney, on the other hand, easily braced her pure-white deck shoes on the foredeck and furled the sail as easily as she had ordered the gourmet food and tipped the porter at the hotel.

KC bit her lip. She *would* learn to sail.

"Liza, you keep an eye on the Fathometer," Patrick yelled. "Let us know if it's getting really shallow."

"Aye-aye," Liza shouted back, climbing eagerly back to the helm.

From her perch, KC could see that the *Bluebeard*

was nosing its way gently over a coral reef. A luminous beach approached. Patrick carefully dropped anchor. It looked as if KC was going to have her first taste of a real-life deserted island.

"We're set!" Jack called out across the water, his hands flashing as he whipped the *Bluebeard*'s nylon bowline around a sturdy-looking coconut palm. The yacht was now secure, suspended neatly between its anchor and the tree.

"Go for it," Mookie yelled, as he and Tony emerged from dishwashing duty belowdeck. A second later they were jumping off the deck and making loud splashes in the shining water. "Primo diving!"

Meanwhile, Winnie had crawled back from the bow into the cockpit and was hovered, gray-faced, over Patrick's nautical map of the area.

KC hopped down next to Winnie. "Come on. Let's explore. It's our first deserted island, Win!"

Winnie frowned and turned the map around. "Which island *is* this?" She squinted up at Patrick, who'd joined Courtney up at the mast.

Liza looked at the map too, trying to comfort Winnie, who was nibbling on her nails and looking anxious. "Come on, hon. Who cares? It's all the same when you're in paradise, right, Captain?" She gave Patrick a sultry smile as he jumped back down into the cockpit and rechecked the stern line.

"Are you kidding, Winnie?" Patrick said, giving the line a cheerful tug. "The Caribbean is so full of tiny islands like this, no map could ever accurately pinpoint each and every one."

"That's what makes it such an adventure!" Courtney called out, slipping down from the foredeck and grabbing the jumbled jib sheet. Swiftly she began coiling it.

"Mmmm," Liza agreed, casting a knowing look Patrick's way, grasping the edge of the helm and stretching her body out.

KC narrowed her eyes and sat down on the cockpit bench. She glanced at Liza, then at Patrick.

Winnie was still panicking. "This is complete and total madness."

Patrick gave KC a look of concern, then stepped over to Winnie. He pointed to a shadowy section of the map. "The geography is always changing around here. Plus, there's so much fan coral in these islands, some of these shores have never been visible. In fact, sailboats are occasionally lost or wrecked and are never found."

"WHAT?" Winnie cried, looking frantically around at the flat, blue water. "We could get lost out here?"

"Don't be silly, Winnie," Courtney reassured her, laying her neatly coiled line down on the seat.

"We've got state-of-the-art equipment on board," Patrick said quietly. "A beautiful radar system and a ship-to-shore radio."

Winnie crossed her thin arms and sulked. A moment later she was dragging herself back down to her cabin.

"I'm going to work on tonight's menu," Courtney broke in with a cheerful smile. "I'll be down in the galley taking a look at those fresh swordfish steaks."

"I'll see if I can help on deck," KC called to Courtney, glancing back at Patrick, who had settled on the edge of the cockpit and was opening a can of soda. For an instant she tried to think of something to say. But before she could open her mouth, Liza began slinking across the boat cushions—right toward Patrick.

KC knew exactly what Liza was up to. And of course Liza was dressed for the kill in a coral-pink bathing suit with a splashy, pink-and-orange-print wrap around her waist. KC watched her climb up to the cockpit bench on her knees, then turn around and sit on the ledge of the cockpit next to Patrick. Liza snuggled up next to him and crossed her legs, her white skin glaring in the Caribbean sunlight. "So, Patrick," she said softly, "how's your first day as captain? Everything okay?"

KC leaned back against the hatch and coiled a loose line around her index finger. She wanted to wring Liza's neck. How could Patrick possibly take her seriously?

Patrick took a swig of his soda and nodded, clenching his handsome jaw a little. "Nice boat. Good crew. I'd say we're doing fine."

"Oh, you're just saying that." Liza inched closer. "I bet you've taken hundreds of tourists out here. You probably always butter them up."

"Nope," Patrick insisted, staring across at the line of vanilla beach, where Jack had banked the tiny skiff. "A lot of folks who can afford boats like this are pretty hard to please," Patrick admitted, turning toward her. His eyes traveled briefly down Liza's full figure, as if he were noticing her for the first time. "Hey, you look great, Liza."

"All dressed up, with nowhere to go," Liza drawled, leaning into his shoulder.

Patrick gave a good-natured laugh, then looked at KC, as if he were trying to include her in their little chat. "Aw, I wouldn't say that. I'd say we were going somewhere in this beautiful boat."

Liza leaned closer and winked. "Are we?"

KC shifted. Patrick wasn't really flirting with Liza. But Liza had practically draped herself over him, and he wasn't exactly walking away.

Liza threw back her head and laughed, nudging Patrick conspiratorially. "Now, look out for my friend KC over there. She's a real take-charge woman back on campus. She'll be taking the helm pretty soon if you don't watch out."

KC was boiling.

Patrick smiled at them both. "That's okay with me. I like it when the crew gets involved."

Liza wet her lips and recrossed her legs so that her toe was tickling Patrick's leg. "You do?"

KC clenched her jaw. She didn't have the stomach to continue vying with Liza for Patrick's attention. Plus, Tony and Mookie had just climbed back on board and were starting to sort through their diving equipment.

"Primo diving situation," Tony gloated, pulling his black wet suit on over his legs.

"Excellen-te," Mookie said, faking an Italian accent.

"Mag-nee-fee-sant," Tony replied, with a huge, silent guffaw.

KC walked toward them. "Where are you going to dive? Why is it so good here?"

"Visibility." Mookie looked at her as if she were slightly dense. "We've got a hundred-plus visibility. And the reef's amazing. Staghorn corals, sea whips, sea fans, brain corals—and a whole school of angelfish. Tony saw a blue-striped grunt—"

"Nah, it's not just that," Tony broke in. "The bottom starts out at about thirty feet right here, then drops off like a knife edge to probably three hundred. I bet that shelf is full of caves."

KC's heart sped up. "I've always wanted to dive," she heard herself say, propelled by her irritation over Patrick and Liza. "I'm a strong swimmer, but I've never lived close to the ocean. And diving lessons are really expensive."

Mookie's and Tony's heads shot up. Then they looked at each other, turned to face her, and locked their elbows together as a sign of solidarity. *"We'll teach you,"* they said in almost perfect unison.

"Really?" KC murmured, suddenly filled with second thoughts as she stared at their wacky grins and silly straw hats.

"Come on!" Mookie cried out eagerly, his sunglasses slipping off his nose. "This boat has a ton of gear."

KC planted her hands on her hips. "Just like that?"

"You'll drown for sure with these knuckleheads," Liza warned, giggling over her shoulder at KC. "There's no way I'm touching that water."

"She won't drown," Patrick said suddenly. "Not if she's a strong swimmer and she's getting the right advice."

"Righto," Tony urged KC, snapping the cuffs of his wet suit and reaching for his flippers. "Come on. We'll show you the ropes."

"No, please," Patrick broke in, getting up and setting his can of soda down on the helm. "Let me."

KC was thrilled. Liza wasn't.

"KC will be okay with Tony and Mookie," Liza whined in the background. "Come on, Patrick. Sit in the nice sun with me."

"Later, Liza. I've done a lot of diving in this area, and I'd like to get KC off to a good start," Patrick said firmly.

"Well, have fun, KC," Tony said, slipping on his air tank. "We're gonna take off, then. We've got some exploring to do. Right, Mook?"

Mookie saluted. "Exploring. Right you are."

"Bye, guys." KC smiled at them. "Thanks anyway. Be careful down there."

"Okay, well, I've got lots to do, Patrick," Liza said loudly, still pouting on the stern. "My nails are a wreck from all this work, and I'm reading a very fine historical novel written by Scarlett Rosamond de Genevievre. You heard of her?"

Before Liza had finished, KC was already following Patrick obediently belowdeck, where he found the diving equipment and began checking it over. She could barely breathe, she was so excited.

"Courtney's rented some first-rate equipment,"

Patrick said quietly, giving her body a shy look as he handed her a thin black wet suit. "This looks like your size."

"Thanks," KC whispered. A small wave rocked the cabin a little, and her chest bumped into his momentarily. "Whoops. Um. Excuse me," she stammered.

"It's okay." Patrick looked down at her in the dim light. "It happens all the time when you sail. You get to know the rest of the crew pretty well."

KC's throat was so tight she couldn't speak. Patrick's face was still a little sweaty from working on deck, and some of his dark hair clung to the skin of his tanned brow. He looked like one of those handsome, intelligent oceanographers they were always photographing for *National Geographic*. Finally Patrick turned and gathered the rest of the diving equipment, and she followed him back up on deck, hardly believing that soon she would be diving into the clear Caribbean.

Nine

"We'll head due south to Sucia Island, Jack," Patrick called from the hatchway later that afternoon. "Anchor there for the night."

Winnie was nestled in a corner of the cockpit, trying to read *Psychology Today,* though the brisk wind was beginning to send her pages flapping in the air. A salty spray flew into her face, and she had to brace her foot against the hatch opening just to stay upright.

She looked back briefly at Jack at the helm, his fingers hooked around the wheel and his dark eyes fixed on a distant point. The breeze picked up even more, turning the blue sea into a choppy washboard.

"Winds are from the east at eight knots," Jack

shouted, his eyes not moving. He let the mainsail sheet out a few feet, and Winnie felt her back press into the cockpit bench as the *Bluebeard* picked up even more speed.

Patrick gave him a thoughtful nod, as if he were beginning to think Jack was a bit of a mystery too. "Good," he yelled back, bracing himself against the inside of the hatch a few feet from Winnie. "We should be there in four hours."

"With luck," Jack said quietly. He pulled his beat-up baseball cap farther down on his head, his eyes fixed on a strip of darkness on the horizon. Winnie followed his gaze and saw it too. The boat bumped against the whitecaps, splashing the top of Winnie's head. A sea gull screamed overhead.

"Hey." Patrick's bobbing head popped up again through the hatch. He grinned across at Winnie. "I'm briefing the crew at fifteen hundred hours. That's now."

Winnie bent her lips into the barest smile. "Okay. I'll be down." Then she slid her eyes back in Jack's direction. It was clear that everyone was expected belowdeck for the meeting while Jack remained at the helm. For the first time since they'd left St. Ramos Harbor, she was alone with Jack. One-on-one with the guy who'd brutally knocked her down and grabbed her in the alley. She braced herself. She wanted to find out what he'd been running from. What if he were some kind of dangerous criminal? For all she knew, he could be ready to throw her overboard when no one was looking.

She bit her lip and wondered if anyone would miss

her. Then she stuffed her magazine between the cushions and walked down the windy cockpit toward Jack. She grasped the edge of the wooden helm and gave him a challenging look.

For a split second, Jack met her gaze. Then he wrenched his eyes back to the horizon. Winnie could see the muscles in his jaw clench.

"Well?" Winnie suddenly said over the wind.

Jack turned the wheel slightly, then gave her a sharp stare. He looked as if he hadn't shaved in a week, but there was still something clean-cut about him. In fact, Winnie realized, if he trimmed his hair and put on different clothes, he would look very different. Maybe even like the rich, preppie types Courtney hung around with at the U of S.

Winnie could tell that Jack didn't want to talk, but she wasn't giving up. She wanted the truth. And why not? Things were basic out here on the open sea. It made her feel like not playing games. There was the water, the sky, and a bunch of people trying to use their wits to stay afloat. There were no tourists taking their status vacations. No imitation-pearl necklaces and cast-off island carvings. No implausibly huge cabin cruisers. It was real—maybe even dangerous—out at sea. And it made Winnie want to be honest.

"Aren't you going to say anything?" she said.

Jack shrugged. "What do you want to hear?"

"Are you kidding? Look at me," she said, holding her free arm out to the side while Jack's eyes traveled briefly down her body. "Don't you remember? St. Ramos's back alley? You knock me down, scare me half to death, then trap me behind a bunch of old boxes while the police look for you?"

Jack looked straight ahead, his eyes half closed against the wind.

"What's going on?" Winnie cried.

He frowned and shifted his position.

"Look, I could have called the police," Winnie ranted. "But like a crazy fool, I didn't. And now you have a cushy job crewing this stupid yacht. So tell me what the hell you were doing back there, and who you are, and why you're here on the *Bluebeard*."

Jack drew in a sharp breath and set his lips. "And who are *you?*" he finally snapped, his dark eyes suddenly clamped on hers.

"*What?*" Winnie cried.

"You heard me," he said grimly. "Who do you guys think you are? A bunch of trust-fund-happy college punks? A few spoiled, fun-loving kids with nothing better to do than hire me to sail your daddy's boat around a bunch of islands?"

Winnie narrowed her eyes. "*One* of us is trust-fund happy. And I'm not her. And I'm not having fun."

Jack's eyes seemed to soften. He looked away, the wind whipping his hair. His fingers loosened on the wheel. "I can see that," he said over his shoulder, barely loud enough for her to hear.

"See what?" Winnie snapped, staring down at the tip of her sneaker.

"That you're not like them."

Squeals of laughter rose from the cabin. There was a blast of music.

"So why are you here?" Jack suddenly asked.

Winnie looked over at him and saw that he was looking at her intently. Suddenly she felt very small and helpless, out there in the middle of the vast ocean. A warm breeze fell against her face and she looked up at the billowing sails above them. Half of her wanted to tell him that she was running away from Josh, from the lost baby—running away from the pain.

Instead she bit her lip and looked down at her lap. Hot tears began to well up in her eyes.

"Okay, then," Jack spoke up, his voice loosening a little. "*I'll* tell you why you're here."

Winnie's eyes darted up. For some reason, she had the feeling he'd been reading her mind. She suddenly felt shy, suddenly terrified. There was something strangely intimate about being together with someone in the middle of a boundless sea. Even when that someone was a complete stranger, and probably an outlaw.

"You're here because *here* is better than being somewhere else," Jack finally said, throwing his head back and letting the wind blow through his scruffy brown hair. Gripping the mainsail winch, he took in the sail slightly. "Someplace even worse."

Winnie pressed her lips together and stood up, grabbing on to the aluminum rail that wound around the back of the cockpit. His words had been like a dart aimed directly at her heart. "Thanks for the free analysis," she said quickly, stepping along the curve of the cockpit seat until she reached the hatch.

Turning to climb down the hatchway, Winnie

brushed a stray tear off her cheek. At the bottom she waited for her eyes to adjust to the yellow cabin light and the closeness of the air. Then she stared at the merrymakers. The big teak table had been extended so that it filled up the entire main cabin, making it practically impossible to reach hers—or the galley. Packed around it were KC, Patrick, Liza, Mookie, Tony, and Courtney—all eating pineapple, skewered chicken, salsa dip, and pitchers of Courtney's mock margaritas. Mookie and Tony had stuck chips into their ears, while KC was trying to inch closer to Patrick without being obvious. Meanwhile, Liza was standing on one of the benches, trying not to hit her head on the ceiling as she kicked her legs up and sang the title song from *Grease*.

Courtney had clamped her hand over her mouth, trying to control her giggling. But when she saw Winnie, a look of pity flooded her face.

Winnie stiffened.

"Come on in, Win," Courtney called gently. "Everybody slide over and make room for Winnie. Patrick's trying to get us to listen."

"That'll be the day," Patrick said good-naturedly. "You all think I just want to make you work. Which is true, actually."

"We'll listen to you, man," Tony guffawed, pulling a chip out of his ear and eating it.

Everyone gagged and burst into hysterical laughter. No one seemed to mind as the *Bluebeard* began to pitch against another series of swells.

"We're going to play charades later, Winnie," Liza yelled across the room. "It's gonna be a scream." She reached out and slapped Mookie on the shoulder, nearly tipping over one of the glasses. "Are you going to be able to keep up with us, you guys?"

Tony raised his glass and closed his eyes. "We live to party."

"Yeah," Liza drawled. "Well, you guys are clearly oxygen starved after being in the ocean all afternoon."

"Not," Tony boomed, as glasses clinked and the noise level rose to hurricane levels.

Winnie turned and scrambled back up the stairs. She knew Jack was trouble, but he was better than the other weirdos she was stuck with. And there was something about him that half of her wanted to know better.

When she stuck her head out the hatch, she felt the cool spray against her face and the comforting roar of the wind. It was the kind of sound that made her feel lonely, but also somehow solitary and safe. The way she felt at the beach, or standing next to the white-water rapids near Jacksonville.

Winnie grasped the railing and crawled around behind the helm again. There was a break in the clouds, and she had to squint against the flood of sunlight that poured over the deck. Winnie drew the salty air into her lungs.

She crossed her legs and stared at Jack's strong back, solid beneath his ripped sweatshirt, fluttering in the warm wind. "A *padlock*? Is that really necessary?" Winnie couldn't help asking out loud.

Jack turned and rolled his eyes at Winnie.

Winnie crossed her arms and braced her shoes against the deck. "Are you afraid of us? Think we're interested in rifling through your things?"

"You figure it out," he said over his shoulder, turning the wheel a little with the heel of his hand.

"Okay," Winnie answered, looking up thoughtfully at a puffy white cloud sailing across the sky. "I think you're smuggling drugs. I think the cops in St. Ramos almost caught you. And I think you lucked out getting a job on the *Bluebeard*. It was a good way to sneak out of town with a minimum of fuss."

Jack gave her a disgusted look. "You've been reading too many cheap novels," he said.

"No, I haven't," Winnie said, shoving her hands under her knees and leaning forward. "I'm a college student, remember? I read nothing but textbooks. Got a contact at Gregory Cays or something?"

"You should be *writing* one of those cheap novels," Jack quipped. Winnie thought she detected a slight smile flicker over his face.

"Well?"

"Well, what?" Jack narrowed his eyebrows.

"Tell me," Winnie said boldly, leaning forward. "About the padlock. About anything."

"Look," Jack said hoarsely, finally relaxing his shoulders and turning to face her. "Here's the deal. My suitcase comes with the lock because I've been crashing in some pretty dangerous dives on St. Ramos. And the cops were after me because I stole some food from one of the vendors in town."

Winnie's mouth dropped open. Jack didn't look like a common thief. "You didn't even have money to buy food?" she asked.

"Nope."

She put her hand on her hip. "You expect me to believe that? A smart guy like you? You can't get it together to feed yourself?"

For a moment, Jack just froze. A stray gust of wind blew in from the south, sending the mainsail into a fit of noisy flapping. It was a moment before he had the sail under control. Then he fell back into the seat behind the helm and held the wheel in place with the side of his knee.

Winnie softened. His faraway look reminded her of herself. "How'd you let yourself get into such bad shape?" she couldn't help asking.

There was a long silence as Jack stared out past the wheel. Then he stuffed his hands into his pants pockets. "Funny, isn't it? Sometimes you just don't know everything is wrong—until it's too late."

Winnie felt her insides quaking. It was as if Jack had said out loud what she'd been thinking ever since the morning she'd packed her suitcase and left Josh. Tears threatened to spill out of her eyes. She pressed her shaking fingers to her face and bent down over her knees.

"Hey, what's wrong? What are you thinking?" Jack asked.

Winnie didn't speak, didn't move. She didn't tell him what was wrong—she didn't have to. Something told her that Jack already knew.

Ten

*L*iza leaned against the galley sink after lunch the next day, trying to get her thoughts straight. Her soapy hands were dripping all over her bare feet, but she was too nauseated to care.

"Feeling sick?" Courtney asked as the boat heeled over slightly. Looking up from her minced shallots, she popped her blond head over to the nearest porthole and looked out. "Looks like the wind has picked up. Want some seasickness pills? They work, but they can make you a little tired and thirsty."

Straightening up, Liza wiped the last lunch plate and gave Courtney a determined look. "I've never been seasick in my life. In fact, I feel like a million bucks. Life in the fast lane. Just the way I like it."

Courtney's cola-brown eyes lit up. Then she reached up and opened a cabinet over the cutting board, taking out a jar of expensive Greek olives. "You're a sport. I knew you'd be, Liza. Well, if you need anything, I'll be in our cabin."

Liza nodded as she slid her elbows out onto the galley counter and stared into the main cabin, steadying herself. Grasping the edge, she sidled around the counter and made her way past the now-folded dining table. She peeked into the forward cabin, where Winnie was reading. Then she looked in the opposite bunk and smiled.

KC, who'd been craftily maneuvering for Patrick's attention since they had first met him in town, was fast asleep.

Aw, look at that, Liza thought. *KC's claws are all tucked up inside her furry little paws. Sleep tight, Little Miss Perfect.*

She took a deep breath and grinned. KC may have gone diving with Patrick yesterday, and gotten very cozy with him around the after-dinner campfire on Sucia Island. But now KC was obviously tired from all that activity. Liza, on the other hand, was fully rested and in tip-top condition. She closed the door and clenched her fists in victory.

Liza smiled to herself. Ever since KC had emerged from her diving lesson with Patrick yesterday, she'd been walking around starry-eyed and superior.

"As if Patrick wouldn't have taken me diving if I'd so much as whispered the thought to him. Give me a break," Liza muttered. She headed back toward the hatchway. The sound of pounding drums and screechy electric guitars thundered through the door of Mookie and Tony's cabin. Liza rubbed her hands together. Even her distracting party boys were busy.

Stealing a peek into a cabin-door mirror, Liza neatened her lipstick. She adjusted the ties under the bust of her sleeveless midriff blouse covered with pictures of little anchors and ropes. Then she made her way confidently up the hatchway and held herself steady at the top. The breeze was snapping through her hair, and the *Bluebeard*'s hull was splashing through the whipped-up sea.

"Ahoy there," Liza called to Jack, who was positioned at the helm, looking stonily into space. She stepped onto a cockpit cushion and grabbed the lifeline railing. Then she squinted at the line of clouds moving swiftly overhead. "Where's Patrick?"

Jack jerked his chin up, motioning to the foredeck behind her. Liza craned her neck. Sitting on the starboard deck, his head buried in a chart, was Patrick. His back was leaned against the side of the cabin, and his deck shoes were braced against the yacht's stainless-steel railing. With his super-dark yachtsman's sunglasses and light, coppery skin, he looked like your perfect rugged, sensitive type. The type she never ran into. Until now.

Liza wiggled her painted toes and climbed toward him, feeling more confident by the second. Tall, elegant KC might be the most gorgeous and sought-after girl on the U of S campus. But it could be that her model-perfect looks weren't going to work out here in the gritty Caribbean.

After all, Liza thought with satisfaction, grasping a shroud for balance, KC thought along one line, and one line only: business, money, and success. She was obsessed. Patrick was an artist, and artists liked people who were a little more exotic, a little more offbeat and quirky.

Someone like her.

"Yoo-hoo," Liza called over the breeze. "What are you up to, fellow sailor?"

Quickly folding his nautical chart, Patrick gave her a surprised yet happy look and motioned for her to sit. Plopping down next to him, Liza playfully turned his baseball cap around backward.

Patrick laughed. "Gee, thanks. Is this how they wear them on college campuses these days?"

"Sure, when it's raining," Liza said. "To keep their necks dry. Then, when the sun comes out . . ." Liza placed one hand on his shoulder and spun the hat back in place with the other. "They wear it like that."

Patrick was grinning at her. "Ah. So that's how they do it."

Liza felt herself blushing. "Actually, I just made it up. Sorry. That's the way my mind works. In fits and starts, like a broken Porsche engine. But when it's running . . ."

He shook his head and laughed. "It really *runs*."

Liza felt dizzy with happiness. Did she and Patrick click, or what? It was the first time since St. Ramos she'd been able to approach him without KC's annoyingly awesome beauty distracting him. And it wasn't easy; after all, she wasn't exactly an expert on men.

Before her freshman year at the U of S, she'd never had a boyfriend in her life. Patrick, on the other hand, probably had strings of girlfriends waiting at every port.

"Weather picking up out here?" Liza made small talk. She looked out at the wide sea and the outline of a green island in the distance. Then she glanced briefly at Patrick's rugged profile. His arms were muscular and tan, but his hands were long and tapered, reminding her that Patrick wasn't just an expert outdoorsman. He was an artist.

Patrick gave her a reassuring smile. "A bit. We might run into a little squall. It's part of the program. Then you can go home and tell everyone about it. I'll even give you permission to grossly exaggerate how treacherous the trip was."

Liza giggled. Then she felt a strange dipping sensation. Was that her stomach that had dropped, or was her head moving sideways?

"Liza?" Patrick looked at her.

Liza brightened. "Oh—um, it's just that the sea we're on . . . it's not a movie set," she said awkwardly. "I mean, even though it seems like one. It's so—so beautiful."

"Yep." Patrick gave her a strange look and began fiddling with his map.

Liza took a breath and pretended to look thoughtfully out to sea. What was wrong with her? Did she need new contacts? She sure was having trouble focusing. Liza shook her head a little. This couldn't be happening. She was in the middle of a *big moment*. At times like this, you simply had to force your brain to kick into gear. Because if you blew it, it was blown forever.

She had to think. She'd *had* a plan. Now if she could just remember what it was. Then she held her stomach and remembered. Late the night before she'd found some expensive-looking art books in the *Bluebeard*'s library. It had reminded her that she'd seen many beautiful paintings in the New York museums. They'd moved her the way they'd probably moved Patrick. She had to make him realize that she was an artist too. She knew what it was like: the hopes, the dreams, the pain.

Patrick looked over, giving her a slightly embarrassed smile.

Liza cleared her throat. For a few moments, the boat heeled over in back of them. Then they hit a series of swells that turned Liza's stomach upside down again.

She reached ahead and clutched the railing. "I love the sea," she began, breathing deeply and trying to remember the name of her optometrist. "Didn't you love the stars last night? You could almost see them reflected in the water, just the way Van Gogh painted *Starry Night*."

"Mmmm," Patrick agreed, craning his head back to look at the mainsail. "I love that painting too."

Liza gritted her teeth and took a breath.

Had it been the chicken? Her mother always warned her about keeping the chicken separate from the salad greens. Chickens carried deadly toxins. Did

Courtney know about that? The way she rationed the water, she probably didn't even wash her hands.

"Don't you just love those chunky little yellow brush strokes he used to show the stars' reflection in the night sky?" Liza said. "Up close, they look so weird. But taken as a whole, they look so real. Just like last night."

Patrick nodded thoughtfully. "You're right, Liza."

Liza felt a bolt of victory. "I guess you could say I'm an artist too," she said wistfully, wondering if Patrick would let her put her head on his shoulder. Maybe she just hadn't gotten enough sleep last night.

Patrick gave her a surprised look. "You paint?"

Liza hugged her knees and looked up at the sky. "No, no. I'm in the theater. We paint pictures with our words, our gestures, our voices. Our *feelings*." She turned to give Patrick a meaningful look, but ended up giving him a strange stare. Why did he suddenly have two noses and four eyes? "We're alike, I guess you could say. I understand what it's like to be passionate about your art."

"I really *am* passionate, too," Patrick said.

"Not everyone understands," Liza explained. "Take—take someone right out of the blue—well, say, KC Angeletti. She's a business major, you know. Very serious. Very concerned with money and numbers. It's all so very *cold*."

Patrick turned and gave her an interested look. "Leave the bean-counting to the bean counters."

Liza's heart shot up to her throat. Then it dropped down again as the bow of the boat hit a swell. She grabbed the lifeline and drew in a lungful of salty air. Her red hair was blowing wildly around her face. The breeze was cool, but her forehead was strangely hot. "Right. And leave us Van Gogh, leave us Monet, Degas, Gauguin. Don't you just love Gauguin's strong colors and bold, primitive shapes?"

Patrick fiddled with his hands for a moment before looking back up at Liza through the wind. The boat hit another swell and he rebraced his deck shoes. "I'm sort of familiar with Gauguin, but probably not like you are, Liza." He cleared his throat and looked a little embarrassed. "I've never been to college. Never even taken an art class."

"Then you're a natural," Liza said, trying to give him a sexy smile with her rubbery-feeling lips.

He shrugged and looked down at his hands. "I'm pretty much self-taught. I read everything I can get my hands on. But out here, what I can find isn't always what I need."

"The *Bluebeard* has a wonderful art library," Liza suggested, her head swooning with victory. She'd reached out her hand and Patrick took it. They were definitely connecting. It was big. Very big. She was about to lead him downstairs when her stomach lurched, and she decided against it.

"I'll have to check it out," Patrick replied. His gaze seemed to hang on hers for a moment before he pulled it away.

"Why did you decide to be a painter?" Liza made herself ask, as a light spray of salt water flew into her face. She pulled her hand away. Her head was beginning to feel light, but she was definitely getting through to him.

Patrick shrugged, then he flashed a smile at her. "Maybe I've always looked at things differently than other people."

The water was choppy and slate-blue. Liza held a hand over her ear to keep out the wind. "Compared to the rest of the U of S student body, I'm kind of different too," Liza said over the mounting wind. "I could probably make it in the serious theater, but you should see the wacky TV shows and offbeat student films I get myself tied up in," she exaggerated.

Patrick was nodding. He rested his chin on his balled-up fist and looked thoughtfully out to sea. "When I think of the money I could be making doing commercial art . . ."

"Stick with it," Liza burst out, just as the boat hit another swell and her stomach did a flip-flop. Her hand instinctively went to her stomach. "Oh."

Patrick blinked.

Liza closed her eyes a little. Could it be she was . . . No.

"You're not feeling well," Patrick finally said, slipping his hand onto her shoulder.

Liza was swooning, but was it just Patrick's nearness? No, Patrick was supposed to make her feel good. This feeling definitely was not good. In fact, it was awful. Rock bottom, ugly, bad, awful.

"Is there anything I can do?" Patrick was half supporting her now. "Let's get you belowdeck. We've got some seasickness medication."

"Seasick?" Liza cried out, reaching for his arm and falling toward the railing at the same time. "I've never been seasick. I happen to be a very healthy person." Tears began rolling down her cheeks. All she wanted to do was throw herself into Patrick's strong arms. She knew now that Patrick would let her. But Patrick was right. She was in bad shape. She was out of control.

Then suddenly Liza felt another swell and a mounting sensation in her stomach and throat. Her mouth was suddenly wet and her knees were buckling. Humiliated and triumphant in one terrible moment, Liza fell to her knees, clutched the lifeline, and finally threw up over the railing of the boat.

Late that afternoon, Courtney was in the galley, happily chopping mushrooms for dinner and remembering something her father told her when she was twelve.

Don't ever give up, Court. If you want something badly enough, just keep working at it. Things will turn out.

Courtney smiled and blew a kiss into the air. "Thank you, Dad. You were right, as usual."

She felt a bolt of confidence as she took in the pleasant scene around her. Tucked into the tiny navigation niche, Jack's serious face was hovered over a detailed nautical chart while he listened intently for the weather reports. Back toward the aft cabins, Mookie and Tony were busily cleaning the head and swabbing down the corridor. Mookie wore one of Courtney's mother's old flowered aprons. Tony was doing the tango with a mop—a Walkman clamped to his head and a snorkel between his teeth.

Courtney hummed a line from *Evita*. The *Bluebeard* surged up and down against the sea. Outside, the waves splashed up against the portholes. Courtney was loving every minute of it. In fact, everything was working out a hundred times better than she ever thought it would.

Patrick was a gem. KC was in heaven. Liza was a scream. And Winnie—well, Winnie was definitely on the mend.

Sliding her mushroom pile over with the side of her hand, Courtney wiped her palms on her apron and grasped the hatch railing. She took the steps two at a time, then stuck her head out into the howling wind.

"Dinner in fifteen minutes," Courtney shouted to KC and Patrick at the helm, their dark hair flapping wildly about them.

"*O-kay,*" KC shouted back, grasping Patrick's shoulder for balance. Her creamy skin was flushed, and her arms were beginning to take on a light tan. Courtney smiled as the two hovered behind the gleaming wheel, their heads almost touching. She could tell that KC had begun to feel the magic of the islands.

Now that she had everything under control, she would probably start feeling it too.

Slipping an elbow out over the top of the hatch cover, Courtney let the stormy wind lash her cheeks. There *was* something magical about being at sea. But everything was different now. When she was a child, all she'd had to worry about was not falling off the boat.

Her parents had taken care of everything else—the food, the sailing, the adventures, the happiness.

Courtney squinted at the thickening cloud cover. Then she gritted her teeth. Soon. Soon she'd get that feeling back. Maybe tomorrow. Just as soon as she was absolutely sure everyone was having a good time. And if they weren't—well, they just *had* to be happy. She just couldn't stand it if they weren't.

A moment later she scrambled back down below-deck to check on Liza.

"Everything okay?" she asked, poking her head into the girls' cabin, where Liza lay next to a bucket and a towel.

"Oh yeah," Liza moaned, her red hair sticky and flattened after hours of seasickness. "Everything's fantastic."

Courtney turned to Winnie, who was curled up gloomily on her bunk, reading. "Winnie? Would you help me with the vegetables?"

"Sure," Winnie grumbled, slapping her book down and stepping carefully down onto the rocking cabin floor. "Whatever."

Courtney and Winnie staggered back to the galley, while the boat continued to pitch.

"Liza's still not feeling well." Courtney tried to sound cheerful. She opened a package of boneless chicken breasts, then handed Winnie a container of fresh peas to shell. "But she's got a lot of spunk. She'll come around."

Winnie took the peas and walked to the other side of the galley counter. "Since when does a spunky personality take care of seasickness?" she snapped.

Courtney clenched her jaw, opened the fridge, and pulled out a container of freshly sliced papayas. Sure, Winnie was going through a terrible crisis, but the island magic would soon work its wonders on her. After all, Courtney was making a special effort to make everyone feel at home on the *Bluebeard*. All they needed was time. Their distrust would melt away like butter after a few more days at sea.

"I can't wait to see how this Greek chicken turns out," Courtney said, changing the subject. "You put lemon, rosemary, and very tart Greek olives in it, and it's just—"

"Really?" Winnie interrupted, snapping open a pea pod and letting the exploding peas fall all over the cabin floor.

"I think it's going to be a lovely night, Winnie," Courtney began again softly, reaching for the pepper grinder.

Winnie reached for another pea pod.

"I think we put a great crew together, don't you?" Courtney continued bravely, putting the chicken into a large casserole dish and sprinkling it with olive oil. "Mookie and Tony are a lot of fun. And I can't believe how lucky we were to find Patrick and Jack. They know their way around this boat like they've crewed it their whole lives."

Winnie's dark-circled eyes flitted nervously toward the porthole as a wave smashed against the side of the hull.

"Did you see KC help Patrick with the rigging this

morning?" Courtney tried again, pulling out another baking dish. "Of course, you've known KC practically all your life, but I can't get over how amazing she is. You could put her on the French Riviera, and she'd outclass and outsmart every woman there."

Winnie rolled her eyes.

Courtney was starting to feel very uncomfortable. What was Winnie thinking? Was she missing Josh? Was she still having terrible pangs over losing the baby? Courtney pushed a lock of blond hair off her face and went on bravely making conversation. She couldn't stand to have Winnie so upset. It made her crazy to think she was in this kind of agony. Couldn't Winnie say something?

"Isn't Liza a nut?" Courtney giggled. "I had such a great time last night on the beach. You know, she really has a lot of potential. When she and Mookie and Tony started impersonating Julie Andrews in *The Sound of Music,* I thought I was going to die laughing."

Courtney glanced over and saw a large tear dripping down Winnie's cheek.

"Winnie." Courtney pushed her chicken dish aside and slid her elbows onto the counter across from Winnie. She tried to look directly into Winnie's eyes. "I know things look bad right now, but I'm certain you're going to find happiness again."

Suddenly Winnie looked into Courtney's face. Her eyes grew round with anger. "Stop it," she said shakily.

"Look," Courtney started again, desperate. "Just let yourself have a good time. Don't fight it."

"No, Courtney." Winnie's voice grew louder. She threw the peas to the floor. *"No, Courtney. I am not having a good time,"* she shouted, nearly knocking Courtney over with the force of her voice.

Courtney gasped. She gripped the edge of the counter for balance. "Winnie, please," she pleaded.

"What are you *talking* about?" Winnie shouted, the veins in her thin neck bulging. "You don't know anything. You live in a fairy tale."

"Wha—what?" Courtney stammered. She got up and backed toward the opposite end of the galley. This was too awful. It was a dream. Winnie could not be this way. She was supposed to be getting better, not worse.

"You're blind," Winnie shouted.

"Blind?" Courtney sputtered back tearfully. She felt helpless. She wanted to help, but she had no idea what Winnie needed.

"You're so sheltered and pampered," Winnie continued to shout. "You couldn't see reality if it came up to you and punched you in the face."

Courtney's face jerked back, as if she'd been physically slapped.

"You think we're your little pets you can stroke and smooth and make all better. But you *can't*!"

"What are you talking about?" Tears welled up in Courtney's eyes. Of course she could make things better. She had before, hadn't she? She'd helped lots of people. It was one of her main goals in life—reaching out and helping others.

"Charity might be okay for the Tri Beta sorority,

Courtney, but it's not okay for me and KC and Liza," Winnie snapped.

"Charity?" Courtney stammered.

Winnie's fists were balled up in front of her, and her eyes were blazing. "A few mushrooms here, a little tarragon there . . ." she ranted. "You think you're going to make this a perfect night. You think you can make everything perfect."

Courtney bit her lip, trying to recover. "I just want everyone to have a good time."

"Well, it's not going to be a perfect night," Winnie sobbed, jerking her head toward the porthole. "In fact, we're probably headed for a major storm. What makes you think Patrick and Jack are going to pull us out of this jam? We don't know anything about them. They could be serial killers, for all we know!"

Courtney pulled in her breath. Tears rolled down her cheeks. Did Winnie know something she didn't?

"As for elegant KC," Winnie went on hysterically, starting to pull herself away from the counter. "She's been trying to act classy since she was in junior high because she's so uptight about being continually *poor*. You think Liza has potential, huh? Yeah, right. She has the potential to be the tackiest freshman at the U of S."

"Winnie, please," Courtney begged as Winnie stormed out of the galley.

Then Winnie abruptly stuck her spiky head back in. "And sure, Courtney, I may eventually find happiness again—if I don't kill myself first!"

Courtney jumped as Winnie slammed the door to their cabin. Then she slipped around the galley table and sat down, burying her face in her hands. A sickening ache filled her body. Something terrible was happening on the *Bluebeard*. Maybe Winnie was right. Maybe she didn't really know what was going on. Maybe she *was* too sheltered and naive to really see people for what they were. Maybe she was a fool. Maybe her life was a waste. She didn't know anymore.

Courtney let the tears fall down her face and she sobbed.

Eleven

KC felt alive.

She nestled her hip on the top of the hatch, closed her eyes, and let the rolling motion of the boat take over her body. The wind lashed her hair. Her cheeks were cold and sticky with salt water. She felt as if she was in a place where everything was happening just as it should, where her body seemed to fit, where she felt really alive—maybe for the first time in her life.

She glanced briefly belowdeck. Courtney had just called them for dinner. She knew her friend needed help. But all she wanted was the wind and the sky—and Patrick.

"Take the mainsail in ten feet," Patrick yelled

through the wind to Jack. "And we'll drop the jib.
Wind's picked up."

KC lifted her head up higher to catch the breeze,
then hung on as the *Bluebeard* righted itself slightly.
The sea was rising behind them, sending the solid boat
surfing down on the swells like a giant, watery roller-
coaster ride she never wanted to end.

KC cupped her hands and shouted at Patrick.
"Surf's up!"

Patrick gave her the thumbs-up sign and grinned.

KC lingered. A ten-knot breeze was right at their
backs, and for the past couple of hours, the *Bluebeard*
had been running with the wind under a soft, gray sky.
Whitecaps flashed on the water's surface. The air was
so fresh and cool, it hurt her nostrils to breathe in
deeply.

A sudden wind knocked her hip into the side of the
hatch. She grinned to herself. The sea didn't scare her
anymore. It was just water. Rolling, clear, beautiful
water. And after a few lessons from Patrick, she knew a
lot about staying afloat. She'd learned to furl the sails.
When they were tacking against the wind, she'd figured
out how to scramble across the foredeck and adjust the
jib sheets. She read the charts. She watched the wind.
Best of all, she had the intoxicating feeling that maybe—
just maybe—she might have some control over her life.

Why was she always worrying about obstacles?
Money. Success. Power. They were all out there, waiting for her, just like any other challenge she would
meet. They weren't problems; they were adventures.
She was sure of that now.

KC finally sprang belowdeck. The boat was pitching and bumpy. But everything down there remained sleek and in place.

"You *called*?" KC practically shouted, leaning over the counter into the galley, where Courtney was thoughtfully brushing rows of chicken breasts with clarified butter. From the pale look on her face, KC thought she almost looked seasick. KC's face, on the other hand, was burning from the wind.

In the background, she could hear Mookie and Tony's boom box blasting through their door. But Liza and Winnie were nowhere to be found.

"Liza still seasick?" KC asked, grinning and popping a Greek olive into her mouth. It was amazing how much time Patrick had for her when Liza was out of the picture. She'd been annoyed at first when he'd paid attention to Liza, but now it was obvious that Patrick had just been being polite.

"KC?" Courtney said, obviously not hearing her. She quietly squirted lemon juice over the dish.

"Yep? Say anything. I can take it," KC chattered back, jumping on the counter.

"Are you glad you came?" Courtney asked, a hint of sadness in her voice.

"What?" KC's mouth dropped open. She stared at Courtney's neat, blond ponytail and crisp white T-shirt. Then she burst out laughing. "Are you kidding? These are probably the best days I've ever had in my life. It's paradise, Courtney," KC gushed. "The beaches, the blue water, the diving, the food, Patrick . . ."

Courtney gave her a slight smile. "I'm glad, KC."

KC squeezed her eyes shut with happiness. *"AAHHH. I love everything."*

"Taste this." Courtney was hovering a spoonful of sauce in front of KC's lips. KC opened her eyes. "Clarified butter, olive oil, fresh rosemary, shitake mushrooms, and Chardonnay," Courtney recited.

KC slipped the entire spoonful in her mouth as if she were savoring another adventure in her wonderful new life. She knew the ingredients in Courtney's fancy sauce probably cost more than an entire week's worth of tuition at the U of S. But she didn't care anymore. It just made the sauce seem even better. "Mmmm. Heaven."

"Thanks," Courtney said wistfully. "Dinner's in ten minutes."

"Good." KC hopped down from her perch, bracing herself as the boat heeled over again. Then, on impulse, she ran around the counter and hugged Courtney tightly. "I'm having a wonderful time, Courtney. *Wonderful.* Thank you so much."

Springing out of the galley, KC staggered over to the forward sleeping cabin and cracked open the door. Inside, Winnie was lying on her side, staring forlornly into space from the top bunk. Liza, pale, but clearly better, was carefully applying a coat of bright red polish to her toenails on the opposite bunk. Clumps of cotton separated her pudgy toes.

"Cozy enough for you?" KC asked, gripping both sides of the cabin door. Though the cabin slept four, Winnie and Liza's heads were practically touching in the tiny space.

Winnie looked at her listlessly.

"Feeling better, Liza?" KC inquired, trying to sound sincere, but biting the side of her tongue to keep from laughing at Liza's carnival-red hair, which was now wound on giant plastic rollers.

Liza gave her a challenging look. "Thank you for asking, KC," she replied. "Actually, I've never felt better in my life. I'm just getting ready for the *night* of my life."

"Really?" KC pretended to look shocked. Then she looked at Winnie. "Dinner's in ten minutes. I'm just going up on deck to tell Jack and Patrick."

Winnie suddenly sprang up, hitting her head on the ceiling. She rubbed it in frustration, then squeezed down into the cramped space between the bunks. On her knees, she yanked open a tiny compartment and pulled out a sequined sweatshirt. "I'll get them. I need some air." Her Mickey Mouse Bermuda shorts were wrinkled and baggy, but she didn't seem to care.

KC made a face and stepped back to make room in the doorway.

"Haven't seen her move that fast in two days," Liza remarked, giving KC a coy look. "I think she's eager to go and brood with Mr. Serious up there."

"Jack?" KC asked.

Liza shrugged and gave her a who-cares look before shifting back to her wet toenails.

KC rolled her eyes and turned to head for the aft cabins, grabbing furniture and wall hooks on the way to keep her balance. Mookie and Tony's boom box was still thundering with old Bob Marley reggae tapes.

Squeezing into the tiny space between the head and the sleeping cabin, she peered briefly through their slightly opened door. Then she stopped. Her jaw dropped open when she saw that, for once, they weren't cracking up, playing an air guitar, or banging aimlessly on Mookie's drum.

Tony and Mookie were actually having a conversation.

KC narrowed her eyes. She slid her back down the wall and squatted on the floor. Through the opening, she could see Tony hovered over a detailed map, making tiny pencil marks. Mookie was busy figuring something on a small calculator. A moment later, Tony reached back to shut off the music.

Instinctively KC moved back, embarrassed. She was spying on them. She started to straighten up and leave.

". . . Tony, but this buried treasure is . . ." she heard Mookie say quietly, before a loud splash outside the hull drowned out his words.

Buried treasure?

KC froze. On the other hand, she thought, sinking back down, she was *definitely* in the mood to spy. Were they joking? Or did Tony and Mookie have a serious side after all? If they did, it was right up her financially-strapped alley.

KC leaned her ear toward the door.

". . . the gold. But diving for it will be a cinch once we . . ."

Gold? Diving?

KC's ears pricked up even more. She couldn't make out their words over the sound of splashing water and wind. They'd done a lot of diving the day before. Were they looking for something?

KC inched closer.

"I checked out Jack's chart," Tony was saying. "Primo situation. At this very momento, my friend, we are sailing through coral-reef city."

"Yeah, man," Mookie answered, "but the reefs that sunk those Spanish galleons could make the sailing wild and woolly for us, too."

Spanish galleons? KC bit her lip. Was this for real?

"Nah, these guys know what they're doing," Tony insisted. "Look, this is the same general area where Frankie sighted the orange sea grass."

"Huh?" Mookie mumbled.

"Come on, man," Tony complained. Through a crack in the door, KC could see him bang once on Mookie's Jamaican drum for attention. "Are you with me on this or not?"

"Yeah, yeah," Mookie said sheepishly. "I'm with you. And I think Frankie's right. The orange sea grass. It's a sure sign of rusting cannons."

KC moved even closer. Mookie and Tony knew where the galleons were sunk? They actually knew where the gold was? This wasn't a joke. They were dead serious.

"That's what Frankie says," Tony said excitedly. "And I believe him. I mean, he's just about the world's leading expert on shipwreck diving. And who knows more about diving than we do? Man, am I ever glad I ran into him in St. Ramos."

"Spanish galleons," Mookie said dreamily. "Loaded

to the gills with gold coins and bricks."

"Yeah," Tony said softly. "It's like a lifetime wake-up call. You know what I mean? It's like, okay, guys, don't blow it and you'll be rich for life."

Rich for life?

KC swallowed. This was unbelievable.

"Frankie knows one guy who made a small find," Tony went on. "Like, it was definitely small-time gold. Eight hundred thousand dollars. That was his haul."

Eight hundred thousand dollars? KC thought desperately. Was it possible? One-tenth of that would take her through college and graduate school with a new outfit for every day of the year.

KC shivered. She desperately hoped that no one would catch her eavesdropping. But she couldn't drag herself away. Sunken treasure? The possibility of being rich for life? She knew how to dive now. There was no way she was going to let this chance slip by. She'd spent her life scraping for things. This could be the break she needed to turn everything around.

"That's why we're here, remember that," Tony reminded him. "Sure, we're having fun with the babes and the good times, Mookie. But we're here to pick up where Frankie left off. And we can do it. We're gonna be rich."

KC peeked through the crack again, just in time to see Mookie and Tony high-five it and break into a fit of silent laughter. Then she pressed herself against the wall of the cabin, excitedly coiling the string on her hooded sweatshirt.

Good old Tony and Mookie, she thought to herself

with a sly smile. *So that's what you're up to. You don't just want enough money to get back home. You want enough money to last you for the rest of your lives. Well, so do I.*

KC made a determined fist. Tony and Mookie were a couple of party boys, but they also seemed to have a lot of good information. Sunken treasure? They *had* to let her in on it. KC had to clamp her hand over her mouth to keep from squealing with excitement. Spinning around, she grabbed the wall railing and started to head back to the galley. But as she did, her head slammed directly into a solid, male chest. She looked up and felt her knees buckle.

"Patrick," KC gasped, feeling her pulse rise. A hot flush began to creep over her cheeks. She wondered how long he'd been standing there. Had Patrick heard Mookie and Tony too?

"Hi," Patrick replied softly. The dim light in the passageway was soft, and his eyes looked curious. He slipped his hands into the pockets of his jeans. "You look like you've got something on your mind."

KC gave him a bold look. "Yeah. Yeah I do. Things are great. I mean, I'm just on top of the *world*." She smiled.

"Umm." Patrick stepped toward her. "I've been looking for you."

"You have?" KC felt like throwing her arms around him.

"Jack and I need you at the helm for a minute," he said slowly. "There's a storm coming up. It's going to be wild." His neck and shoulders were graceful beneath his soft, worn sweatshirt. His face was ruddy from the winds. KC felt loose-limbed and free, as if she could do anything, say anything, and end up just exactly where she wanted to be.

"Good," KC said. The boat heeled over a little and KC had to brace her foot at the bottom of the wall, but she couldn't stop grinning at Patrick. Then, without realizing what she was doing or why, she placed her two open palms on his chest and slid them slowly up to his neck.

Without a word she slipped her hands lightly around his face and kissed him, just as she felt his arms circle tightly around her waist.

Twelve

"Limbo!" Tony cried out after dinner that night. He leaped out of his cabin, grasping a thin wooden stick.

"*Par*-ty!" Mookie shouted, squeezing his close-set eyes together and shaking his uneven bangs.

"*AAAAHHGGG!*" Liza shrieked, squirming out from behind the dining table as the *Bluebeard* made another high-seas lurch. A glass toppled over, and a sickening shudder went through the boat. "Patrick and I get to hold the limbo stick. But where? There's no room."

KC stretched her long arm out and delicately plucked the stick out of Tony's hand. "Patrick," she began, pulling him out from behind the table. "Come on. It's you and me in the galley."

"No, no, anything but this," Patrick was protesting as KC dragged him off.

Winnie looked around nervously. Outside, the wind was howling and waves were slashing up against the portholes above them. Didn't anyone mind? Didn't they care? The weather report was really bad for tonight. Shouldn't they all be making emergency plans or something?

Courtney punched the power button on Mookie's boom box. Earsplitting reggae music thundered through the cabin as the boat lurched back and forth. "Come on," she shouted, swaying her hips a little to the beat. "Let's flip down the table and make room for limbo."

The wind screamed outside, and something jolted the floor. Winnie clutched the table and tried to slide out, but another crash shoved the edge of the galley counter into her stomach.

"Whoa," KC cried, pressing against Patrick and coaxing him into a dance. "This is *wild*."

"Patrick-*meister*," Mookie shouted giddily. "The Pat-*man*. The Pat-a-*reno*."

Winnie felt something in her throat clutch—the music, the lurching boat, the craziness. All of a sudden, she felt as if she were being swallowed up. She wanted land. She wanted two feet on solid ground. She wanted to go home.

Another loud vibration and crash knocked her into Patrick and KC. A picture fell off the wall, and the forward cabin door swung crazily back and forth.

"Patrick," she shouted over the music. "Is everything okay? I mean, it seems really rough out there."

Patrick and KC were pressed together like sardines, but he still managed to twirl her around with one finger, then reach behind and grab Liza by the waist. "No problem," he shouted back. "Squalls like this are par for the course in these islands. Stop worrying." He let go of Liza, then leaned forward as he dipped KC backward, holding her cabin door open to make room for her head. "Jack's got it under control."

Winnie sucked on her bottom lip, trying not to cry. Then she staggered a few feet to the hatchway and pulled herself up. She yanked open the hatch cover and felt her heart drop into her stomach.

Outside, the sky was black, and the wind was so strong, it nearly knocked her down. All of the spikes in her hair suddenly stood straight up as the wind rushed up from behind. A wave of salty spray splashed directly into her face.

"Oh, my God!" Winnie cried out into the raging night. Her eyes were stinging with salt, but up ahead in the dim light, she could see Jack clinging to the helm as he stared intently at the taut mainsail above them.

Winnie's mouth went dry. Desperately she shut the hatch cover, then stumbled toward the helm, half pushed by the howling winds. Sea spray had already drenched her T-shirt. Through the grayish light, she could see Jack reach back for the mainsail winch. He pulled it in as far as he could, then watched carefully. Winnie gasped. He was soaked to the bone, and his face was dripping with water.

"What's going on?" Winnie shouted over the roaring wind, clutching the side of the helm and trying to stand upright. A sudden jolt threw her onto the cockpit seat behind the helm.

Jack looked back and wordlessly shook his head. His eyes were clearly worried, and Winnie could see that both his fists were clenched.

"Is it bad?" Winnie cried, as another groaning gust of wind blew through and the boat gave a sickening thump.

"Hang on to the wheel for me," Jack yelled, pulling her forward and draping her against the helm. "I'm going to reef the main until this storm blows through. Hold the bow into the wind. It's all we can do now. Just pray we don't run into any coral reefs. This area is full of the stuff."

Winnie's mouth was dry with terror. She stared at Jack, wondering if he really cared about what happened to the *Bluebeard*. She cupped one hand around her mouth and shouted, "What about Patrick?"

"Hang on to the wheel!" Jack shouted back, scrambling up toward the mast, clinging to every available shroud.

Her heart in her throat, Winnie grabbed the wheel harder and tried to see ahead through the sheets of rain that swept across the deck. She could barely see the white foredeck and Jack's dim figure against the mast. It was as if they'd suddenly been swept up into a huge, wet wind tunnel. Hold the bow into the wind? How could she? The wind was coming from all directions now.

Winnie was trying desperately to steel herself with courage. Her skin was soaked with freezing salt water, and the wind was howling into her ears like a huge monster ready to eat them all alive. She clung to the wheel and braced one foot against the side of the cockpit bench. But a moment later there was an enormous, groaning sweep of wind that heeled the boat over sharply, sending Winnie's sneakers sliding to the side.

"Help!" Winnie screamed into the wind as she fell on her back, leaving the wheel to spin crazily on its own. A wave roared over the port deck, and the whole area was suddenly flooded with six inches of water. There was a dull, heavy moment before her worst nightmare came true.

CRRACCKKK.

Winnie screamed. The boat had hit something in the water. Was it the coral reef Jack had been worrying about? The terrifying sound of crunching onto something below split through Winnie's head. Up ahead she could barely make out Jack's furious look as he struggled from the foredeck back to the helm.

The boat gave a sickening groan before jerking aimlessly to the side.

Suddenly the hatch cover burst open and Patrick dragged himself on deck, shouting into the confusion of wind and water and darkness.

"She's hit coral—JACK!" Patrick screamed.

Winnie clung to the wheel in terror. Liza, Courtney, and Mookie emerged behind Patrick, screaming at the tops of their lungs and diving for the life jackets under the cockpit seats. But another jerk of the boat sent them sprawling to the wooden grate on the floor.

"There's water in the cabin!" Courtney yelled over to Winnie, grabbing on to the sides of the hatch, her face contorted with anguish. "Oh, my God!"

"*Jack!*" Winnie shouted, watching Patrick tumble back belowdeck. "*We've got to radio for help!*"

Letting go of the wheel, Winnie crawled across the cockpit toward the hatchway. Jack was crawling along the foredeck toward her. Lunging for the hatch cover, Winnie yanked it open, then stumbled down into the navigator's niche under the hatch steps.

In the ominous darkness, Winnie desperately scanned the high-tech panel with her fingers. Seawater lapped around her ankles, and Patrick was nowhere to be found. Then she felt the black radio's coiled wire hanging from the wall. Quickly she grabbed it and clicked the receiver. "HELLO? HELLO?" Winnie shouted. Then her photographic memory clicked in. Girl Scouts. Seven years ago. Seamanship badge. There was something about sending distress signals at sea. "*Mayday. Mayday. Mayday. This is the* Bluebeard. *This is the* Bluebeard. *We have struck a reef about thirty miles southeast of Sucia Island. We're going down. Please—send—HELP.*"

Winnie felt a hand grab the radio. The boat's lights switched wildly off and on. She looked up through the hatchway steps and saw that it was Jack. "Jack!" Winnie cried. "I'm trying to get help."

She looked at Jack's taut face between the steps. A sheet of rain blasted through the hatchway. His dark eyes were flashing at her and his lips looked like two thin blades of flesh. Winnie gasped. To her horror, she saw that he wasn't making a move for the radio. He was just holding it in his hand as if he wanted the *Bluebeard* to go down without a call for help.

"Jack!" Winnie cried as she grabbed the radio from him and the boat heaved over on its side. The dinner dishes crashed to the floor of the cabin.

The hull seemed to dig deeper into the reef. Winnie fell over into the galley just as Jack jumped down and grabbed the radio from her again. Everything was swirling and splashing around her, and she could hear the others screaming abovedeck. In a burst of motion, she threw herself against Jack and struggled for the radio. But the boat lurched again and together they fell sideways into the galley. A sheet of water sprayed into Winnie's eyes and she could feel Jack's arms still clinging to her from the back. She gasped. It looked as if the radio had been pulled out of the wall.

Winnie struggled against Jack, grabbing on to a handle on one of the galley cabinets. "Get away," she cried in confusion, as Mookie's limbo stick and one of Courtney's Greek olives swept past their tangled legs on the floor. Her lips were blue with cold, and salt water had soaked her entire body. It seemed certain that the boat was going down. In a moment she'd be going down too.

It was impossible, Winnie thought, her heart breaking. But it was true. She twisted around, trying to loosen Jack's powerful grip. Then, in the half-darkness, she could see that he was looking at her. His eyes were flashing with fear the way they had that afternoon in the back alley.

She remembered the statue in St. Ramos, dedicated to the sailors lost at sea. Her heart seemed to beat in slow motion as she read the words again in her mind: *There is a destiny that makes us brothers—none goes his way alone.*

Jack pressed his lips together and pulled her to his chest. Winnie looked up at his tight face again. Was he her brother—or her enemy?

"Winnie!" KC was screaming into the wind. *"Courtney!"* She was crawling on her hands and knees up the cockpit seat, her cheek pressed by the wind onto the cushion. A moment before, the *Bluebeard* had slid farther up the slope of the reef, sending its bow into the air and its stern deeper into the lashing water. The forward thrust of the boat had been violent enough to throw the entire crew overboard. Had it?

KC yelled again. But she wasn't getting any answer through the darkness and the wind.

Reaching up, KC grabbed the boat's aluminum lifeline. Then she struggled to rise up high enough to see forward. "Patrick!" she yelled. Her throat was raw from shouting over the wind, but she was desperate to know where he was.

A blurry block of orange descended toward her. She blinked the rain out of her eyes and coughed. It was Mookie, followed by Tony.

"Man," Tony shouted at her over the wind. He and

Mookie were wearing orange life vests, as she was. Both were clinging to the port-side railing, trying to check out the damage. Courtney was behind them, closer to the bow, but KC could barely see anything except a blur of wet hair.

KC's chest was heaving with panic, but she bit the inside of her mouth and made herself think. If Patrick wasn't on deck, he must have gone below to radio for help. Something told her that she had to find him.

"I'm going below to look for the others!" KC screamed back over her shoulder. The wind streaked through the two masts, sending weird howling noises through the air that made KC's blood run cold. She knew their lives were hanging by a thread, but she forced herself not to think about it. The only way she could cope with the horrible moment was to think about reaching the others.

She tumbled down onto the cockpit floor, landing hard on her shoulder, then slid back down toward the helm. Crawling up the slope of the deck, she was finally able to grab the slippery hatch cover and pull it open.

"Patrick!" KC shouted as she tumbled inside the cabin, slamming her shin against a step. The boat was tilted at a steep angle, so that most of the water had drifted down into the aft cabins and half of the galley. A gaping crack had split the hull where the main cabin area bordered the forward compartments. Water poured in through the bottom of the crack, and sheets of rain blew wildly into the cabin's teak inner walls. She grasped the edge of the dining table and pulled herself forward. "Patrick! Winnie! Jack! Liza! Please, answer me!"

The boat shuddered, and KC looked up just as she glimpsed Patrick's white shirt, soaked with seawater, streaked with seaweed, and sticking to his back. She gasped. He was backing out of the forward storage area, awkwardly clasping his two oil canvases, which were strapped together and wrapped in layers of plastic sheeting.

"The paintings!" KC called out, struggling to move forward to help. Through the spray, she could see Patrick lift one edge of the package toward her, a desperate look in his eye. KC drew in her breath. Those paintings meant everything in the world to him. Her fingers grasped one corner of the package. Then she held on and dragged it over the cabin table and toward the hatchway with all her might.

"I need to get them on deck!" Patrick shouted.

KC tugged harder, then somehow managed to find the middle step in the hatchway. With Patrick supporting the other side of the canvases, the two of them struggled up on deck, shutting their eyes against the hurricane-force winds.

"You've got to save them!" KC screamed.

"Look out!" Patrick shouted. He was lying on his side with a stricken look.

"Oh, no." KC saw that the crack in the hull was starting to widen, steepening the angle of the boat. She slipped, then held out her hand to help Patrick. But a moment later a sheet of water blasted over the deck, wrenching the paintings from Patrick's grip.

"NO!" he screamed as the paintings began to slide down the deck toward the surging water. *"NO!"*

Meanwhile, Liza lay limply on the tilted floor of her cabin. She'd run into the head to vomit, then had crawled back out at the sound of the terrifying crack. When she heard KC and Patrick screaming in the main cabin, she'd tried to reach them, but a gush of water had knocked her back into her room.

"Please just let me die," Liza moaned out loud, covering her wet face with her hands. By this time, she was lying in two inches of seawater. She moved her legs listlessly, trying to brace herself. Then she reached up and grabbed on to the brass doorknob on the swinging cabin door.

". . . them on deck!" she heard Patrick shouting over the wind.

"On deck, on deck," Liza mumbled to herself, pulling on the doorknob, then falling blindly into the dark main cabin. She moved one knee forward first. Then the other. Her only thought was to get up the hatchway. There she could at least breathe the air and see the sky—before the boat went down.

Sick at heart and even sicker to her stomach, Liza continued to crawl and sob in confusion. Why was this happening? Only an hour ago, she'd been sailing through paradise with the most beautiful guy she'd ever seen. She'd been nibbling Greek olives, doing the limbo. Now she was about to buy it at the bottom of the dark ocean. How could life be so cruel?

Finally Liza clutched the top of the hatchway and

staggered up into the cockpit, where she could dimly see KC lying down, but struggling to get up. There was a huge wave of seawater, then a scream above her.

Liza wiped the water off her face and squinted through the rain. It was Patrick, up on the port deck, lunging for a large, square package wrapped in some kind of plastic.

"The paintings!" Liza shouted, throwing herself toward the helm, which was sunk in two feet of water. "Your art—you can't let them go!"

"It's too dangerous! Hopeless!" Patrick cried out in the darkness.

"I've got it," Liza screamed, hoisting her knee up from the cockpit seat onto the slippery stern. The boat was about to sink, and everyone was probably about to perish on the reef. The last thing she needed to worry about was a painting. Right?

"LIZA!" she could hear Patrick shouting behind her.

Then she saw the paintings. They were still on board, jammed up against the railing but hanging by a thread. The package was narrow enough to slip through the railing posts at any moment, and the plastic sheeting was beginning to unravel.

They aren't just things, Liza thought suddenly. *They're Patrick's paintings. His hopes are in there, his heart, his love.*

A wave crashed down on Liza, hurling her against the stern railing and banging her head. Her body was now half submerged in the crashing sea. She grabbed one of the aluminum posts, her mouth full of saltwater.

Just as she looked over dizzily, the paintings began to tip precariously, then loosen and drop.

"Uugghh!" With all her might, Liza stretched out to grab the closest corner of the package. She had to show Patrick how much she cared. She had to show him what she was capable of doing—just to prove how much she loved him. Maybe everyone else was content to die in the storm, but she wanted it to mean something more. A second huge wave swept across the stern as she reached again, and Liza felt the sickening sensation of her fingers loosening from the rail. A surge of something powerful broke her loose from the boat, sending her plummeting into the dark water.

There was a sudden quiet as the water closed over her ears. It was almost enough to make her want to give up. The roar was very distant. Then she felt a tightness in her chest. Air! She had to have air!

In a flash, she saw Alistair's weathered face hovering in front of her. *Destiny,* he was saying. *Destiny is not a matter of chance, you know. It's a matter of choice. A matter of choice . . . A matter of choice.*

Liza moaned desperately. She did not choose this. She did not want or deserve this! With all of her might, she flailed her arms in the water and kicked herself up.

"AAAGGHH!" she screamed as she rose up out of water. Above, she could see Patrick's anguished face at the railing. In front of her she could see the ragged, plastic-covered painting, still half floating in the water. "I can't swim!" she managed to scream at him, before sinking back down again into the muffled quiet.

A moment later she heard a splash. Someone had jumped into the raging sea. It was probably Patrick, she thought. He was jumping in to save—not her, but his future as an artist.

Then she felt a strong arm hook her around the chest and drag her to the surface. She gasped and twisted around, trying to see Patrick's face. Behind him, the last visible corner of the paintings sank into the ocean.

"The paintings!" she screamed. "Your art!"

"Hang on!" Patrick yelled back, turning her on her back and holding her chin above the whipping water. She could feel the strength of his body beneath her, pulling her toward the ladder. "Okay, now. Grab on to the bottom rung."

Liza clasped something metal, and with the last ounce of strength she had, heaved herself back up on deck. The wind had died down slightly, making it possible for them to crawl toward the foredeck and away from the sinking stern.

"Hold on," Patrick shouted again, bracing them both against a cabin porthole. Together, they felt the *Bluebeard* crack a final time against the coral, sink slightly, then go quiet.

Liza was sobbing. "Oh, my God. Oh, my God. The paintings. KC, Courtney, Winnie. The others . . . Where are they?" she babbled on, unable to get her thoughts in focus.

Patrick's arm circled her and he drew her shaking body close. After a few minutes, the wind died down, and it looked as though part of the *Bluebeard* would stay above water for the time being. All around them, they could see tangled line and cracked chunks of fiberglass hull splashing up against the toothy coral reef they'd smashed into.

"What are we going to *do*?" Liza wailed.

Patrick held her closer. "We'll get out of this. We will."

"We're shipwrecked," Liza sobbed. "We're lost at sea. And your paintings . . ."

"Yeah, the paintings," Patrick murmured sadly.

"Your whole future," Liza cried out. "Your whole future is sinking to the bottom of the sea."

Thirteen

ourtney stirred. In the distance, she could hear sea gulls squabbling, the rush of seawater pouring in and out of the reef, and the slow flapping of the *Bluebeard*'s flag. Her mind felt slow and thick. She tried to remember. What was it? There was darkness and water, howling wind, a loud crack. Then everyone shouting . . .

Courtney's eyes opened suddenly. Still lying stomach-down on the foredeck, her hands were clasped around the bottom of the mast. Her knees ached and her fingers were stiff with cold.

Am I the only one alive? she thought desperately, lifting her head. She breathed again as she looked to the left. The black sea was beginning to take on a silvery light. In the dimness, she could see Liza and Patrick braced against the port side of the cabin, asleep. Mookie and Tony were huddled down in the half-sunken cockpit. Winnie and Jack sat silently together at the bow, already awake and staring at the rising sun.

Her eyes trailed down the boat, which was now only half floating. During the storm, it had hooked itself onto the top of a sharp reef, ripping its hull open about a third of the way down from the bow. Now it was heeled over on its side, and the stern was sunk about five feet below water.

Courtney dropped her head back down. For a moment she lay in shock, her cheek pressed into the smooth fiberglass, staring numbly at a single chunk of hull that had splintered off into the water. It rocked back and forth against a bank of spiny coral sticking up from the water.

Patrick, Liza, Mookie, Tony, Winnie, Jack . . .

Courtney stiffened. "KC," Courtney tried to call through her hoarse throat.

There was a creak and a groan. KC's head rose slowly up from the cockpit. "Courtney?" she whispered. Her curly dark hair was clinging to her scalp in clumps, and her lips were blue-gray with cold. "Are you okay?"

Courtney nodded and blinked the tears from her swollen eyes. Then she collapsed back down, burying her face into her elbows. "Everyone's here. Everyone's okay. Oh, my God. Everyone's okay," Courtney sobbed.

She let out a long, shuddering sigh. All night long she'd been lying on her stomach, clinging to the mast and praying for dawn. At one point everyone had been accounted for in the wind and darkness. But no one knew how much time they had before the wreck of the *Bluebeard* crumbled into the water, or if they were near land. Courtney now realized that she must have slipped into unconsciousness several hours ago.

"We struck a fan-coral reef," Jack said quietly over his shoulder. "It stretches out about a quarter mile off the beach. We managed to plow right into the tooth-iest section. But we're close to land."

"Land?" Courtney whispered. She tried to stand up on her knees. A bolt of pain shot through the back of her neck where the boom had struck her during the storm. "Land," she repeated, forcing herself up. She grasped a line that had tangled around the bottom of the mast. It was almost too much to believe. After all, believing too much had been her first mistake: believing she could throw a crew together in half a day, believing that the seas would be as forgiving as they had been for her parents or for Captain Hark. Believing—even—that her friends would be grateful.

Then she looked. About five hundred yards off the starboard deck, she could see a small, round island taking in the sun's first yellow rays. Waves rumbled onto its white beach. The sand swept up to a dense forest of palm trees. Higher up, layers of cliffs looked out over the reef.

"It's true," Courtney whispered, a flood of tears rushing down her cheeks. Everyone would be okay. They might be lost and shipwrecked, but she could handle it now. Soon they'd be on land again, and she would get everyone back to safety. She *would*.

"Land?" she could hear Patrick groaning behind her. She looked back as his rumpled head lifted from the port-side deck. His wire-rimmed glasses were bent, and there was a bloody gash on his forehead. All of the confidence and joy was drained from his face. She watched as he turned her way, then spotted the island. He pulled a waterproof chart book out of his wind-breaker and leaned his elbow up onto the foredeck. "I guess it's light enough to read this thing now."

Winnie had swiveled around from her perch on the bow, her dark eyes fixed on Patrick. "It was light enough last night in the party room to read the chart book, Patrick," she said quietly, bitterly. "Why didn't you read it then? Too busy doing the limbo?"

Patrick's eyes narrowed, but he continued to stare intently at the map. "Jack and I knew precisely where we were, Winnie. The storm drove us off course, not the lack of a chart."

"Yeah, man, but you're the one who's supposed to be in control of this rig," Tony complained, sticking his head up from the cockpit. "What a drag. We're stuck out here, and there's no way anyone's—"

"Cut it out," Courtney said sharply.

"Cut it out?" Winnie mimicked. "Courtney, you're the one who organized this little adventure. You spent an hour talking me into it back in Springfield."

Courtney shuddered. "I'm sorry, Win. . . ."

"Oh, sure the boat's really big and safe. The captain's really experienced. The weather's always fine," Winnie mocked her. "I thought you knew what you were doing. Why didn't you tell us that we'd be risking our lives?"

"Yeah, some party," Liza complained, sticking her head up from the port-side deck. Her face was as white as flour, and her black mascara had melted into two dark tracks down her cheeks.

Courtney shook her head at Liza and Winnie, then gazed at the jewellike island. She had to get off the boat.

There were footsteps from the hatchway, then Tony popped his head up from the cockpit, running a hand through his wet, dark hair. "I just went below. The radio's gone, and the radar is broken."

Patrick was shaking his head over the chart book. "It's impossible to tell exactly where we are. This could be one of hundreds of islands."

Winnie abruptly stood up on the bow and gave everyone a challenging look. "I sent out a Mayday last night while we still had the radio. And I gave our location."

Courtney's heart speeded up. Maybe help was on the way, after all.

Patrick's eyes were round. He looked at Winnie, stunned. "You knew how to do that?"

Winnie crossed her arms and shivered. "I'd watched Jack use the navigational equipment. And the radio's pretty self-explanatory."

Liza laughed derisively. "Yeah. There's an ON switch and an OFF—"

Courtney felt her blood start to boil. "OKAY!" she said abruptly, clenching her fists together, unable to hold back. "Look, Liza. We should be thanking Winnie for having enough sense to make the call."

"Forget it," Winnie snapped, looking grimly toward the island. "Who knows if anyone heard us? There were probably a lot of Mayday calls last night. The whole *world* was probably Maydaying it. We're probably the only people left on earth."

There was a stony silence. Courtney bit the side of her mouth and looked away. The sea rushed forward through the jagged reef, then back again like a million tiny trickles moving all at once. Her father always used to say you could really find out about a person after a few days at sea in close quarters. Now she knew he was right.

She cast a longing look at the white beach. She really did have to get over there, fast. If she didn't, she was going to say things she didn't mean—she'd tell them they were ungrateful, lacking character, spoiled, spiteful. But the last thing she wanted was to get into a petty argument now. She'd only regret it later.

The air was starting to warm up, and Courtney watched as a white pelican soared above the boat, then swooped down and scooped a fish out of the blue water.

Patrick finally cleared his throat. "Even if someone *did* get the Mayday, it could be days before we see a rescue helicopter."

Jack rose up from his perch on the bow and cast a long glance down at the ruined *Bluebeard*. "And even longer if the boat sinks before a rescue party can spot it from the air."

"Okay, look," Patrick began, clenching his jaw and talking through his teeth. "We still have our little dinghy. And if the outboard still works, we should be able to unload the food and gear we'll need for the island without any problem. But we're going to have to move quickly. The *Bluebeard* could sink in five minutes, given the right current."

"Good idea," KC said brightly, giving Patrick a brave smile. "We'll camp on the island tonight, and look for rescue helicopters tomorrow."

Courtney gave KC a tired look, then pointed her head toward the island. "I can go ahead and check out the island. After all, it may be inhabited."

Liza rolled her eyes. "Right. I can see it now. We walk down the beach, and—what do you know? It's a Club Med," she drawled. "We'll be ordering little crabmeat sandwiches and fruit platters before lunch. Dip in the pool, anyone?"

Courtney's eyes widened with rage.

"Okay," Patrick broke in. "Look. Let's not start beating each other up, okay? We're all in this together now. And we all want the same thing: to get to safety as soon as we can."

Everyone nodded.

"Now, I'll keep watch on the boat," Patrick continued, biting the side of his thumb and staring intently into space. "Winnie, Jack, and Liza—you can ferry supplies from the boat to the shore. And Courtney— you take KC, Tony, and Mookie. See if there's anything on the island—a settlement, fresh water, fruit, anything."

Everyone nodded again, suddenly grateful to be doing something.

Courtney stood up and headed down to the stern, picking her way through the dangling sheets and tangled lines. To her relief, the *Bluebeard*'s tiny dinghy was floating unharmed in the blue water, still tied to its cleat. KC, Tony, and Mookie followed her and climbed in while she held the edge of the boat steady. Then she swiftly unraveled the line from the cleat and hopped in. She yanked the outboard's throttle and revved the engine. "One of us will come back with the boat in a few minutes," she called back to Patrick, before pointing the bow toward the quiet beach.

Courtney headed full-throttle across the water toward the tiny island, trying to forget the pointless bickering on board. It was too much to take. After all she'd done for her friends, why were they suddenly blaming this accident on her? Her only consolation was the island itself, which lay ahead, shimmering in the sunshine. Little blue waves rose and fell and lapped on the shore, and the wind ruffled the coconut palms that lined it. Everyone hung on as the skiff bumped into a small cove. It seemed impossible that they weren't on an innocent day-trip to a pretty island—instead of a last-ditch effort to survive with only a few days' worth of food and supplies.

"Take the bowline, Tony," Courtney called out, cutting the engine. She lifted the outboard up and beached the bow straight into the powdery-white sand.

"Looks deserted to me," Mookie said dully. His

straw hat was soggy, and there were long, wet strings hanging from his jean cutoffs.

"But it's really pretty," KC said cheerfully, as if they were planning a picnic. Courtney pressed her lips together. Didn't KC understand what was at stake? They were shipwrecked on an unknown, deserted island with only a small chance of a quick rescue.

Tony scrambled to shore, the white sand sticking to his wet legs like powdered sugar. Then KC, Mookie, and Courtney followed.

"Oh," KC gasped, jumping out of the boat and landing shin-deep in the clear, glittering water. "I never thought I'd be setting my feet on land again."

"You can say that again," Tony said softly, dragging the skiff up farther on the beach.

Courtney stepped down into the soft, white sand and let the water lap around her ankles. She shaded her eyes and looked down the curve of the unspoiled beach. A straight line of low green shrubs gave way to the springy tops of the palm trees, which swayed softly in the morning breeze. Aside from the gentle sound of the low waves washing up on the beach, everything was completely quiet.

"Look at this, you guys," KC called over to Mookie and Tony from a huge bush at the top of the beach. "Wild hibiscus. Look at these huge, red blossoms. This place is wonderful. Let's hope the rescue party doesn't come *too* soon."

Mookie and Tony dug their heels into the sand and headed off to join her. Courtney rubbed the back of her neck, irritated. She looked down at her filthy shirt and scratched, bruised legs. Why was KC suddenly so friendly with Mookie and Tony? She needed KC now, but she was starting to feel more deserted than even the island seemed to be.

Spotting a clearing in the woods at the other end of the beach, Courtney turned and began trudging away from the others. The warm sand felt good under her bare feet. The rhythmic to-and-fro of the gentle waves soothed her. Above, she could hear the chattering of tropical birds in the cool branches.

"Wait up, Courtney," KC yelled behind her a few minutes later.

Courtney looked back at KC, who was waving a branch laden with flowers. Then she squinted ahead at the unknown forest. To reassure herself, Courtney dug into her pocket and found her pocketknife. The sun was starting to feel hot on her back, but the island was fragrant with the smell of dusty palm leaves, hibiscus, frangipani, and mossy rocks at low tide.

Courtney angled her footsteps away from the water when she spotted the natural clearing again. It was a grassy, open area sloping up from the sand, overhung with flowering brush and tall palms.

Squaaaawwk! a single bird called out.

"Look out for the legendary parrot-o-saurus," Tony panted, catching up to her. "Prehistoric giants left over from the Pleistocene age, these deadly creatures can reach heights of more than fifty feet and are fueled by huge carnivorous appetites."

KC and Mookie joined them from behind, giggling.

"Shhh." Courtney put a finger to her lips, pausing in the shady green glen. In the distance she could hear something.

"What is it?" KC whispered.

Courtney, KC, Mookie, and Tony walked slowly up the clearing, a gentle canyon about two hundred yards across, carpeted with soft green grass. Banked up on each side was a thick tangle of trees and vines. Courtney walked carefully ahead, then stopped as the sound became clearer. She recognized it. It was the sound of trickling water. She stuffed her hands in her pockets and stepped a few feet to the right, where, behind a grassy bank, she finally spotted a crystal-clear stream. Courtney took a deep breath. It was about ten feet wide, meandering gently through the low grasses.

"The island has fresh water," she called back over her shoulder. Then she reached down with both hands and splashed it all over her face and neck, letting the cool drops spill down the front of her shirt.

"Hey, that's great," Mookie replied, stepping into the water and dunking his head into it.

Courtney continued eagerly up the stream, brushing away stray branches that hung over a path that seemed to lead alongside it. As they moved deeper into the shady woods, she breathed in the rich, damp smells and looked up at the sunlight filtering down through the canopy of trees. The soil felt cool under her toes.

"*Bali-Haiiii,*" Mookie began singing. "*Bali-Haiiii.*"

"Mookie," KC protested. "You're off-key."

"Then you sing it," Mookie complained.

KC gave a silly giggle. "I'm tone deaf, actually."

"Shhh," Courtney quieted them again. Far off, she could hear another sound, more like the roar of surf, though they were too far from the beach for them to hear the ocean. The clearing went higher and higher toward the roar. She pushed ahead, dodging rocks and pushing away the thick, waxy leaves that bobbed in her path. A few moments later the roar was deafening and the air felt damp and cool. The vegetation thickened, and Courtney made a final push through the brush until the whole air exploded in a noise of thundering water.

Courtney stood still. They were standing on the edge of a deep, green pool, fed by a crashing, fifty-foot-high waterfall.

"How beautiful," KC called over the roar, slipping past her and dipping a toe in.

Courtney nodded wordlessly, feeling her tense neck muscles relax for the first time in days. The hidden pool was large—about thirty feet across—and almost perfectly round. The stony ledge the waterfall poured over was deep green with moss. Pink bougainvillea and blood-red hibiscus sprang up about the brush. Tiny, orchidlike flowers bloomed on the water's edge.

"I can deal with this," Tony said appreciatively, climbing up next to KC. "If you're going to get shipwrecked, this is definitely the way to go."

Courtney nodded, her mind suddenly clear. "You're right, Tony," she shouted over the roar. "We're going to be okay on this island for a while. But we're going to have to move fast and get our stuff unloaded. The *Bluebeard* could go under at any time. And our supplies are still on it."

KC linked arms with Mookie and Tony. "Let's get back to the boat."

"I'm going to scout this area," Courtney said quickly. "I'll see if I can get up high enough on those cliffs to see the other side of the island."

"See you," KC yelled over her shoulder as she and the guys hopped back down the clearing.

Courtney watched them go, then stepped out onto a smooth rock and sat down, absently picking a small pink flower that grew by the water's rippling edge. The spray from the waterfall felt good on her face. Her skin smelled of sweat and boat grease. Her scalp itched with salt. She dipped her legs into the clear water and wiggled her toes. Then she stood up and looked around. KC, Tony, and Mookie were definitely gone. Quickly she tore all of her clothes off, put them on the rock, and slipped into the cool water.

Courtney kicked fiercely ahead, as if she could loosen her tangled thoughts and leave them behind in the cool water. She dove to the bottom and felt her hair fluttering against her nape. Then she did a somersault and floated on her back, staring up at the blue round of sky nestled in the canopy of trees.

For a while, Courtney tried not to think of anything. The water lapped at her ears. The tumbling waterfall sparkled with light through the trees. Flowering shrubs nodded in the slips of breeze.

"Insurance," Courtney suddenly said to herself, stroking on her back through the water. Her father had been paying insurance for years on the *Bluebeard*. He'd lost the sale, but he'd get his money back once he filed the claim.

Her breathing slowed, and Courtney rolled over in the water, taking a few lazy breaststrokes toward the waterfall. "The Mayday call." She continued to talk aloud to herself. "Winnie actually made the call. They're bound to come. And maybe KC is right. Maybe we *should* hope that help doesn't come too soon."

Something made Courtney stop thinking. She lifted her head up and tread water, looking at the pool's brushy bank. Then she froze. There, barely visible in the tangle of vegetation, was the top of a blond head. It moved, then ducked down. Someone was there, spying on her.

Courtney tried to think. She remembered Mookie's scraggly blond hair. "Mookie!" she called out. "It's not funny. Why don't you just go back down to the boat with the others?"

She slipped down in the water again, furious. What was the problem? Just last fall, she'd gone skinny-dipping in a mountain lake, only to find that Marielle Danner, a snotty Tri Beta, had taken photographs of her to smear her reputation. Why couldn't people leave her alone?

A moment later she resurfaced and smoothed the water off her face, looking back toward the brush. "Mookie?" she shouted. "Are you gone, you . . ." Suddenly Courtney's mouth dropped open. Through the bushes, she could see the barest outline of a face. A face that *wasn't* Mookie's. A face that she didn't know.

Courtney's heart jumped. She turned and darted away, heading back for the rock on the other edge of the pool. She clutched her clothing on the rock, then looked cautiously over her shoulder.

By this time, the guy had risen slightly above the thick leaves, so that his tanned face and bare, golden chest could be clearly seen. For a split second, her eyes meet his. His thatch of golden hair caught the light. His blond beard glistened, and his lips tensed, before he ducked back down again and disappeared without a sound.

Courtney hung for a moment on the rock. She felt angry, but she also knew that a part of her felt strangely drawn to the stranger's intense stare. Finally she heaved herself on the rock and yanked her sticky clothes back on, not knowing whether to run away or to follow the guy into the unknown jungle. For a while she just sat there, feeling her wet hair soak into the back of her shirt. Then she turned and headed quickly down the clearing. She ran across the sand into the cool sea, where she stood perfectly still, staring at the *Bluebeard*'s broken profile on the distant reef.

She caught her breath, digging her toes into the wet sand and staring at the waves, trying to get a grip. From what she'd seen, the island was clearly deserted. So who was the bearded stranger? Had she really seen him? Or was she in some kind of shock from last night's violent shipwreck?

Had the face at the waterfall been only a dream?

Fourteen

"o, ho, ho, and a bottle of rum," KC sang, dragging the *Bluebeard*'s tiny dinghy up on the beach, her eyes sparkling with adventure.

Winnie shaded her eyes and squinted into the morning sun. An hour ago, they'd made their first landing on the empty beach. Since then, she, Patrick, and Jack had been scouting the area for a protected tent site, while KC, Mookie, and Tony ferried supplies from the *Bluebeard*. Meanwhile, Courtney was still off exploring.

"Look at our haul, Win." KC dropped the bowline into the sand. She rubbed her hands together and dragged her pretend peg leg behind her. "We pillaged the shipwrecked *Bluebeard*! We have enough capers, herbed vinegar, and Dijon mustard to last us for a lifetime."

"Yahoo," Tony yelled.

"Gourmet city!" Mookie agreed.

"The tent site's over there, where Patrick is working," Winnie said dully, pointing down the beach to a sandy area surrounded with low brush. "He says it's pretty protected. Jack's going to build a storage area just this side of it. Did you guys remember the ax?"

Tony glanced down the beach, dropping a toolbox down to the sand. "Yep," he said shortly. "Anything else, boss?" he muttered, starting off down the beach.

Winnie opened the toolbox and took out the ax, while KC and Mookie carried duffel bags filled with blankets, clothing, tarps, and sleeping bags.

Winnie headed toward Jack, her feet slipping against the sand. Her stomach growled with hunger. Her elbows were scraped and raw from her fall during the storm. Then her eyes fixed on Jack, who was clearing brush near the storage area, carefully ripping away branches with his bare hands. Lying next to him in a huge, soggy pile were the *Bluebeard*'s vast mainsail and jib sail, which he had salvaged from the sinking deck. According to Jack, they had enough sailcloth to build two sleeping tents and a storage shelter, for which he was now trying to build a frame.

Winnie pushed ahead, grimly watching Jack's slow, careful movements. All of this survivalist activity was starting to make her nervous. Why weren't the white sails being used to make a huge SOS on the beach? A rescue helicopter wouldn't be able to see their tiny beach camp, but it could see a huge sail spread across the beach. They could use rocks and sticks to create an SOS sign on top of it.

They were in peril, Winnie thought nervously. Couldn't anyone see that? Only a few hours ago they'd all thought they'd be dead by morning. And they could have been, easily. It was a dangerous time, and it called for some drastic action. But everyone was acting as though this was some kind of Boy Scout Jamboree.

Winnie dug her heels in and stalked straight up the beach toward Jack. The others trekked past her toward the sleeping-tent sites, where Patrick was busy leveling sand. Finally Winnie stopped. She dropped the ax and glowered at Jack, remembering the way he'd grabbed the radio from her during the storm, the way he had attacked her in the St. Ramos alley.

Jack looked up at her through his jet-black sunglasses. Then he grabbed another branch and ripped it. His St. Christopher medal lay shining in the sun against his grubby gray sweatshirt. "You get the ax? I want to make some posts for the storage tent."

Slowly Winnie reached down and picked up the ax.

"Thanks," Jack said curtly, stepping forward to take it from her.

Winnie tightened her grip and held the ax up in front of his face. "Hold it right there," she barked. The sharp edge of the blade glinted in the sunlight.

Jack stepped back a little and crossed his arms over his chest. Then he rolled his eyes. "Okay. What?"

Winnie narrowed her eyes into two hard slits. "Tell me the truth."

Jack took off his sunglasses and let them dangle around his neck. "The truth about what? What the hell is your problem, Winnie Gottlieb?"

Winnie jerked the ax up in the air. "My *problem* involves the radio that you grabbed from me, *Jack*," she snarled.

Jack dug one foot in front of him and looked up at the sky. "Oh yeah, right. I staggered down the hatch to make a Mayday call and saw you standing there like a zombie with the radio in your hand."

"I was making a Mayday call!" Winnie screamed, as two sea gulls squawked and flapped away.

"How was I to know that?" Jack yelled back, his dark eyes flashing at her as he leaned forward, nearly touching her nose with his. He didn't seem to mind the glinting ax hanging over her head. "I was trying to get it away from you so *I* could call."

"Then why didn't you?" Winnie cried, suddenly sinking down onto the hot sand.

Jack raised his hand to his face and wiped away the sweat. "I—I just saw you standing there looking so scared, and I—I guess I just sort of froze for a moment," he said quietly.

Winnie's lips parted. She could feel her pulse rising strangely, as if he'd flicked a switch inside of her. She wanted to drop the ax on his foot and walk away. But something made her stay. "You froze," Winnie repeated, rubbing the back of her neck impatiently.

Jack cleared his throat. "And then the boat heeled

over and we fell into the galley. You grabbed it from me, and I tried to get it back. I didn't know you'd made a call. I didn't know you knew how."

Winnie slowly raised her head. "You didn't want to be rescued," she said intently. "You took the radio from me, then you ripped it out and destroyed the radar."

"It was destroyed in the storm!" Jack came back.

"You're lying," Winnie snapped at him. "We're stuck here on this horrible island all because of you. All because *you're* running away from something. Probably the law. And you're perfectly willing to drag us along with you."

Jack yanked a branch away, sending a flutter of green leaves onto the white sand. His gold earring glinted in the sun, and Winnie could see the sweat running from his scalp down the strong lines of his cheek. She saw it again: the lost, confused look, the anger. Maybe it was in the taut lines of his mouth, maybe his eyes. But whatever it was, it made her nervous and angry, and most of all, it scared her to death.

"I'll lose my mind if I don't get home soon," Winnie said abruptly. "I'm not equipped for this."

Jack kicked the sand. "Don't see why going home would help."

"Oh, you don't, do you?" Winnie exploded. "Well, what if something happens to one of us? What if we're never rescued and we die of starvation? Is that what you want?"

Jack looked at her again, his lips tightening. "Look, like I told you before, you have no idea what I want. You know nothing about me. Okay?"

Winnie stood up. "But I'm going to find out, Jack Frederick Cruz," she snapped, turning and marching down the beach away from him.

"There's something about you that makes me nervous," she muttered to herself as she trudged toward the others. "And I'm going to find out what it is."

The next day, Liza and Patrick sat quietly on the beach, watching the wreck of the *Bluebeard* crumble slowly into the clear water.

Patrick shook his head and leaned back on his elbows. His bare torso shone in the sun, and his jeans were caked with clumps of sand. "Too bad. She was a fine boat."

Liza shifted a little, then glanced over at his slightly stubbly cheek. Her eyes roamed down his well-defined chest, long arms, and tapered fingers. Since Patrick was a sailor, she should probably act as if she, too, were devastated. But actually, she wasn't that upset. She felt much safer on dry land. And now that she wasn't seasick, she could spend her time focusing on Patrick, instead of obsessing on how to keep from vomiting on him during casual conversation. "Yeah, I loved being on the open sea," Liza lied, pretending to adjust her position on the soft sand, but actually trying to inch closer to him.

Patrick nodded slowly, as if his head were very heavy. Then he shifted onto the elbow farthest from Liza and bit his thumbnail.

Liza's eyes darted nervously to the side. When she'd found him here a few minutes before, he'd invited her to sit down. But now he looked distant.

"There goes the bow," Patrick said softly, looking out at where the final white triangle was slipping into the blue ocean. "We'll be harder to find now."

"They'll find us," Liza leaned over and whispered into his ear. "And our camp is decent enough." She rubbed her arm muscles. "God, I haven't worked this hard in ages."

"Yeah." Patrick looked back over his shoulder at the camp they'd begun constructing yesterday, and had just completed that afternoon. Using the *Blue-beard*'s sails, two white lean-to tents had been set up on opposite sides of a clearing just off the beach, supported by the surrounding coconut palms and yards of boat line. Between them, a partly covered central cooking area had been organized, complete with a campfire pit, a makeshift table that was now stacked with their food supply, and a Coleman stove. A few yards down the beach, the low-lying storage compound had been set up, stocked with the boat's tools, diving equipment and air compressors, plus fishing gear and bottled water.

"You're upset," Liza said soothingly, stroking the side of his arm with one knuckle. "You lost your paintings. All that work . . ."

"Nah, nothing to it," Patrick said with a sigh. "You don't want to hear my sad tale."

Liza sat taller. Actually, she *did* want to hear every single word of his tale. Every thought, every nuance, his teeniest, tiniest thoughts. After all, this was her first chance to talk with him alone since the storm. She'd spent hours trying to recover from shock and seasickness, and then as soon as she felt well enough to stand, they'd put her to work. They'd put KC to work too, for that matter. And whatever feelings were brewing between KC and Patrick on board—well, they certainly weren't going anywhere at the moment.

Liza needed some answers.

She carefully cleared her throat. Then she looked down at her painted toes and dug them into the sand. "I—um—never did get the chance to thank you, Patrick."

"Thank me? For what?"

Liza stirred. She thought carefully. "Well, for saving my life, of course."

Patrick tilted his head toward her. "Oh, that."

Liza let out a half-laugh, relieving at least some of her pent-up tension. "Well, you have to admit it, Patrick. You *did* jump in and save me. I don't know how to swim and—and I would have drowned without your help. So I'm thanking you."

She looked shyly at him. Her heart speeded up when she saw that he was staring at her. He had a curious expression on his face, as if he were searching for something behind her words. "I mean it," she blurted.

"I know."

Liza was starting to lose her patience now. Maybe Patrick was like one of those great books with the fascinating covers you couldn't wait to dig into, until you discovered that it was impossible to read. "Well, what I'm trying to say, Patrick, is that I'm sorry you had to lose your paintings. I mean, even after you pulled me out, you stayed with me. You didn't go after them."

Patrick made a fist and rested his forehead on it. "I don't know why I did what I did, Liza," he said softly.

Liza felt a flicker of hope. Could it be true? Did Patrick really sacrifice his paintings for her—because he cared? Slowly she felt a warm glow spread through her body. She looked across at his strained expression. Patrick might be the shy, artistic type, but she knew chemical attraction when she felt it. There was no denying it any longer. Patrick was crazy about her.

"Patrick," Liza said suddenly, rising to her knees and slipping her bare arm around his solid shoulder. "Oh, Patrick, thank you," she whispered, before she found his lips and kissed him with all the hope and tenderness she had.

Liza felt him kiss her back, then pull away slightly. She pressed again gently, not knowing where to go or what to think. Patrick still seemed distant, but then, he wasn't pushing her off, either.

"Patrick!" she heard KC's voice call from behind them.

Liza looked up, then Patrick shifted and looked around too.

Liza watched victoriously as KC's mouth dropped open, then closed again into a line of pure contempt. "Never mind," she snapped, before turning away sharply and stalking back to the covered eating area.

Liza looked back at Patrick, then smiled with satisfaction at the gently rolling surf. After a moment she felt Patrick stir, then stand up.

"I'm taking off," Patrick said tersely.

"You're what?"

He pointed inland. "Those cliffs up above our camp. I want to check them out. See if I can get a view of anything useful."

Liza scrambled to her feet, raking her tousled hair off her face and brushing the sand off her shorts. "I'll go with you."

"No." Patrick shook his head. "Really. You stay here and rest. You need it."

Liza gave him a desperate smile. "I feel great. Never felt better. Hike? I was made to hike. I can hike forever. They call me Miss Sierra Club back in Rocky Mountain country."

Patrick was hurrying forward into a sandy clearing that headed inland. "It would be fun, Liza. But I want you to get some rest, okay? Eat something."

Liza dug her feet into the sand and rushed ahead with a joyful leap. Was he kidding? Did he actually think she wanted to hang around camp with KC, Courtney, and the others, when she could have him all to herself?

No way, darling, Liza thought, grabbing her sun hat from a bush and skipping ahead into the brush with Patrick. *You don't know Liza Ruff. I've gotten this far with you; I'm not giving up now.*

Fifteen

KC's head was on fire. She turned on her damp sleeping bag and stared bitterly up at the sailcloth tent ceiling, still lit with the late-afternoon sun. Her heart was beating with fury, but her eyes were as dry as two stones.

Barely two hours before, she'd seen Liza and Patrick kissing on the beach. KC kicked her foot in the air. "Patrick Hanson," she whispered with disgust, "at least I know now that you're a louse."

She yanked the sleeping bag's zipper back and forth, still scolding herself for having been misled by the cozy sailing lessons, the magic of her first scuba dive. She had thought Patrick cared. She had thought he was different. She had even risked her life to try to save his paintings. How could he?

Her trip to the Caribbean suddenly took on a whole new meaning. It wasn't about meeting a gorgeous guy—it was about one thing and one thing only: *surviving*. She rolled over on her side and stared intently at her blistered hands. She knew she would survive this shipwreck, and then go home and survive the world back home . . . in style.

Because she would be rich.

There was a moan, and KC looked across at Winnie sprawled on her back, rolling her head back and forth in her sleep. Next to her, Courtney slept quietly, a sheen of sweat covering her forehead. Meanwhile, Mookie, Tony, and Jack were supposed to be napping in the guys' tent. Everyone was completely exhausted from the shipwreck and the work setting up camp. Patrick and Liza, on the other hand, had left the beach shortly after the infamous kiss. And they had not returned.

KC sat up and buried her hot face in her hands. Chemistry. That's what she thought she and Patrick had. She'd look into his green eyes and see his smile, thinking the smile was meant for her alone. She'd hear him talk and think his words were for her. Every glance, every gesture—she'd thought it was for her. How could she be so stupid? It hadn't been anything but her own imagination building something that wasn't there.

KC picked up Winnie's baseball hat and fanned herself. Then she heard a rustling outside the tent.

Falling down on her hands and knees, she crawled

across the sandy tent floor in her bathing suit. Then she pulled the door flap aside a half-inch and peered out. A few yards away, slipping out of the other sleeping tent, she could see Tony and Mookie. Tony was crouched down, touching a finger to his lips, while Mookie tiptoed quietly behind him.

KC froze. She stared as the two headed down to the beach.

They were up to something—something she could sink her teeth into. Money.

Quickly slipping on her sneakers, KC tiptoed out of the tent and darted across the clearing until she was hidden behind a low bush. To her right, she could see Tony and Mookie moving down the beach toward the storage tent, murmuring something intently between themselves. KC strained to hear above the droning of insects and the steady, distant rush of waves. She knew it had to be something about the treasure, and she was determined to find out. Frustrated, KC stuck her head out of the bush and watched the two disappear inside the storage-tent flap. Seeing her opportunity, she sprang up and hurried through the soft sand, collapsing on the ground near the back of the tent.

". . . know it was," Tony was whispering loudly. "I saw it when we were ferrying stuff back to the beach."

"Man," Mookie came back softly. "You think you saw it, but maybe you're just *wishing* it, man."

"Look," Tony insisted. "It was rust-colored sea grass, okay? The kind nature doesn't make. The kind that comes from iron. And it's right off that big old reef."

KC covered her mouth, muffling her gasp. She could hear air tanks knocking against one another in the tent, then the sound of wet suits being zipped. Mookie and Tony had spotted the sea grass and they were going to investigate the area for a sunken ship, possibly laden with gold.

Mookie broke the silence. "Can you believe Patrick? First he tells us not to go diving because we might miss the rescue helicopter. Then *he* takes off."

Tony let out a soft chuckle. "Looks like old Liza finally broke him down, huh? To hell with your big diving ban, Patrick. We're going anyway, Captain."

KC carefully crouched down in the sand, then crawled around the tent on her knees until she had a clear view of the beach. She watched patiently until Tony emerged with Mookie, wearing everything they needed for scuba diving except their fins, which they held, along with Mookie's fishing spear and Tony's diving light, as they scurried down to the water. As soon as they were gone, KC made her move. She slipped into the storage tent and grabbed the wet suit she'd used only once before.

I can do this, KC thought grimly, pulling the wet suit over her one-piece bathing suit. Near a pile of tools, she found the bright yellow buoyancy-compensator vest, and quickly packed the air tank and regulator onto it, checking the oxygen level. "Full," KC muttered, noticing the arrow pointing to the blue part of the gauge.

Grabbing a pair of fins and a mask, KC poked her head out of the tent, then ran across the beach to the water, the heavy air tank banging painfully against her back. She looked up just in time to see Tony's and Mookie's heads drop below the surface.

"Gotcha," KC whispered to herself, sitting down long enough to pull the fins on and clamp the mask to her head. Then she waded into the crystal-clear water and slipped the regulator into her mouth, trying to stay calm.

Breathe normally. In and out. Don't go down too far, she reminded herself. *And remember, you're a beginner. That tank will last you less than a half hour.*

"Thank you for the lessons at least, Patrick," KC muttered between gritted teeth. Then, taking a deep breath, she lowered her knees and slipped down into the clearness of the aquamarine waters.

Once submerged, KC kicked off the sandy-white bottom and moved quickly ahead, trying to keep her breathing normal despite her excitement. Up ahead, through a cloud of tiny parrot fish, she could see the distant outlines of Tony's and Mookie's air tanks and fins. She kicked steadily ahead, trying not to linger as her body slid over the starlike corals below. Now and then, the feathery orange and white gills of a tube-worm waved in the water like a peacock fan.

After swimming for ten minutes, KC began to see the faint outline of the submerged *Bluebeard,* collapsed, defeated, and now resting on the sandy ocean floor. She could see how it had plunged into the toothy coral, then fallen back down its slope.

Shaking her head silently, KC kicked ahead. Tony and Mookie were now out of sight. But she saw a narrow, ten-foot-wide gap in the crimson reef where they must have slipped through to the other side. She angled her body away from the shipwreck and darted back. Then she swam through the coral opening, being careful not to scrape against its dangerously sharp edges.

The opposite side of the reef was clearer and calm. Giant orange sea anemones clung to underwater boulders, their fingers waving slowly in the water. Schools of tiny purple fish fluttered and darted. KC could have watched the beautiful scene all afternoon, but she was intent on something far more important.

She kicked away from the reef, then stopped. An eerie feeling crept over her. Was it the shadow of something just out of her field of vision?

She twisted around.

A sound, perhaps? Or just the rising rhythm of her own heart in her chest?

There was a sudden movement behind her. She panicked as she felt something grasp her waist, then her neck. She struggled. There was a third arm. KC's heart stopped. A tentacle? It was grasping her under the arm, then around the knees. A giant eel? An *octopus?*

Suddenly there was a cloud of bubbles and a pair of masks. The hands left her body. All she could see were Mookie's and Tony's faces in front of her. She'd been discovered, but they didn't seem to care. She tread water and stared as they shook their fingers at her and planted their hands on their hips in mock admonition. Mookie held up his fishing spear victoriously. On the end was impaled a medium-sized flat-fish that KC assumed was headed for the camp stove that night.

KC gave them a sheepish wave.

Tony kicked toward her again and pretended to be a fish nibbling on her knee. Mookie swam up to her and crossed his eyes behind his mask.

KC felt herself relax. Good old Tony and Mookie. Did they ever let anything bother them? It didn't look as if they were trying to get rid of her. Maybe they figured they could use another diver for the treasure hunt. Her heart speeded up. Tony was motioning for her to follow him. She readied herself to kick forward, but felt a tug on her arm from behind.

She swiveled around. The ocean suddenly felt quiet and big. She looked into Mookie's mask, but his face wasn't cross-eyed and silly anymore. It was terror-struck. Slowly he raised his hand and pointed down the reef. KC couldn't breathe.

Only about twenty yards away from them, a large, gray shark was swimming slowly their way.

Winnie was running down a long, dark alley. She could hear her feet pounding against the cool cobblestones. Her chest was begging for air. There was light at the end of the tunnel, but the harder she ran, the farther away it seemed. She squinted and saw that KC, Courtney, and Liza were all there at the end, urging her to run faster. Then she blinked and the image faded. Instead, she saw Josh at the end. He looked sad and distant. She tried to run into his arms, but something stopped her. She swung around. It was Jack, sitting quietly in a chair where the tunnel branched off. The light was soft. She could hear waves and steel drums. He called her over. "Why are you afraid, Winnie? Why are you afraid? Afraid? Afraid? Afraid?"

Winnie sat up and blinked. She looked around the tent, then rubbed her eyes and fell back onto her sleeping bag. From the weird, flat light in the tent, she could tell it was still midafternoon. Courtney was sleeping peacefully across from her, but KC was gone.

"I don't know why I'm so afraid," Winnie whispered, a tear rolling slowly down her face and into her ear. She stared up at the white sailcloth and listened to the squawk and trilling of birds in the jungle behind her. The muggy air seemed to press down on her. She could feel the sweat bunching up the spiky mess of her hair.

She sprang up and crawled outside, squinting at the gray, glaring sky and wispy low clouds. Down the beach, the blue waves rolled continuously back and forth. Up above, the palms stood perfectly still in the shimmering heat.

Winnie stood up, her hands still shaking from the vivid dream. Then she wiped her sweaty palms on her shorts and took a few steps toward the beach. To the left was the low-lying storage tent. To the right, propped up against the trunk of a palm tree, was Jack, sound asleep.

For a moment Winnie just stood there in the sand, staring at the slow rise and fall of his bare, tanned chest. His face was hidden beneath a beat-up straw hat, and his feet were dug into the sand.

You have no idea what I want. You know nothing about me. Jack's angry words echoed in her mind.

"You're right," Winnie murmured. "And now I'm

going to find out." She turned back to the sleeping tents. The air was slow and hot, but her mind was suddenly racing with purpose. "Jack and his secrets," she muttered to herself. "His big, obvious padlock. His big, dramatic you-don't-understands. It's almost as if he's begging someone to find out what makes him tick."

Grabbing the ax from the eating table, Winnie darted over to the guys' tent and quietly stuck her head inside, expecting to see Mookie and Tony. She gritted her teeth with satisfaction. The only thing in the tent was a few scattered sleeping bags, a backpack, and a neat bedroll in the back. Winnie crawled forward, breathing in the tent's damp, sweaty, male smell. Her heart thumping, she shoved aside the sleeping bags and packs, then the bedroll, revealing Jack's beat-up but expensive-looking leather case. She looked carefully back at the tent flap, then ran her fingers along the suitcase's heavy stitching and brass trim. She stared at the steel padlock that had been put through two brass eyeholes under the handle.

"What are you hiding, Jack Frederick Cruz?" Winnie said, sitting back on her heels and pausing as she gripped the ax handle. It was such a small suitcase to answer such a big question. And why did she even care? She was wrong to be in the tent, wrong to want to smash the lock. But somewhere, deep down, she had the strange feeling the case held more than the secret to Jack. Winnie wiped a bead of sweat from her brow, her thoughts swirling wildly in her head. Why did she have the eerie feeling that Jack's answers were somehow all tied up with hers?

Winnie took a deep breath, raised the ax up into

the air, and smashed it down on the lock. It snapped open. Panting with excitement, she lifted the suitcase lid and gasped. The inside of the case was packed with neat stacks of crisp twenty-dollar bills, a Rolex watch, and a black-and-white photograph. Her heart falling, Winnie picked up a stack of bills and flipped it absently with her thumb. Of course she'd suspected Jack of being a criminal, but she didn't want to believe it. She wanted to believe his story about needing a padlock in the cheap St. Ramos dives he stayed in. But this? It looked as if Jack had enough money to stay in the finest hotels in the Caribbean.

Sadly Winnie picked up the photograph and realized that it was a formal portrait of Jack, standing in what appeared to be an ornamental garden. She looked closely. The face looked strangely familiar, but everything else was completely different. Wearing an expensive-looking suit and with neatly clipped hair, he was posing stone-faced in front of a large home, leaning against a garden bench.

She put the picture away and stared quietly at the money. She'd wanted to believe him. There was something about Jack that . . . Winnie tried to think. Well, maybe there was something real about him. Something human. A part of her wanted to stay away from him, but another part was urging her closer.

But now . . . this. What was he doing? Petty thefts? Drugs?

Winnie suddenly stiffened. Through the thin tent walls, she could hear the sound of footsteps pushing across the soft sand. Quickly she shut the lid and turned around on her knees. But it was too late.

Winnie stared at Jack, horrified. For a moment he just crouched stiffly in the tent flap, his mouth open and his eyes full of fear.

Whah whah WHAH WHAH. A distant beating sound began to draw near. Winnie looked up. Jack looked over his shoulder.

Whah whah whah whah WHAH WHAH.

Winnie's heart jumped. "It's the rescue helicopter! Oh, my God. They've found us!" she screamed, leaping up and dashing past Jack through the tent flap. "Courtney! The rescue helicopter is here!" she shouted in the other tent, before she ran with all of her might toward the beach, waving and jumping wildly in the air.

Sixteen

....

Courtney tried to open her eyes. There was an echo in her head. A faraway sound. She blinked, but her lids felt heavy.

"Courtney!" she heard the call again like a splash of cold water. "There's a helicopter over the beach."

Courtney struggled to get up on her elbow. The air was hot. Her head felt like a heavy bag of sand. She looked over at the tent flap, where Winnie's panicked face hovered. "Wha—what?" she mumbled.

"It's a rescue party," Winnie yelled. "Get up fast! It's flying up and down the beach looking for us, but they can't see us. Our camp is in too far. *Come on!*"

Courtney sprang up and burst out of the tent, following Winnie, who was racing back to the beach, waving her hands over her head wildly. Meanwhile, a bare-chested Jack was down by the water, staring calmly at the sky.

"It's gone," Jack shouted back at them.

"NO!" Winnie screamed, running out into the water, yelling and trying to look in all directions at once.

Courtney looked worriedly up at the cloud cover. Between the wisps of low-lying clouds and their protected camp, it could be hard to find them. "They'll circle around again. They'll see us if we stay right here."

Winnie was screaming hysterically into empty air, waving her thin arms. She ripped off the grubby T-shirt she wore over her bikini top and waved it in the air. "Help, help! We're down here!"

"Forget it," Jack shouted, stuffing his hands into his hiking shorts and looking down at his feet. "It's gone."

Courtney could see the tears streaming down Winnie's face as she continued to jump up and down. "We should have put a signal on the beach!" Winnie screamed. "We should have used the sails for an SOS instead of for tents. It's your fault, Jack!"

Jack turned away.

Courtney looked around, still trying to get her groggy thoughts together. Patrick? Liza? Mookie? Tony? Where was everyone?

Winnie raced past her toward the tents again. "I'm going to make a signal with the sleeping bags and tarps," she shouted. "I'm going to find the others,"

Courtney shouted back. She looked at Jack, who had turned to walk down the beach, away from the camp.

Courtney frowned, then scrambled back up the beach to a clearing behind the tent site. Since yesterday, she'd suspected it sloped up into the cliffs. And from the cliffs, she might be able to sight the others—if not wave down the helicopter herself.

Grabbing her deck shoes from the tent, Courtney jammed them on her feet and began running inland. She ran carefully, trying to watch for holes and rocks. Any injury on an island as deserted as this could make things very difficult—even dangerous, since they had no doctor or real medical supplies. She ran up a hundred yards from their camp through the vibrant hibiscus and broad-leafed brush, feeling the sweat pour down her forehead. The humid jungle floor was carpeted with grasses and thick, flowering bushes, but as the hill sloped up, the air became drier and the vegetation thinned out. Courtney was puffing hard, but trying to control her breathing so she didn't run out of energy.

Finally the hill steepened. Courtney scrambled up, now above the junglelike canopy that fringed the island's white beaches. At this height, scraggly palms dotted the hillsides and the dry grasses whipped in the wind. Even higher above her, the reddish, rocky cliffs loomed. Panting, Courtney balled up her fists and urged herself on toward the high inland cliffs, swirling with the dartlike white terns that nested there. The damp clouds were blowing only shreds of moisture now. If a helicopter flew over, she knew she could be seen.

Still straining upward, Courtney's calf muscles were

beginning to burn. Her throat was raw, and the high island wind was whipping her hair over her face. Stepping onto what seemed like a narrow animal trail, she began a slow, zigzagging climb through a series of sandy boulders. The terns shrieked warnings above her head. Tiny rocks slipped beneath her feet, and she could hear them pinging down the steep, rocky hill below. Courtney dug her toes into the path, half listening to the sound of the falling rocks, and half straining to hear something else. Was it a pounding? A helicopter? She stopped, trying to hear through the blood rushing in her ears.

Then she realized that what she'd been hearing were footsteps—right behind her.

"Patrick? KC? Jack?" Courtney called back over the crest of the hill. She was high up now. Below, she could see the cove, and even the high reef where the boat had gone down. The wind flapped through her hair. "Hey, guys?"

The steps grew louder, and Courtney looked down breathlessly as a head emerged over the crest. Her heart stopped when she saw the thatch of blond hair and the golden beard glinting in the sunlight.

It was the guy from the waterfall. He hadn't been a hallucination, after all.

"You . . ." Courtney drew in her breath. "I *did* see you. . . . I . . ."

The guy moved slowly ahead, not saying a word. His eyebrows drew close and his lips parted, as if he were just as stunned to see her. For a moment she stared at the piercing blue of his eyes, which were fixed on her with an expression of anger and frustration. Courtney ran her eyes down his tanned and dusty body. The guy was barefoot, and wore a pair of blue shorts that were so shredded they were practically falling off his tall, muscular body. His hair tumbled down his shoulders, mixing with the hair of his beard. His arms were muscular, as if he were used to heavy outdoor work, but she could see that his hands were clean and well-shaped. Around his neck he wore a handmade string of tiny white shells.

Courtney felt a chill run through her body. The guy looked as if he hadn't seen a soul in years. And now he was staring at her with an expression so wild and free, he almost looked like an animal hunting for easy prey.

Desperately, Courtney looked up at the sharp red cliffs behind her. Then she looked down at the rolling hills leading back to the jungle and beach. She knew that if she had any chance in the world, she had to dodge him on the path and somehow outrun him to safety.

She lunged to the right, digging her shoe into the dust. "I, uh, please, uh . . . let me by," Courtney stammered.

To her horror, the guy suddenly reached one arm out as if to stop her. Courtney fell against it, then tried to pull away. "No!" she shouted. "Let me go!"

She felt herself tipping toward the edge of the cliff, then the guy's strong left arm grabbed her. Their feet scuffled on the dry path. She righted herself, then grabbed his smooth arms and tried to push away. "Let me go!" she screamed, wrenching herself around.

Suddenly she felt her foothold on the edge of the path weaken. There was a crumbling sound, and she began falling backward. Her hands were still instinctively clasped around the stranger's arms, and as she fell, she felt him falling with her. Courtney closed her eyes as her head thudded against the side of the cliff and sharp gravel scraped against her back. Together, she and the stranger were tumbling over each other helplessly. She slid, still trying to shove him away. Her knees banged against the hard gravel. Her necked whipped as she rolled. She looked down as a boulder loomed below. Then she jerked her head up again, staring into the guy's face closely for the first time.

Courtney felt everything fall into slow motion. The beautiful face, the blue eyes, the glint of golden hair. Then the painful thud of her head against a rock, and blackness.

"I'm gonna have a heart attack," Liza moaned, lifting her purple sneaker one more time and setting it down a few inches farther along the dusty trail.

"We made it," Patrick said quietly, leaning his forearms on his knees and staring out over the rolling view of blue ocean. "This is the highest point on the cliff. Check it out. We're practically right over the water."

Liza stopped and raked her hair back with all ten broken nails. She looked at the waves crashing on the black rocks below, then down at the smooth stretch of beach beyond it, where they'd camped. Her sleeveless blouse was gritty and stiff with salt water. Her feet were blistered, and her lungs felt as though they were going to burst. Worse, her shoulders were so sunburned, little white blisters were beginning to pop out on the stretched red surface of her skin. "Yeah, now that's a million-dollar view a developer would kill for, huh?" she panted, collapsing down on the ground next to Patrick.

Abruptly Patrick stood up and shaded his eyes with one hand. "Damn," he whispered.

Liza looked up. "What?"

Patrick's lips were pressed into a tight, angry line. He stretched out his arm and pointed. "Out there, on the reef. Divers. One, two . . ."

"Tony and Mookie?" Liza strained to make out their tiny heads in the aqua water near the reef.

". . . three," Patrick finally said. "I told them not to go diving. We need to be watching for rescue helicopters and boats. Damn it!"

Liza frowned. "That third diver must be KC," she said with a sidelong glance at Patrick. "Remember? You taught her how."

"Yeah," Patrick said angrily. "How could they be so stupid? I told them to stay *near the camp*."

Liza narrowed her eyebrows and squinted up at Patrick. She'd never seen him so angry and upset. He'd always been the perfect gentleman. A model of a cool, calm captain. Liza sighed, distracted. Her eyes roamed up from his fingers and leather watchband to his bare arm and muscular shoulder. She took in his strong jawline and the dashing blackness of his sailing sunglasses. Maybe it was all that exercise, maybe it was all the fresh air, but she was suddenly feeling very good. She could positively feel the blood coursing through her veins and down to the tips of her toes. Sure, Patrick was mad and everything. But they were alone in paradise. What more could she want?

"Patrick?" Liza asked. She raised one hand and placed it on his thigh. Then slowly she began walking two fingers teasingly down his leg toward his knee.

"Uh, yeah?" Patrick muttered, his eyes fixed on the three distant divers as they came up from the water, then descended again.

Liza walked her two fingers back up his thigh again, staring intently at the little shreds on the seam of his jeans. "How do you feel about me? I mean, do you feel the way I do?"

She raised her face shyly. She could see the muscles clenching in his jaw. For a moment, all was still. Then, all in a rush, Liza saw a swiftly moving helicopter heading right for them on the cliff.

The tiny craft swooped down over them, then zipped down toward the beach, where it razed the coastline, then raced inland again.

"HEEEYYY!" Liza screamed, jumping up and tearing off her blouse. "Over here!" She waved it wildly over her head, her stomach doing a flip-flop. Were they going to be rescued, after all? "Patrick! Do you think they saw us?"

"Liza," Patrick murmured, placing his hand on her bare shoulder and turning her toward him.

Liza looked down and bit her lip. All she had been wearing under her blouse was her pink bathing-suit top. She shivered. Patrick was slowly drawing her closer, rubbing her bare back with the palm of his hand. "Patrick?" she whispered.

"Liza," he whispered back, running his hands down the outside of her bare, sunburned arms, sending prickles all over her body.

Liza's eyes darted frantically between the helicopter's path and Patrick's gorgeous face. "The helico—" Liza squeaked out the barest protest before he bent his head down and kissed her deeply on the mouth.

She let her head fall back a little, feeling as if she were going to faint. His hands were all over her now, and the vision of rescue was gradually fading into the back of her consciousness.

"I can't stand it anymore," Patrick murmured into her ear, before biting it gently. "I've been trying to keep my distance, Liza."

Tears began to fill Liza's eyes. Was it true? Was he crazy about her *too*? "I didn't *know*, Patrick," Liza said, delirious with joy, feeling her knees buckle and hearing the crash of the pounding surf below.

Patrick nuzzled her neck. "That night on the boat, when we talked about our art—I knew it then."

"Oh, Patrick," Liza moaned, grasping his neck and kissing him more deeply than before.

"I knew I loved you when I saw you slipping away from me during the storm," Patrick went on. "But I just couldn't tell you. Even after that kiss on the beach, I just didn't know how."

Liza pressed against his lips harder and clamped

her body to his, hearing in the distance the to-and-fro of the helicopter below them. Together they fell back onto the soft dirt. There was no holding back anymore, Liza realized. She loved Patrick. She needed him. And as for being rescued by the helicopter, well . . . Liza didn't care if they ever went home again.

Back down on the beach, Winnie was still running frantically back and forth, waving her Mickey Mouse Bermudas in one hand and her skimpy top in the other.

"HELP!" she shouted until her throat was raw. She watched as the helicopter sailed a half-mile down the beach, then circled aimlessly over the water for a few minutes before heading inland. "OVER HERE," she screamed again. Her lungs felt as if they were tearing up inside, and her throat was ragged and raw. She thought about cave people hundreds of thousands of years ago, living in wild places like this. *They had probably screamed like that,* Winnie thought frantically, *just before they were attacked by wild beasts and eaten alive.*

She ran into the water, every muscle in her body shaking. A wave poured in, then drew back, sucking her feet into the white sand. She knew they should have set up some kind of signal on the beach with the sails. She knew why Jack didn't want to attract attention: He was a criminal. The suitcase full of money proved it. But what about the others? What about Patrick?

"The sails," Winnie said suddenly out loud. She twisted around and stared at the long white storage tent Jack had made from a huge length of the mainsail.

Suddenly Winnie turned and ran up the beach. With all of her might, she ripped the sail from its makeshift frame. A large chunk of it ripped away from the structure and Winnie thudded back into the sand. Then, with her last remaining ounce of strength, she yanked the end of it out from under the felled trunk of a coconut tree.

The helicopter had to come back, she thought. It was probably circling around the island now. And when it did return . . .

Winnie grasped a corner of the sail and ran back down the beach toward the lapping water. The white cloth fluttered behind her like a huge white wing. She looked around. Where *was* everyone? Why weren't they here to help?

She heard the scream of squabbling sea gulls, then her name being shouted above the roar of the waves. Winnie ignored it, continued to run up and down the beach with her vast, white SOS banner floating behind her.

"Stop!" she heard Jack yell as he drew close behind her. She whirled around and looked in horror as he grabbed the other end of the sail and pulled it down into the waves.

"LET GO!" Winnie screamed at him, yanking the soggy end out of his hands and running faster. But it was hopeless. Jack's grip was too strong, and the sail finally slipped out of her hands.

"Winnie!" Jack shouted. "It's useless. They can't see us."

"Thanks to you, you *thief*!" Winnie screamed back, running away from him as the helicopter dipped over the opposite end of the beach.

"Look," Jack shouted breathlessly, running behind her. "We'll get picked up. I promise you, Winnie. Pleasure boats come by here all the time, believe me."

"I've never believed anything you said," Winnie yelled over her shoulder. She wiped her face with the back of her hand, then kept running. She could have run and run forever. But she felt him behind her. His feet splashed in the water next to her and his hand fell heavily on her shoulder, slowing her down.

"Get your hands off me," Winnie screamed. "I saw the suitcase full of cash. I saw the stolen watch."

"Winnie, stop!" he shouted. "Look, it's not what you think. I just can't be found by the Coast Guard, that's all."

"What?" Winnie screeched incredulously, just as she saw the helicopter make a final dip over the end of the beach, then angle off toward the horizon. She staggered in the water, drawing in air and beginning to cry all at the same time. "Look what you've *done*," she yelled at him. "Now we're stuck, all because you don't want to turn yourself in, you slimy thief. Or smuggler. Or whatever you are. Happy now?"

Winnie tried to whirl herself away, but Jack quickly grabbed her by the shoulders. "Look, Winnie," he said shakily. "Look at me." Winnie looked up at him, feeling the water swirl around her ankles and the hot wind blow in her hair. His hard face and dark eyebrows were the same. But now there was something else—a loneliness, a pain behind his eyes she'd never noticed before, maybe because she hadn't wanted to look too close. His tiny gold earring glinted as a cloud moved away from the sun. "I'm not a thief, Winnie," Jack said, just as a wave poured in around their knees. "And I'm not a smuggler."

Winnie grabbed his hands and flung them off her shoulders. "Then what are you, Jack?" she shouted. "What the hell are you?"

"I'm a liar," Jack said simply, not moving. "A coward." Winnie searched his face, unable to speak. "I'm sorry, Winnie." Jack bent his head back until he was looking straight up into the clouds, his face filled with pain that looked a lot like her own. "I'm sorry I caused so much trouble, because you don't deserve this."

Winnie felt her lips part in wonder.

"I'm sorry, Winnie, that I ever came into your life."

Seventeen

KC's adrenaline was racing through her veins like a knife.

Desperately, she tried to slow her breathing so that she could conserve precious air in her tank. But she was too intent on getting away from the lethal shark that had been trailing them in the water for almost the last ten minutes.

She kicked madly toward the reef, trying to get downcurrent. Though Mookie had immediately dropped his spear and fish when they spotted the shark, the huge beast still seemed interested in him. KC gulped. The shark was no baby. It was at least eight feet long, and its thick gray skin was covered with the scars of a long-lived fighter. For a few minutes, they'd dodged it behind a large coral formation, but seconds later, its enormous row of sharp teeth had loomed around the corner. The only thing they'd been able to do was play a deadly game of tag in the shadowy water.

And time was running out.

KC glanced briefly over her shoulder, where her air tank's gauge needle was dipping precariously into the red danger zone. Five, maybe ten minutes was all she had left. Then she felt a hand on her shoulder. Whipping around, she saw Tony's outline behind her. He was shaking his head frantically and signaling for them to surface. Instantly, she understood. They didn't have enough air to play tag. All they could do was surface and pray.

KC lunged ahead and grabbed Mookie, motioning for him to surface too. Behind his mask, she could see his eyes were round with terror.

Everything's going to be okay, Mookie, KC began to chant inside her head. She remembered Patrick's orders to surface no faster than the rise of her own bubbles. Clasping Mookie's fingers with her right hand and Tony's in the other, they slowly moved up toward the shimmering ocean ceiling. Once they were on the surface, KC reasoned that they could quickly reach the beach. The three kicked patiently up, and KC could feel her eyeballs about to burst from the strain of looking in all directions for the dreaded shark. Bolts of light played eerily on the scarlet coral formations. Schools of yellow-tailed parrot fish slipped past them in perfect formation. But KC barely noticed, her heart was pounding so furiously with terror.

Then KC saw the shark again, swimming toward them from the right. For a moment, she stopped breathing. This time, the shark wasn't here for a casual look. He was swimming at full speed, his tail whipping purposefully, his blunt nose pointed directly at Mookie.

NO! she thought wildly. She clung to Mookie's elbow, armed with the desperate thought that maybe the shark would be more afraid of three people than just one. But a moment later the shark's jaws lunged for Mookie, and KC could feel the quick jab in her side as Mookie took the blow. A trail of bright red blood began to stream from Mookie's arm, and KC watched in horror as he buckled over in pain. She sickened as she watched the shark dip below them, retreat, then circle around again. Tony's grip loosened from her left hand, and KC looked back long enough to see the panicked look in his eyes behind his mask.

She looked forward again and clenched her teeth. The row of razor-sharp teeth was charging toward them now. But instead of terror, KC felt a strange moment of calm flood through her. She could feel her leg muscles, strong and supple, beneath the neoprene suit. She could feel the quickness of her mind. It was snapping into gear. Now that they were cornered, it seemed as if her final reserve of strength began to take over. Everything was humming. Everything was ready. She could take anything now.

Without thinking, she let go of Mookie, then grabbed Tony's heavy diving light from his hand.

Clasping it with both hands, she held it out in front of her of face and locked her elbows straight. Then she kicked out toward the attacking shark and aimed the light directly at its vicious mouth. There was a powerful thud as she rammed the bright, heavy light into the shark's snout with every ounce of strength she had. KC's wrists almost snapped with the blow, but her body surged back. She quickly righted herself and kept the light in front of her chest. She took a deep breath, then looked around, treading water, readying herself for another attack.

She felt Tony's hand on her shoulder, then followed his pointing finger with her eyes. The shark was retreating. It was swimming rapidly through a break in the reef. And then it was gone.

KC felt her body sag with relief. The shark actually had been frightened by the blow! With one hand, Tony took the heavy light from her. Through the mask, she could see the tears in his eyes. He was shaking his head, then slapping her a five in the water. Together, they swam over to Mookie, who was beginning to droop from shock. A red cloud surrounded his arm as they began to gently haul him up to the surface. KC felt the sunlight blazing into her eyes as her face broke through to the surface. She ripped the regulator from her mouth and sucked in fresh air. Blue water lapped around her neck, and she saw the white beach lying blessedly close to where they'd surfaced.

"Ugh," Tony gasped, as he too breathed in air and pulled Mookie up by the elbow. "Come on, man," he panted, looking over at Mookie's drained face. He ripped off Mookie's regulator and mask, then flipped him over on his back. "We're getting you to the beach. You're okay, man."

KC swam around to Mookie's other side, then made sure his chin stayed above water as she and Tony pulled him toward shore. Soon the gentle waves began nudging them to safety, and KC felt the land beneath her fins. They'd drifted down the beach away from the camp, but it would be only a short walk back.

"Ohhh," Mookie groaned, staggering with KC and Tony's support to the sand, where he collapsed on his back. "Damn spearfishing . . ."

Tony quickly pulled off Mookie's BC vest, then examined his torn sleeve, revealing a small gash on the outside of his arm. "Surface wound, Mook," Tony reassured him. "I know it hurts like hell, but it's not bleeding too much now. You're gonna be okay. We're just going to let you rest here for a minute, then head back down the beach."

"Thanks—to—KC," Mookie whispered, his eyes drifting up to her.

Tony held out his shaking hand. "You think fast, KC. I—I still can't believe you did that."

"We did it together," KC said, taking Tony's hand in both of hers and clasping it, just as Mookie sat up and placed his own lanky hands over theirs. Together, the three of them raised their hands and brought them down again in a show of solidarity and victory.

KC dumped her vest and unzipped the top of her wet suit. She shook her hair out and fell back on her elbows, letting the sun bathe her face. Dry land had never felt so good.

"Why were you following us?" Mookie said softly, wincing as Tony carefully helped him slip out of his damaged wet suit.

KC bit her lip and gave them a sheepish look. She gazed out at a gentle wave rolling up the beach, then sinking peacefully back down again. She wasn't going to lie to them. They were solid now, the three of them. "I followed you because I knew you were looking for the sunken Spanish galleon. I overheard your plans back on the *Bluebeard*."

Tony and Mookie looked at each other with wide eyes, then turned back to stare at her in amazement. "Man, you stay on top of things, don't you?" Tony said in awe, checking Mookie's wound again. "Look," he said, glancing briefly at Mookie, "if you're interested . . ."

"Yeah," Mookie whispered. "If you're interested, you know. After what you did for me . . . Hey, I'm your slave."

"Yeah, your wish is our command," Tony agreed, pushing his dark hair off his high cheekbones.

"Okay. I want in," KC said boldly. "I'm not an experienced diver, but I'll do my best. Look, I need the money. I'm willing to work for it."

Tony rested one elbow thoughtfully on his knee. "We really do think we've found a site. Now, there may be gold there, and then again, it might be a complete and total bust. But we're going to try. We'll need another diver, KC. If we find gold, it's going to be some heavy-duty work to bring it to the surface."

"So if you want in, KC," Mookie said quietly, "you're in. Full partner."

KC's heart was in her throat. Her dream. Her dream was getting closer. She'd never felt as strong and free as she did that moment. She held out her hand. "Here's to our partnership."

"And friendship," Tony said, shaking her hand vigorously. Slowly he drew out a small laminated map he kept in a waterproof belt around his waist. "Here it is. The map that's supposed to lead us to the treasure. We think the reef on this," he pointed to the map, handing it to her, "is the same reef right out there."

KC shivered.

Mookie reached over. "Trust. Here's to trust, man. That's what it's all about."

"Where am I?" Courtney groaned. Her fingertips felt the scratchy blanket beneath her. There was the earthy smell of the jungle and the sound of a hundred singing, squawking island birds. She stirred and tried to lift her head, then dropped it back down again.

The pain in her head came like a black wave on the beach. There were no memories at first, only images. The waterfall, the bearded guy with the golden hair, the struggle on the rocky cliff. Then the fall. Then . . . ?

"What happened?" she stammered, opening her eyes. The light was dim and she could barely make out the crisscrossing of a palm-thatched ceiling. She struggled to remember.

She heard the scraping sound of a match. There

was a burning scent of sulfur, then a flickering light with a hand attached to the end. Her gaze followed the light to a candle. Behind it, in the gathering light, she could see the round, metal end of a gun, pointing directly into her face.

Courtney gasped. She struggled to sit up, but the pain in her head and back and elbows was too great. Falling back again, she stared up into the narrowed blue eyes of her attacker. "Put that gun down," Courtney said softly. "Please."

The guy's eyes closed slightly, taking her in. She could see the revolver trembling in his hand, but his expression remained as hard as a stone. She glanced down. She was lying on a small canvas cot. Her eyes lifted to his thick beard and wild hair. The necklace of white shells rose and fell with his tanned chest.

"Why are you pointing that gun at me?" Courtney whispered, her throat tightening. "Who *are* you?"

The guy stared back at her, squinting a little as she spoke. She could see his nostrils flare slightly as if angered by a brief, passing thought. His wild hair made him look like the illustration of Robinson Crusoe she used to see as a child in her parents' library. But, like the picture, there was something civilized, even refined, in his eyes.

"C-can't you speak?" Courtney started again, her voice getting quavery. She wondered if he spoke French or Spanish. Perhaps Dutch? "Do you speak English?" she whispered. *"Parlez-vous français?"*

There was a long silence as Courtney lay there helplessly, feeling the waves of pain in her head and wondering if she'd ever get out of this alive. It seemed that no matter what she did on this trip, things kept spiraling downward. Perhaps it was only logical that she'd end up with a bullet in her head on a deserted island, she thought bitterly. The whole trip had been cursed from the start.

"Okay, look," Courtney began again, gathering strength. She lifted her hands up and pretended to draw in the air. "If you can't speak, can you draw? I want to know what you want with me."

"Yes, well, I'm not letting you go. So you can put that out of your mind for now."

Courtney's eyes widened. The guy could speak, all right. His clipped British accent made him sound as if he had come straight out of a royal garden party. "I—I don't get it," she stammered. "Why the gun?"

The guy huffed through his nose and threw his head back slightly. The candlelight flickered against the rough wooden walls of the room. "You really are quite amazing, you people. You're very smart, the lot of you."

"Who? What people?" Courtney struggled, shoving her hair back off her grubby face. "What are you talking about?"

"I'll give you fair warning," he snapped back, bracing his feet. "I'm not afraid to use this gun. I know that you and the others are running drugs. I've been watching it for months, and I'm sick of you using this island. So you're just going to have to wait until the authorities arrive. Because they will, you know. They were here a few hours ago with a helicopter. They're onto you."

Courtney sat up abruptly, gripping the edge of the cot with her scratched fingers. "I'm not a drug runner," she said firmly, feeling an indignant flush rise to her face. "If you were watching us so closely, you would have seen that our boat was wrecked on that big reef out there night before last. All we want to do is get home safely. Why are you so convinced that we're criminals?"

The guy gripped the revolver tighter and gave her a grim smile. "Because the only people who come to this island are criminals."

Courtney let out a gasp of exasperation.

"Let me tell you how it goes," the guy began in a tone of exaggerated patience. "You hide the drugs on the rental yachts, so you can avoid customs on the main islands. Then you rendezvous here with your partners and pass on the goods. Tell me, how am I doing so far?"

"Not great." Courtney shook her head in frustration. Was he crazy? Did he have some kind of tropical fever? Maybe he'd been alone on the island too long.

"Now all you're waiting for," the guy went on, crossing his legs on the overturned box he used for a chair, "are your mates. Let me see. If all goes according to schedule, they should be here pretty soon in their ultralight, ultrafast speedboats. Wouldn't want any of the authorities to catch up with you in these waters, would you?"

"Huh?"

"I've had enough. I'm taking my island back."

"*Your* island?" Courtney gasped. There was a moment of silence as Courtney's eyes drifted past the guy's blond head. She took in the dimly lit room. Its ancient plank walls flickered in the candlelight. Peeling, floor-to-ceiling shutters were hung with rotting mosquito netting. Through a wide door, she could see a larger room, outfitted with a neat makeshift camp table, hung with simple cooking utensils. A broad desk had been placed near a big window at the far end, where another lighted candle stood. Courtney could see stacks of books, a microscope, drawing and writing supplies, and a row of jars filled with small, delicate flowers in all shapes and sizes.

"Orchids?" Courtney asked softly, drawing her knees up to her chest.

She watched his face soften slightly. His grip loosened on the gun and he threw a terse look over his brown shoulder. "Yes, they are."

"Mmm," Courtney said, trying to think of something—anything—to distract him and make him put the gun away. She had to convince him that she was not a threat.

Then his eyebrows narrowed imperceptibly. His eyes lifted to hers and she saw that they were absolutely blue beneath his sun-bleached eyebrows, like the turquoise colors in the sea. "How did you know they were orchids? I mean, they're a very rare and small variety."

"My mother used to raise orchids," Courtney said simply. "Not all of them were your junior-prom variety, I guess you could say." She paused, waiting for a reaction. "I've been thinking about that, because . . ." She stopped again and looked boldly into his eyes. "Because I saw some lovely small orchids at that little waterfall up from the beach. Remember? When you saw me—swimming?"

He cleared his throat and looked away.

"So," Courtney began carefully, looking down at her bruised knees and rubbing them. "You're English. The English are crazy about orchids. Are you studying them?"

The guy sat up straighter and pointed his gun again. "Don't try to change the subject."

"Look," Courtney burst out. "My name is Courtney Conner. I'm a junior at the University of Springfield. Okay? I'm majoring in international relations, and I've been on spring break with my friends, trying to get my parents' boat delivered to Gregory Cays. Except that it cracked into a reef night before last, and we're stuck here until someone can help us."

The guy's face softened.

"What do you want me to do?" Courtney begged him. "Do I seem like I'm tough enough for the drug trade?"

Slowly the guy lowered his gun. Then a smile crept over his face. He sighed and scratched his chin. "Yes, actually I think you'd fit in quite nicely. But I'll believe your story for now." Then he rose and walked through the semidarkness to a wooden box, where he placed the gun and padlocked the lid.

Courtney sighed with relief.

"My name is Huxley Jonas," he said, walking back to the cot and extending his hand. Even with his wild hair and beard, there was something precise about him that put her at ease. "How do you do, Courtney?"

Courtney shook his hand, then dropped her head in fatigue. "Hi, Huxley. Why don't you start by telling me what happened up there on the cliff?"

Huxley walked over to the window nearest them and stared out into the darkness. Courtney could see that his back was dark brown from months of constant sun. His hair was bleached into strawlike streaks. "You startled me, for one. Then you came hurtling down on top of me and it looked as if you were going to fall."

"You terrified me," Courtney interrupted.

Huxley looked down at his shredded shorts and worn sandals. Then he ran his hand over his wild mane and chuckled softly. "Yes, well. I must have."

Courtney's face softened into a smile.

"Then you grabbed me and I managed to fall about fifty feet down that cliff with you," Huxley explained, sitting down again and resting his elbows on his knees, which were as scraped and bloodied as her own. "You'd hit your head. I could see that. You woke up for a few minutes, but slipped back into unconsciousness again. So I had to carry you back here."

Courtney started. "All the way up that steep cliff?"

Huxley fiddled with the lobe of his ear and grinned at her. "Let's just say I'm still recovering."

Courtney stared at him wordlessly. Then she rose and walked through the room. She looked at his neat desk and the bunches of tiny orchids. Some were a small white variety with a birdlike shape and yellow petals. Others had brilliant orange-red and scarlet flowers.

"It used to be part of an old sugar plantation," Huxley explained, taking a candle and lighting several more until the room was filled with a soft, yellow light. "At least I think so. And this place is high up enough. Out of the jungle, you see. So there aren't as many insects. One of the colonial families must have lived here."

"Ages ago," Courtney whispered, running her hand along a panel of the ancient wall.

"Yes. It's completely deserted now." Huxley crossed the room and opened a far door. Outside in the moonlight Courtney could barely make out blowing grasses and a few palm trees. "There are no paths leading to it anymore." Huxley pointed his head out the door. "So I'm completely hidden from the dangerous types wandering about out here. I do have a little fishing boat, but it's pretty well hidden."

Courtney wound a lock of hair around her finger and walked back through the room, looking at Huxley's tidy desk. "How did you find this place?"

Huxley came back in and sat on the other edge of his large desk. He reached toward a delicate orchid and stroked one of its petals gently. "By accident, actually. I'd been camping on the island for four months before I stumbled onto it."

Her eyes darted up into his face. "Four months? You've been here alone for four months?"

Huxley crossed his arms over his chest and chuckled softly. "Six months, actually. I've been in *this* place for the last two."

Courtney was horrified. "What do you *do* all day?"

He shrugged and looked down. "Read, contemplate, think. Actually," he said, reaching for a jar containing a delicate branch of tiny white orchids, "my official business is a horticultural study I began two years ago back at Oxford. We'd heard that many of the orchid species that are native to Mexico and South America had migrated to the Caribbean area and were flourishing and had even crossed with . . ." He stopped himself and looked down bashfully. "But look at me. I'm going on."

Courtney laughed softly and sat down in his desk chair. A lock of hair fell across her cheek, tickling her. The candlelight danced on Huxley's face. "Six months alone to think?" she said wistfully, running her fingers down the spine of one of his books. "I can't remember the last time I spent five minutes by myself."

"I'm planning to spend the entire year here," Huxley said quietly. "I want this time to live as simply as I can with my own thoughts. No distractions, no obligations, just living. I want to find out who I am."

Courtney searched his eyes. The room was peaceful and quiet, and though there was a sudden silence between them, she didn't feel the need to speak. She thought about her own life and the overflowing leather organizer she couldn't make a move without. There were tiny little pencil notes crammed inside of it: meeting dates, exam dates, social dates, study dates, and volunteer dates. She had short-term goal lists and long-term goal lists. To-do lists. Note-writing lists. Shopping lists. It had all led to something. She was always perfectly sure of that.

But now she couldn't remember what it was.

"I want to show you something," Huxley said softly, pulling aside a blanket he'd hung over a door frame.

Courtney pushed away from the desk and followed his slim, muscled back. Outside, she breathed in the fragrant evening air. Huge frangipani bushes rustled in the gentle breeze, their pink-white blossoms nodding in the darkness. The tall grasses tickled her legs, and the salty smell of the ocean blew through her hair. From this point, she could see that they were high on an inland hill. In the distance, she could see the shimmering ocean.

"See the moonpath?" Huxley whispered, moving a little closer to her.

She stared straight ahead at the moon ahead of them in the starry sky. Huxley was right. Its silvery light seemed to cast a path directly toward them, across the water and up the hill through the grass.

"I have no idea who I am," Courtney said suddenly, her eyes fixed on the moonpath.

After a moment her eyes drifted over to his and she saw that he was staring at her in the darkness. For a long moment, their eyes locked. Huxley took a step toward her, and his arm brushed hers. Courtney shivered. She was being pulled toward this stranger just as surely as the moonpath was being pulled toward them.

"I know," Huxley murmured, suddenly stepping away and crossing his arms over his chest. "Not many people do know themselves. They don't know what they really feel, or what they really want, or what makes them happy. It's too hard to separate yourself, sometimes, when you're surrounded. . . ."

Courtney felt herself reaching out to touch the side of Huxley's bare arm. "When you're surrounded by people who need you and rely on you and . . . I just don't know anymore," she whispered. "I just don't know."

Huxley touched her hand. "You can stay here tonight, of course," he said, his steady eyes filled with regret. "But tomorrow, I'll show you the way back to shore."

"There's no hurry," Courtney said quickly. At that moment she would have done anything just to talk with him a little longer. She needed to know what he'd discovered, learn what he'd learned.

"Courtney," Huxley said, raising his hand. "I took a vow of solitude, and I can't turn back on it now. Don't you see?"

Eighteen

"So we missed the rescue helicopter yesterday," Tony mumbled into the breakfast campfire the next day. "And now I know what it's like to be attacked by an eight-foot-long shark."

Mookie rubbed his bandage, then gave Tony a small shove in the side. "Right. You were attacked."

"Where's Courtney? Didn't she come back last night?" Winnie stuck her head out of the tent, rubbing her eyes sleepily.

"No," KC said quietly, shoving a stick in the fire and staring out at the sun just beginning to rise over the horizon. "She's been gone since yesterday afternoon." The sky was a blazing tangerine, and a flock of tiny, black-headed birds were chattering noisily in the brush behind them. "She completely disappeared. I woke the others a few minutes ago. She never came back."

KC gave Patrick and Liza an irritated glance. Across the fire, they were cuddled up on a rock together, a sleeping bag pulled over both their shoulders. Meanwhile, down the beach, Jack stood quietly at the water's edge, staring out at the sunrise.

"Where could she be?" KC suddenly burst out, springing up and pacing toward the tent and back. "Winnie? Which direction did you say she headed?"

Winnie shuffled sleepily toward the fire and plopped down on an overturned box. "It was just after yesterday's nap. Jack and I heard the helicopter, and I woke Courtney up to let her know about it. But when we couldn't find *any of you people* . . ." Winnie looked bitterly around the group. "Courtney ran up there, behind the camp, saying she wanted to find everyone."

KC bit her thumbnail. "What if she fell? What if she's up there injured?"

"If anyone can take care of themselves, it's Courtney Conner," Liza said quickly, looking up at Patrick and batting her eyes. "She's extremely self-sufficient. I bet she had lots of Girl Scout badges when she—"

"Shut up, Liza," KC barked.

Liza shot her a hot look.

KC glared back. She'd never hated anyone as much as she hated Liza Ruff at that moment. How could Liza make jokes about Courtney at a time like this? She could be seriously hurt. She could have wandered into some dangerous types on the island. Anything could have happened. "We're going to split up into search parties."

"You bet," Tony said eagerly.

Winnie nodded. "Oh, God. Poor Courtney."

Liza put her hands on her hips, letting the sleeping bag fall away from her sunburned body. Her sleeveless blouse had been tied like a scarf on her head, and she wore nothing but her bathing-suit top above her grubby shorts. "Patrick's still the captain, KC. He's the main man, hon. The one in charge."

"Fine," KC snapped back, digging her heels into the sandy ground, suddenly feeling a million miles away from Patrick. It was as if her attraction to him had been a dream, or a two-day junior-high crush that disappeared as quickly as it had come. "Then *Patrick* can lead a search party on the north side of the island. Liza and Winnie, you go with him. Mookie, Tony, and I will look on the south side. I'll go ask Jack to keep watch here. How's that sound, Patrick?"

Patrick stood up, hooked his thumb into the collar of his shirt, and slung it over his bare, bronzed shoulder. "Good thinking, KC," he said carefully, his green eyes looking directly at her. He pushed his wire-rimmed glasses up on his nose and looked down at Liza. "Come on, Liza. The north end it is. We'll meet back here at sunset. If Courtney is found, the signal will be the sail on the beach. We've got enough rocks to pin it down."

"We should have done that in the first place," Winnie said bitterly, pulling her sandy T-shirt over the bathing suit she'd slept in.

"Have a piece of cheese, Winnie," Patrick said with

mock patience, holding up a plate. "Courtney picked it out herself at a nice place in St. Ramos."

"Come on, you guys," KC snapped, taking a piece of cheese and biting into it hungrily. Tony and Mookie leaped up. "Let's go."

The sun had risen by the time KC, Mookie, and Tony climbed through the clearing in the jungle behind the camp. KC stepped carefully as the slope steepened, trying not to think about Patrick, trying to focus on Courtney. Yesterday's cloud cover had disappeared and the blue sky was stretched tightly over them. Once they were in the open grasses, she could feel the hot sun blazing down on her back. She pushed ahead, knowing that she wouldn't stop until Courtney was found. Courtney Conner, the sorority princess who had turned out to be one of her most loyal friends. Courtney had wanted so much for everything to work out. Now KC knew that she was going to have to make it happen for her.

KC stopped and looked up at the red cliffs toward the center of the island. To the left, she could see another, lower set of cliffs overlooking the ocean. "Which way, guys?" KC panted.

"Let's go up," Tony said, wiping the sweat off his forehead with his arm. "We might be able to see something from that height; get our bearings. Then we can move down and explore the lower cliffs and beaches."

Mookie nodded, and KC let Tony take the lead. For several hours, they climbed through the high grassy hills, dotted with stands of palms and low-lying brush. They even hiked up to the highest, windswept point on the island. But there was no sign of Courtney anywhere.

"Let's explore down through that wooded area, then angle over to the cliffs. There might be a way down to the beach from there," KC suggested. The afternoon sun was beating down on her head now, and she knew they'd have to find water soon. "Come on," she yelled over her shoulder.

She marched down an open field, feeling the sharp rocks stabbing through the bottoms of her sneakers and the dry grasses whipping her bare ankles. Large, speckle-breasted birds clustered on the tallest palms squeaked and buzzed at them as they passed. As they approached the ocean cliffs, the arrowlike terns swooped and dived.

Along the cliffs, KC, Tony, and Mookie picked their way through prickly bushes covered with tiny scarlet blossoms. From this point, they were looking directly east, and they were only about a half-mile south of the reef and their camp on the beach. KC hurried ahead, anxious to check for the sailcloth on the beach. But when she reached the edge of the cliff, she spotted something else—something she hadn't been looking for, something she hadn't counted on in her wildest dreams.

"Tony, Mookie!" KC screamed over her shoulder, pointing down the cliff. "Look!"

Mookie and Tony stumbled through the brush, terror-stricken. "What? What?" Tony yelled. "Is it Courtney? Did she fall? Is she alive?"

KC stretched her arm out, still pointing. "Don't you see? Look there, in the water. This side of the reef. Look at the sea grass."

Mookie gasped. "It's that rusty color Frankie was telling us about."

Tony was laughing giddily. "Sticks out like a sore thumb, doesn't it?"

KC reached for Tony and Mookie's treasure map tucked in her back pocket. She pulled it out and unfolded it. "So that's where we are. This *is* the island your friend Frankie had explored for treasure." Quickly she found the island reef detailed on the map, matched it, and marked the location of the sea grass.

"We're there," Mookie whispered.

"Once we find Courtney, we dive for the Spanish galleon and look for gold," Tony shouted, punching his fist in the air.

KC upturned her palm and Tony and Mookie slapped it down.

Then she looked away from the cliff, tucking the map back into her pocket. But as she did, her eyes instinctively roamed the hills above them, looking for a glint of blond hair, a flash of white shorts, anything that could be Courtney, whether alive, injured, or even dead.

Suddenly her gaze came to an abrupt halt. Standing on a rock outcropping in the hill was Patrick. She could see Winnie and Liza searching the brush behind him. But he was standing quietly by himself, staring intently down at her. KC clenched her teeth and shoved the map farther down in her pocket. "Patrick," she whispered to herself bitterly. "You're interested? Forget it, pal. I know a friend when I see one. And you aren't it."

Winnie sat up in her sleeping bag and stared across at the luminous Caribbean sea. The moon sent a silvery light on its smooth surface. Closer to the beach, she could see the glowing white lines of the waves as they broke and spilled toward her. There had been no sign of Courtney that day, and no further sign of the rescue helicopter. After a dinner of mango, rice, and fresh fish Jack had caught, they'd dragged their bags out of their oven-hot tents and collapsed, exhausted, onto the beach.

It was midnight. Winnie was alone. She felt the cool breeze on her face and listened closely to the smooth rise and fall of the waves on the beach. The dark sky was thick with millions of stars. A huge, vast universe, Winnie thought, her heart filled with longing. She and Josh used to drive up into the mountains near Springfield to look at the stars. Back then, the stars had seemed so close she could practically reach out and burn her fingertips on their fiery light. Now they seemed a billion light-years away. And she felt completely alone. She reached her arms out to each side and dug her hands into the soft sand, then let it trickle slowly out between her fingers.

There was a rustling behind her, then a snap near the tent.

"KC?" Winnie called softly. Her mind began to race. *"Courtney?"* she cried, rising to her feet. "Courtney, are you back?"

She stepped through the soft, cool sand toward the tents. Tiny birds rustled in the bushes. A log dropped farther into the campfire, sending up a tiny shower of sparks. She opened the flap to the girls' tent, then the guys'. But both were empty. The snapping sound had probably been the fire, but it had put her on edge.

Winnie walked slowly back out to the beach, rubbing the back of her neck. She scanned the long line of the sand until her eyes rested on the dark outline of someone sitting alone at the water's edge. She walked closer, slowly recognizing the stern profile and the still, sad posture of someone in trouble. She felt a strange pull in her heart. It was Jack.

Winnie moved forward, then crouched next to him on the sand. She stared at the sharp angle of his jaw and the wave of his thick hair. His body was compact and muscular, like hers. She could almost feel the energy trapped inside of him like a spring. She waited, hoping he would say something first. But his head dropped slowly, and after a while, she heard him sniff.

"Jack?" Winnie said softly. She looked at his back beneath the soft sweatshirt. It was beginning to shake. He made a fist with one hand and drew it up to his bent forehead. "Are you okay?"

She heard him sniff. Then cough. "I have to stop running, Winnie," he said in a cracked voice.

Winnie slipped a bare leg out in front of her and sat down. Then she bent her head forward and tried to look into his face. "Running from what, Jack?" she asked as gently as she could.

Jack drew his wet face up, then turned and looked at her. She pulled back a little. He looked so sad, so lost. "I hate myself like this," he said. "I can't stand it."

Winnie's eyes widened. "Like what?"

He shook his head slowly, grabbing a fistful of sand and tossing it into the air. "You wouldn't believe me if I told you. Why should you?"

"Try me," Winnie said, throwing a handful of sand to match his, and wondering how she could even begin to help him—she couldn't even help herself. "I might believe you if for once you told me the truth," she continued. "I mean, you've been lying to me all along. I see those tight lips of yours and your solitary walks and your padlocked suitcase and—"

"Okay, okay," he breathed.

Winnie moved a little closer. "Look, Jack. If you're in some kind of trouble, why don't you just come out and tell someone about it? I mean, you're not the only one with problems around here, you know."

Jack just stared at her in the bluish moonlight. Then he looked over her shoulder, pushing his hair back with his hand. Winnie stared at his finely shaped forehead and the dark eyebrows that framed his brown eyes. His face was wider and more intense than Josh's, but he had the same sensitive eyes. The kind of eyes you could actually read if you looked closely enough. Finally his gaze drifted back to her. "I told you the police were following me because I stole some food."

"Uh-huh."

He shrugged. "I lied."

"Why?" Winnie asked quietly.

Jack buried his face in his hands. "It's a long story."

Winnie took a breath and sat back on her elbow. Then she took a finger and drew a line in the fine sand. "I'm not going anywhere."

"My dad," Jack began shakily. "My dad—he's something, you know." He leaned his head back and looked up at the stars. "Oh, man oh man, what a guy."

Winnie's eyes grew hot. Why did she think she knew what he was going to say even before he said it?

"He's the one who taught me how to sail, of course," he said with a bitter edge to his voice. He stroked his chin thoughtfully and looked out at the water. "When I was twelve, I was sailing yawls like the *Bluebeard* single-handedly. My dad was the one who sat up on the foredeck and gave directions. Long hours at the helm. Hours practicing my knots. It built character."

Winnie bit her salty lip. "Yeah, I see."

"After all," Jack went on shakily, falling onto his back and sticking his hands behind his head, "his sons would be the ones to take over his big old Texas oil business. *They'd have to have backbones of steel.*"

"Oil?" Winnie whispered, lying down on her side next to him.

"Heard of Geo-Cruz Oil?"

Winnie thought a moment. "Yeah, I think so."

"That's us."

"Oh." Winnie nodded, staring down at the gold loop glimmering in his ear. If Jack was an heir to the Geo-Cruz fortune, he'd probably grown up with unbelievable wealth.

"Dad was particularly happy when I got into Harvard, where I'm a freshman majoring in engineering," Jack said sourly. "Or rather, *was,* since I hopped a plane to the Caribbean three weeks before exams.

Just like that. Told my roommate to cover for me. Took a quick trip to the bank to take out the twenty-six hundred dollars I had in my savings account. And I was off."

Winnie reached out and stroked the side of his arm with her little finger. "Why?"

"Because it was too hard!" Jack suddenly burst out, sitting up and burying his head in his hands. "I was taking too many credits, I guess. One of my courses, a weird calculus seminar, was giving me major trouble. I'd never been behind like that. I'd always aced everything. Everyone expected it. Dad did. I did. I just didn't know how . . ."

"To ask for help?" Winnie finished his sentence as fresh tears made him stop. Jack nodded, unable to speak.

"I'm sorry, Jack," Winnie said gently. "I'm so sorry."

"They're looking for me," Jack choked out. "I was on my way to find my brother down here. He runs the Caribbean oil interests. But then I found out that Dad hired a private detective after I didn't show up for exams. I'm a damn missing person now, Winnie. I feel so stupid. Police, Coast Guard, investigators. They're all after me now. I'll never live this stupid stunt down."

"That's why you didn't want to use the radio during the storm," Winnie breathed.

Jack jumped up and walked toward the water. Winnie followed him, letting the warm seawater lap around her ankles. "I ripped out that radio, Winnie. You were right. And then I smashed the radar in. I'd rather have my parents think I'm dead than know the truth."

"That you dropped out," Winnie said softly, touching his shoulder.

"Yeah," Jack said hoarsely, staring out to sea. "That I dropped out when things got tough. But I screwed everything up for all of us—you, me, everybody."

Winnie stood perfectly still. She stared at the stars, which arched down until they seemed to touch the water at the horizon. To the left, the moon stood high and bright, blazing down on the white beach. She thought about Josh and the lost baby. She thought about everything they'd been through, and how one day she had stuffed her clothes in a suitcase and walked out of his life. Things had been easy for her, too, before Josh; grades, friends, even her therapist mom. Of course, she hadn't realized it back then. But it had been easy, all right. Compared to being married, her life had been a piece of cake.

Jack touched the tip of her hair lightly, then pulled his hand away. "What are you thinking?"

"I ran away too, Jack," Winnie said simply, kicking her foot out and watching the sparkling curve of water. He looked at her, surprised. "I met a guy at school last fall," she said, trembling. "Josh. Josh Gaffey. I fell in love with him and we got married."

"Married?" Jack pulled back a little. "You're married? I thought you said you were only a freshman in college."

"I am," Winnie replied in a tiny voice, kicking the water again. "God, I don't know. We did it on impulse one night when we were driving through Nevada. It was wonderful. The happiest . . ."

"What went wrong?"

Winnie felt her heels sink into the sand as the wave drew back. It made her feel heavy and sad. "I don't know, Jack. Maybe we just didn't trust each other. We didn't listen. We'd *talk*, but we didn't listen. Not really. It's so hard, Jack. You wouldn't believe. It takes so much patience."

Jack crossed his arms over his chest. "I guess I wouldn't know. I mean, I've had girlfriends, but I never really met anyone who . . ." Winnie looked over as he lifted his eyes and gave her a funny look.

"Then we found out I was pregnant," Winnie said abruptly, as if she wanted to shock him with her own anger and pain. She had the sudden yearning to show him he wasn't alone. She was suffering. Millions suffered.

"Pregnant?" Jack whispered, wide-eyed.

Winnie held her stomach and bent over. "And then I lost the baby when I was only three months along. A motorcycle accident. I told Josh they weren't safe, I told him to get rid of it. But he wouldn't and one night we went for a ride and I hit the tree and . . ."

"Winnie!" Jack cried out, grabbing her shoulders as she began to fall forward into the water.

"I can't face anything now," Winnie sobbed, leaning into Jack. "No one understands. They think they do. Or they try. But they don't. And I can't live with it."

Winnie was crying hard now. She felt Jack lift her gently, then her arms slipped around his neck. Her cheek pressed into the soft front of his sweatshirt, and she cried like she hadn't cried since the day she left Josh. Everything, every emotion she had, was emptying out.

"I want to go home," Winnie cried. "But I know it'll be hell back there, too. I don't know where I belong anymore."

"Winnie," Jack was saying softly. "Winnie." He lowered his head, trying to look into her wet eyes. "Winnie." His gaze locked on to hers and his face drew near. Suddenly his lips were on hers and her arms were tightening around him.

"Jack," Winnie breathed, pulling away, not ready to believe what had happened. Her knees were buckling and her heart was filled with terror, but as he bent down to kiss her again, she felt something small and warm and hopeful begin to flicker inside her heart.

Jack's arms tightened around her back. "I need you now, Winnie. It's all happening really fast. But I know that I need you like I've never needed anyone before."

Nineteen

"Patrick?" Liza said suddenly, realizing she'd
dozed off in her sleeping bag. She sat up
like a shot and looked over at the spot next
to her on the beach where she'd put a bag down for
Patrick. But it lay as cold and flat as a day-old pancake.

Liza squirmed out of her bag and stood up.
"Patrick?" she called down the moonlit beach. "Pat—
rick," she whimpered, looking sadly at the waving
palms against the starry sky. By now the low clouds
that had hidden them from the rescue helicopter that
day had cleared. The moon had drifted way over the island. She'd been asleep for hours!

"Where *are* you?" she sang out over the waves
through her cupped hands. She set off down the

beach. What was the problem? Mr. Patrick Perfect was turning into a major disappearing act. Was he shy? Was he having second thoughts about their date for the night? He'd kissed her that afternoon like she'd never been kissed in her life. Did he actually think she was going to forget about that?

Where was he?

Liza continued up the beach, impatiently shaking the sand out of her bathing-suit top. Near the campfire, she could see KC, Mookie, and Tony sacked out in their bags. To her left, on the beach, half hidden by the low brush, she could see Jack and Winnie.

Liza stopped and pursed her lips. Jack and Winnie were lying fast asleep on a zipped-open sleeping bag, their arms clasped around each other. "Misery loves company," Liza muttered to herself, shrugging and shaking her head in disbelief. "Couple of wackos."

She tiptoed toward the tent, but stopped when she noticed the yellow glow of a flashlight beneath the stretched sailcloth. "Courtney?" she whispered excitedly. "Courtney? We've been looking all ov—" Liza stuck her hand in the tent flap and pulled it back. Instead of Courtney, she was staring at the back of Patrick's creased white shirt. Liza frowned. He was hunched over, facing away from the tent flap, tucking what looked like a small, shiny map into KC's rucksack. He shifted slightly, and Liza could see his profile in the dim light.

Liza gasped. Patrick was holding a small, hand-held radio. Her thoughts began to race. Hadn't the radio been destroyed in the storm? If they had a radio, why was everyone so worried about getting rescued?

She stepped back in confusion. "Patrick?"

Patrick turned around and gave her a shy, relieved smile. His thumb clicked a switch on the radio, and he slipped the antenna down with the flat of his hand. Then he stuck the radio carefully into the front pocket of his windbreaker and took her hand. "Hi. I was just headed out for our camp on the beach."

"What are you doing in here?" she whispered back hoarsely. "And what's with the radio? You actually have a *radio*? Where did you get it? Does it work? Did you reach help?"

Patrick pulled her down and looked intently into her eyes. Then he bit his lip and looked away. "I'm sorry, Liza. I . . ." He pulled her shoulders around so they were facing each other on their knees inside the tent. Then he clasped her tenderly to his chest. "Please, forgive me."

Liza's mind was whirring with confusion.

"Yes, I've had this radio all along," he said. "It's just that my paintings . . . My art . . . Everything is gone—and I—just can't face the world yet. I know it's wrong, but I didn't want to be rescued. Back in the real world, I'm going to have to start all over. And I'm going to have to say good-bye to you."

"Oh, Patrick," Liza murmured, pressing her body against his chest and kissing him on the lips. A moment later she pulled away and looked, horrified, into his eyes. "But what about Courtney? She's been gone for almost an entire day. She might not survive if she's injured out there somewhere, Patrick."

Patrick nodded, stroking the side of her arm. "That's why I finally used the radio, Liza. It took some soul-searching out there on the beach, but it was the only thing I could do."

"But . . ."

"Then I found out that KC has a map of the area," Patrick went on, nodding toward KC's rucksack. "I don't know why she didn't tell us about it. But I used it to describe our location to the Coast Guard. They'll be here tomorrow."

Liza began to melt again as Patrick leaned over and nuzzled her neck. She leaned into his chest, taking in the reassuring look in his eyes. She started to pull him down next to her on Courtney's sleeping bag.

"Wait." Patrick pulled back a little. "The Coast Guard wants me to stand by."

Liza bit her lip with disappointment. "Oh. Okay."

Patrick looked down at Liza. He reached down and held her chin tenderly in his hand. "I guess they want to ask a lot of routine questions about the *Bluebeard* and exactly where we're located, who we are, all that kind of bureaucratic stuff. You know how it goes."

"I do?" Liza came back in a tiny voice.

"Get some sleep." Patrick pushed her shoulders down gently. "Big day tomorrow." He gave her the thumbs-up sign. "Rescue. Maybe we'll get a headline or two, huh?"

"Yeah," Liza said sadly, watching him back out the tent flap and slip out into the darkness. "Good night, Sweet Prince," she whispered to herself, crawling on her hands and knees toward the opening so that she could watch him disappear into the night.

The last thing she saw was the back of Patrick's white shirt, heading quickly for the storage tent.

Courtney took a deep breath, then let it out again, slowly. She opened her eyes, calmly taking in the dim images in the room: the paned door, the table leg, a cup sitting on a chair. An orchid in a glass.

She ran her fingertips along the edge of her silky grass mat. Outside, the night was velvety black and stirring with a thousand waking birds. Inside, her mind was at peace.

Courtney turned her head and stared at Huxley sleeping at the other side of the room. His blond hair was spread out on his rough pillow, and his expression was innocent and peaceful. She'd spent the entire previous day with him, rather than returning to the beach. It was wrong, she knew. Her friends were probably crazy with worry. But for once, she decided she would let them do the worrying. For once, she was going to let time stop. She was going to find out what it was like to live moment by moment, without worry, without purpose, without responsibility.

Yesterday, after eating a simple breakfast of rice, coconut, and Huxley's fresh mint tea, she had sat quietly for an hour staring at the ocean. Then she read from one of Huxley's books.

I went to the woods because I wished to live deliberately, to front only the essential facts of life, and see if I could not learn what it had to teach, and not, when I came to die, discover that I had not lived.

"Thoreau," Huxley had said, looking up from a detailed drawing he was making of a small yellow orchid. "American writer and my mentor this year, as you can see."

"Yes," Courtney had whispered. "Yes, I see."

Later that day, she'd watched Huxley examining the root structure of a large white orchid he'd collected the day she'd seen him at the waterfall.

"It's a *Catasetum phileatum*," Huxley had explained. "See the spikiness in the petals here? It's been found in Trinidad and Venezuela, too. Very rare and beautiful, don't you think?"

Now Courtney lay quietly on the mat, watching the morning light slowly turn the walls from black to a faint blue-gray. She couldn't ever remember time unfolding so slowly and naturally. A faint yellow dawn appeared in the window, and Courtney rose to meet it. She grasped the handles to the tall, paned doors that led outside. She would watch the sun rise. She would take note of every color and every sound. She would remember the feeling of silence in her mind, then carry it with her always.

Pulling open the door, Courtney began to draw in a deep breath. But a faraway flapping noise made her look up. For a split second, she saw something fluttering above. She held her gaze, then felt her heart beginning to pound. Up above, the sky was beginning to thicken with the fluttering black things. She stepped back.

Bats!

Courtney felt for the door handle. Scores of bats were swooping down from the sky, apparently headed for an open window in the building's attic. But before she could get the door closed, a single bat missed its target and flew right above her head into the room.

"Agghh," Courtney shrieked as the bat flew over her head. "Huxley, wake up! There's a bat in here."

Huxley leaped out of bed and spotted the bat on the ceiling near the opposite wall. "Calm down, Courtney. Bats are harmless," he said, going over to put a comforting arm around Courtney's shoulders. "They get a bad rap—totally undeserved."

"Yes—yes. I guess I know that," Courtney said, though she was still trembling. "It's just that I've never had a close encounter with one before."

Huxley laughed. "They come in here all the time when they return from evening feedings. But I'll shoo this little guest out since you're so scared." He opened the door on his side of the room, and Courtney watched in fear as the squeaking, hairy bat fluttered, panicked, and finally flew back outside into the dawn. "Oh," Courtney breathed, standing in the middle of the room, shaking. "I'm sorry. I—I don't usually frighten easily."

Huxley smiled and clasped her tightly to him. Courtney slowly circled her arms around his waist, resting her cheek against his bare chest. She could feel his heart beating, then a slow laugh starting inside him.

Courtney pulled back a little and smiled at him.

He released her and fell back onto his mat, then turned on his side, looking at her. "I wouldn't have believed it. You really do seem like you're not afraid of anything."

Courtney pulled her mat closer to his, then lay down on her stomach, letting her hair fall over her shoulders. "Yeah, well, maybe I'm too afraid to wonder if I'm afraid. I just kind of charge ahead. You know."

Huxley cleared his throat. "No, actually, I don't know."

Courtney shook her head and smiled, flustered. There was something so offbeat and endearing about him—a combination of wildness and gentility she couldn't resist. "Oh, well, it's an American tradition. You should try it. The idea is you sort of barrel through life and try to accomplish as much as you can."

"And then?" Huxley wanted to know. He searched her eyes.

Courtney bit her lip. "Well, then you feel good, I guess. Because you end up with interesting work. And you've helped people."

"But how do you have time to feel good if you're spending all of your time at it?" Huxley teased her gently, looking down and fiddling with the shells on his necklace. Behind him, Courtney could see the building's overgrown garden take on the morning light. A wild parrot squawked loudly in the brush.

Courtney closed her eyes and nibbled on her thumbnail. "I don't know, Huxley. I just don't know."

"Well, maybe it's about choice. Maybe you have to choose one thing, maybe two, then do those things well. And save some time to do what you did yesterday, for instance. You seemed to do some reflecting yesterday."

Courtney nodded. "Yes. Yes, I did. For the first time in a long time. It's just that my life is so busy—I get interested in things, people. I get caught up in righting the wrongs. Trying to help. Even this trip . . ."

"What about this trip, Courtney?" Huxley asked, reaching out and touching her hand.

Courtney felt her face tense. "It's that I wanted to share it. I wanted to make some friends of mine feel better about their lives. My friend KC has had so many frustrations this year, with her father dying and all of her financial problems. And Winnie lost a baby and separated from her husband. Then there's Liza. She drives us all crazy, but I really wanted her to feel accepted."

"You can't do it all," Huxley said, bringing his face closer to hers.

Courtney gently pulled her hand away, then laced her fingers together and stared at them. "I know. Whether we have a good time or bad, whether we get out of this jam or not—I guess it's not all up to me, is it? I mean, I can't control everything. If things go wrong, I'm not necessarily the guilty party here, am I?"

"No."

"Thanks for letting me off the hook, Huxley," Courtney whispered, smiling across at him.

"I can get sidetracked too," Huxley admitted, sitting up cross-legged. He picked at the worn threads hanging from the hem of his blue shorts. "My parents are good people and all, but they pushed. They both teach at university, so they wanted me to have an education too. There was always something they wanted me to learn: piano, cricket, Dickens, Newton, botany."

"Some schedule." Courtney giggled.

"Yes, well." Huxley scratched his ear, grinning at her. "It got to the point where I had to say, Look, Mum, Dad. I'm going off to think about his. I want to make some choices."

"So you came here," Courtney said.

"Yes." Huxley's eyes softened. "And I don't want to waste this year. It's precious to me. I can't get sidetracked at this point, Courtney."

"I don't like to get sidetracked either," Courtney said, looking into his eyes. "But every once in a while, I'll see a detour along the way. And sometimes I wonder if I should take it. I mean, maybe I'm missing out."

Courtney watched as Huxley's face drew near. His hair was golden in the morning sun, and his eyes were a brilliant, piercing blue. Her throat tightened as he touched his lips gently to hers. She reached her hand up and stroked the side of his face. His beard was soft and tickly. "Huxley," she breathed.

A moment passed before either one of them moved. They lay there side by side in the growing light, staring into each other's eyes. Then finally Huxley broke the spell. "You are very beautiful, Courtney Conner. And I like you so much." Suddenly he pulled away and rolled over on his back. She watched the gentle rise and fall of his chest. He shook his head slowly. "This is very hard."

"Why?" Courtney asked, her eyes stinging.

Huxley clasped his hand to his forehead. "It's

about choice, Courtney. I made a decision to be completely alone this year. I need my mind to be free, just this once. Don't you see?"

Courtney felt her heart drop. She did see. But it wasn't fair. *She* was ready to make a detour. In fact, she wanted nothing more than to stay with Huxley for the rest of his year on the island.

Twenty

"Shh," Tony whispered, climbing out of his sleeping bag and shoving his sneakers on his bare feet.

KC crouched low and looked at the quiet tents on either side of the campfire. The lemon-yellow light of dawn was reaching across the beach, and she could hear the occasional squawk of an awakening bird.

Mookie stirred in his bag, and KC placed a hand on his shoulder. "Mookie," she said softly, putting a finger to her lips. "It's time."

Mookie nodded intently, and together the three of them crept out toward the storage tent. Inside, KC was shuddering with excitement. Since they'd sighted the rust-colored sea grass from the cliffs yesterday, she'd been on pins and needles. She, Tony, and Mookie were determined to check out the possible shipwreck site, despite Patrick's urgent reminders to stay out of the water. Before they went to sleep after dinner, they'd made a plan to rise at dawn and investigate the site with their diving lights.

"Go!" Tony whispered hoarsely as they ran across the sand. "The tanks are all ready."

KC hurried. She'd barely slept that night, thinking about the strangely stained sea grass. Was it really the sign they'd been searching for? Could they really be that close to a centuries-old treasure they could claim for themselves? She pulled back the flap to the storage tent and tiptoed in behind Tony, her heart full of longing. She felt as if she were on the verge of something impossibly huge. A life turning point.

"Treasure," KC whispered out loud, running her hand over the piles of diving equipment spread out on the tent floor. To her, treasure wasn't something she could look at or hold in her hand, like a coin. It was something more. It was a feeling she wanted to have. A life without the constant worry of not having enough. It meant staying in school, having a life, a future. To her, treasure was nothing less than freedom itself.

"Your stuff is right over there," Tony said, hurriedly pulling on his wet suit, then his BC vest.

KC groped in the tent's dim light. "Yeah. Okay." She found her wet suit where she'd left it draped over the toolbox, drying with her mask and fins.

"I filled the tanks last night," Tony whispered, double-checking his air tank's gauge. "Good thing we were able to salvage the spare oxygen tank off the boat. So they're ready to go."

KC glanced over at Tony and Mookie, who'd quickly suited up and were already heading out of the tent. "Wait," she whispered. "I don't have my tank on yet."

"Hurry," Tony breathed, his face furrowed and intent in the darkness. "If Patrick finds us, we have to call the whole search off. And the rescue party could get here before we have another chance."

"Okay, okay," KC gasped, zipping up her wet suit to the neck, buckling her weight belt, then groping for her air tank.

"We'll keep watch out here," Mookie whispered as the two ducked outside.

KC nodded, feeling for the tank Tony had put out for her. Her heart was pounding. Had Tony and Mookie forgotten? She wasn't an experienced diver like they were. "My tank," she cried softly to herself. Then she clenched her teeth, trying to think. If she was going to be a full partner in the treasure dive, she was going to have to act like one. She turned, remembering the spare tanks filled and ready to go by the tent entrance. Quickly she grabbed one and attached it to her BC vest and regulator. Then she checked her equipment, grabbed her mask, fins, and diving light, and headed out onto the beach.

"Come on," Tony whispered as he began to run, crouched down low over the powdery sand. "I want to approach this site by water. We'll use up more air this way, but if we run down the beach, the others could see us. We'll swim just beneath the surface and check every few minutes for the landmark on the cliff."

KC and Mookie nodded, grasping their masks. Yesterday they'd noted a large, flat-topped boulder on the cliff just above the point where they'd spotted the orange sea grass. Now all they had to do was find the boulder, then descend and begin swimming away from shore.

At the water's edge, they quickly slipped on their fins and turned on their air-tank valves. The water was warm and lapping around KC's legs. The sun rose higher in the sky, sending streaks of orange light toward them. As soon as they were chest deep in the water, they quietly slipped beneath the surface.

KC took quiet, even breaths as the water closed over her head. She was determined to keep up with the other two, and conserve precious oxygen. Holding a lightweight diving light in one hand, she kicked forward strongly, feeling her body soar over the white sand bottom. When they reached the reef, they swam quickly through it, as they had before. But this time they weren't so lighthearted. Their eyes searched anxiously for sharks. KC's stomach was churning. The coral formations were as beautiful as ever, but KC wasn't looking at them. Her eyes kept searching through the blue-green water for a sharp outline, a bow, a mast, a cannon.

Tony continued to quietly surface, then descend again as he searched for the landmark boulder in the cliff. After ten minutes, he swam to the surface for a final time, then dropped back again, giving her and

Mookie the thumbs-up sign. Once Tony had sighted the boulder, the three of them quickly shifted direction and headed straight out from the beach.

KC kicked her long legs hard, shining her light steadily ahead, plugging her nose and breathing to gently pop her ears as they descended. Her eyes struggled to take in everything, desperate for a sign. But after swimming away from shore for only a few minutes, KC saw something that made her stomach tighten. Up ahead she could see ribbons of light playing in a huge meadow of green and rust-red sea grass. She looked over eagerly at Mookie, who gave her an "okay" sign. Then she steadied her light and continued to swim toward it. A few seconds later she saw something that made her stop dead in the water. She knew she wouldn't have to swim any farther.

It was the ancient shipwreck!

KC's eyes began to tear beneath her mask. She could barely hold her light steady. Dead ahead of them, half buried in the sand and grass, KC could clearly see the outline of an ancient ship's bow.

It's all coming true. True. True. True. The words whirled through KC's mind.

Up ahead she could see Tony and Mookie wildly gesturing, holding their diving lights victoriously in the air and embracing. She kicked forward toward the eerily beautiful site. Light played on the ghostly, bluish outline of the collapsed ship, heeled over on its side—a huge gash in the middle of its hull. Though its wood was rotten and its deck had collapsed in the middle, much of it was still intact. She stared at the tiny, square portholes, the maidenhead figure on the bow, and the broken stump of a mast that had cracked in a storm centuries before.

KC shook her head, realizing that the ship had crashed into the same reef that had destroyed the *Bluebeard*, though the *Bluebeard* had come to a rest on the other side. She wondered if any sailors had survived. If some had managed to swim to shore, had they lived on the island? Had they perished there?

Mookie was waving them over to where the sea grass had turned a deep rusty color. Just as Frankie had explained, the rust appeared to be coming from the huge iron cannon that lay corroding off the ship's starboard deck. KC stared in amazement, swimming down the line of the hull toward the massive stern. It was amazing that the ship could have remained intact for centuries. She couldn't wait to slip inside and see what its cargo had been. If it were gold down in the ship's hold, her life was about to change forever.

But as KC began to turn away, something caught the corner of her eye. She twisted around in the water, then looked down and blinked. Sloping down from the reef was a bank of white sand. And lying on its side, KC saw the familiar stainless-steel wheel that had once been attached to the helm of the *Bluebeard*.

KC swam toward it, noticing other stray items from their boat strewn in the sand. Though they were some distance from the wreck of the *Bluebeard*, the violent storm had swept some of its contents for some distance, especially things that had been on deck. There were broken pieces of fiberglass from the hull, a section of shiny railing. But it was a large, flat item half-buried in the sand that caught her attention. She could see its square corners and clouded plastic wrap. There was tape wrapped around it, but it was badly unraveled and waving in the water's current.

Patrick's paintings! KC realized with shock.

Eagerly she swam forward, remembering how desperate Patrick had been to save them. Six months of work. His art and his future. Were they salvageable? She grabbed the edge of the package, hoping to drag it ashore. Surely Patrick would forgive them for diving if she rescued his valuable artwork. But as she pulled the paintings up, the sheeting broke away and the two frames separated slightly.

KC stared in horror. From what she could see, the canvases were completely blank. She tried to think. A white canvas? Two or three days underwater could wash away the last traces of a pastel or a watercolor. But Patrick had said the paintings were oils.

With her fingers, KC pried at the package a little, trying to see if smaller paintings were perhaps stored between the two frames. She shone her diving light into the small space. In the faint, bluish light, she could see that it wasn't empty. She squinted. It almost looked as if something was stored inside.

KC felt a hand on her shoulder and whirled around. It was Tony, swimming limply and grabbing his neck with one hand. But when she started to give him a playful nudge, she realized that he wasn't kidding around.

Tony was out of air!

Quickly KC pulled him over and glanced at his air-tank gauge. According to the needle, Tony still had three-quarters of a tank left. She yanked her mouthpiece out and let Tony breathe. But as she did, she saw something else over his shoulder. Mookie, who had begun swimming toward them, had suddenly stopped kicking and was tapping frantically on his regulator.

KC looked at Mookie in horror, taking the mouthpiece from Tony and taking another breath for herself. She gave Tony the mouthpiece again, grabbed his arm, and began dragging him through the water toward Mookie.

By the time KC reached him, Mookie was beginning to kick and flail in panic. Gripping Tony's arm with one hand, she grabbed Mookie's with the other. Then she handed him the air. Surrounded by a swirl of released bubbles, Mookie finally breathed and nodded. Then KC motioned for them to surface, and the three slowly kicked up, sharing the air as they went.

KC glanced nervously at Tony as they slowly rose. Unlike Mookie, who had recovered quickly, Tony's eyes were still drooping and he looked only half conscious. It was clear his oxygen had run out long before Mookie's. KC clasped his arm tighter, wondering how much longer her own air would last. Then she remembered. Tony and Mookie had taken the air tanks they had clearly set out for themselves in the storage tent. But she had taken a spare. Had their tanks been tampered with the night before?

KC felt sick. Her lungs were bursting, and Tony was almost completely limp at her side. She and

Mookie had to get him to the surface, but they still had another fifteen feet, then a swim to the shore.

Come on, Tony. KC's mind was racing. *You can make it. Hold on.*

She looked up at the approaching surface, which was now shimmering with sunlight. Dizzy from lack of oxygen, she was starting to have difficulty seeing how far away they were. Her muscles felt heavy and limp. Then in the distance she heard something—a whining sound that grew into a roar. Looking up again, KC could see something approaching on the surface. It was the gray outline of a powerboat, and it was racing right over their heads.

Twenty-one

Winnie clasped Jack's hand as they climbed the steep path up from the jungle. Together, they had risen with the sun and slipped off alone, hoping to spend the entire day looking for Courtney. The cool, low-lying brush waved through their legs, and small, warbling birds flushed into the air as they passed.

"You okay?" Jack looked back at her, pushing his hair off his face with his free hand. His dark eyes had softened, and Winnie could almost feel the current running between their interlocked fingers.

Winnie nodded as he picked a red bloom from a bush and placed it behind her ear. Then he cupped her face in his hands, bent over, and kissed her gently.

"I think we should walk along these east-facing cliffs, then see if we can keep moving along the coastline," he suggested, turning back up the path. "If Courtney had run up here to wave down the helicopter, she would have stayed near the water."

"Yeah, you're probably right," Winnie said, lightly jogging to keep up. She was worried about Courtney, but there was also something deep inside of her that knew Courtney was okay. Something had happened, that was for sure. But then Winnie herself had been shipwrecked and missing for three days now. Back home her mother and her friends were probably thinking the worst. But she was okay. In fact, she was better than she'd been in a very long time.

"Come on," Jack urged her, slipping his dark glasses on as they rose out of the jungle vegetation. "This looks like a path."

Winnie's mind leafed back through the night before on the beach. They'd talked in a rush for what seemed like hours. First Jack, then Winnie, then Jack again until their separate stories seemed to converge into one. They were both running from lives that had spiraled out of control. But somehow, Winnie thought, just being able to explain it to Jack gave her the energy to go on.

Winnie smiled to herself and hurried ahead, grabbing his hand from behind. "I've changed my mind. I don't want to be rescued. I want to stay here for the rest of my life with you. We can build a little grass shack right up there." Winnie pointed to a level area above them, surrounded by a grove of coconut palms. "We'll watch the sun come up over the Caribbean every day, just like we did this morning."

Jack pulled her close and grabbed her other arm, pressing her chest against his. His dark eyes flashed down on her and the morning breeze whipped his hair. "Winnie. We're going back. We're both going back to face our lives, deal with the people we've hurt or have hurt us, and then we're going to go on."

Winnie felt her head shaking from side to side. Tears sprang to her eyes. "I want to be with you, Jack. I'm not ready to say good-bye."

"We *will* be together, Winnie," Jack replied with a force in his voice that made her knees buckle. "Whatever it takes, we'll be together. I'm not going to let you go."

Winnie slipped her arm into Jack's as they continued up the hill toward the cliffs they hoped would lead them to Courtney. The sun blazed down on their heads, and the rocks were sharp beneath their feet. After a half hour, they could see the broad, blue Caribbean spread out to their left.

"Look," Winnie pointed out. "We're not that far from the beach. There's a kind of path that leads down to it right here."

Jack nodded, following her gaze down a sandy path that meandered down through a gently sloping section of the cliff. "She might have walked around to the other side of the island along the beach. Let's . . ."

"What?" Winnie whispered. Jack was looking up toward the water, his face suddenly dead serious.

"Look," Jack said quietly, his lips tensed into a narrow line. "A boat."

"What?" Winnie exclaimed, her eyes wildly scanning the water below. A second later she spotted an unusually long and narrow speedboat cruising over the reef near their camp. *"Hey!"* she started to yell, waving her hand over her head. *"Up here."*

Winnie stiffened when she felt Jack grab her wrist and pull her arm down. "No, Winnie!" he shouted.

"What?" she shouted back, making a fist. "First you tell me you're ready to go back and face your problems, and now you're hesitating."

Jack held on to her wrist. "Listen to me, Winnie. That boat down there, it's not a rescue boat. . . . Look, I've been in the Caribbean long enough to know about the drug trade. That's a special kind of boat, usually used by drug runners."

Winnie stared at him. "How can you tell?"

Jack ducked down on the trail and motioned for her to crouch. Then he pointed to the boat, which had made a complete turn and was heading back toward the camp. From this location, Winnie could barely make out two people in it. "See how narrow and lightweight it is?" Jack said. "It's specially designed to move quickly through reef waters, faster than police boats. And it's made out of extremely lightweight plastic. Undetectable by radar. They cost a fortune. No one needs a boat like that unless they're running drugs."

Winnie was confused. "But what are they doing here, Jack? I mean, it's just us. We don't have any drugs."

"I don't know, Win," Jack murmured, tightening the fist that rested on his knee. "But whatever they're here for, they're probably ruthless and armed."

Huxley pushed a heavy branch out of his way. He bowed slightly, holding the branch for Courtney. "After you, miss. One mango tree. Our breakfast is nearly ready."

Courtney stepped through, laughing. After their early-morning bat visit, they'd decided to have breakfast out by the cliffs. Up ahead she could see the huge mango tree Huxley had told her about. Heavy with the fat, oval fruit, she could see that many of them were red-ripe and ready for picking.

"One for you," Courtney said softly, reaching out and twisting the waxy fruit off a branch. "And one for me."

Huxley held out a basket made from latticed palm leaves. "I don't know what I ever did without you."

Courtney's smile suddenly grew serious. She lifted her eyes up from his smooth, tanned chest to his blue eyes. "I could say the same about you, Huxley."

He lowered their fruit basket to the ground. Then he reached for her hand and took it gently in his own. "Courtney, I don't know what to say, except that in six months . . ."

"You'll write?" Courtney murmured, her eyes closed. She felt like crying, but she didn't want to spoil their beautiful morning together on the island. She never wanted to forget it. The soft morning breeze, the sun on her face, the flowers, the red-throated birds that sprang up from the brush as they walked.

"Yes, I will write," Huxley said, lifting her chin up.

"And if I can't get out to the States to see you . . ."

Courtney smiled. "I could definitely come to London to see you, if that's where you'll be."

"I'll be there, Courtney," Huxley murmured back, his eyes fixed on hers. "I'll be there." Picking up their basket of fruit, Huxley pulled her toward a clearing behind the tree. "Come see my lookout. We can have our breakfast with a wonderful ocean view."

Courtney followed him down a grassy path until they reached a rocky ledge overlooking the water. "It's beautiful," she exclaimed, stepping out and looking for a place to sit. "I didn't realize we were that close to the water. Can we climb down to the beach from here?"

Huxley pointed. "There's a path right there that leads to it. In fact, I keep a small skiff hidden down there for fishing. Bit steep, though."

Courtney stared as Huxley suddenly ducked. Instinctively she stepped back into the brush. "What is it?"

"Look," Huxley said with disgust, pointing to a long, narrow powerboat that was pulling up to the beach. "Now you'll see what I mean. Look at those fellows. Drug runners."

"What?" Courtney gasped. "But this has to be near our camp on the beach."

"Well, then, Courtney, this might interest you," Huxley said, peering over the rocky ledge. "Our druggie friends seem to have a mate waiting for them on the beach. Take a look."

Courtney's eyes were wide. She crawled forward over the ledge until she could see the white beach below. Then her mouth dropped open in disbelief.

Walking out slowly from the beach, his white shirt blazing in the sun and his hand extended in greeting, was Patrick.

As the boat pulled closer, Courtney slowly raised her hand to her mouth. Operating the drug runner's craft was a slender woman in a wet suit and a burly, middle-aged man wearing a straw hat and a loud, red-print shirt.

Courtney gasped. "That—that man."

Huxley narrowed his eyes. "You recognize him?"

"Yes," Courtney said with a cry of alarm. "That's Thomas Curio. He owns a yacht-charter service in St. Ramos. And—and the guy who's meeting them on the beach is Patrick. I hired him to skipper the *Bluebeard*. Thomas Curio recommended him for our trip to Gregory Cays."

"God." Huxley sank his forehead into his hand.

Courtney's head was spinning. Her eyes were glued to the turquoise water below as Patrick waded out to grab the boat's bowline. "Are you sure that's a drug-running boat, Huxley?" Courtney pleaded. "Patrick almost looks like he's meeting them."

"It's a rendezvous," Huxley said sharply, his voice rising. "These people. Lowlifes! I'm going down there, Courtney. I've had enough."

"Huxley!" Courtney cried. "It could be dangerous. And you're not armed."

"I don't have time to get my gun," Huxley shouted over his shoulder, scrambling down the path ahead of her.

"Wait!" Courtney sprang up and followed him.

"I'll go with you. This has to be some kind of a misunderstanding! Patrick's not a drug runner! It's just not possible."

"Yoo-hoo!" Liza called out, sticking her head out of the tent. *"Patrick!"*

She stepped outside and examined her sunburned shoulders. Then she stretched her arms above her head and gazed at the morning sunlight filtering down through the coconut palms. The air was soft and fragrant, and suddenly she was glad Patrick had ordered her back to the tent last night. It felt good to be so rested. Patrick had been right. She'd needed a good night's sleep. And today, the rescue boats would be there, thanks to him.

"Everybody *UP!*" Liza yelled with glee, clapping her hands together and glancing at the cold campfire. She stepped toward the beach, looking for both Patrick and the others. "Hey, where is everyone? Let's get a fire going. Breakfast! Frosted flakes! Pop Tarts! Weird fruit!"

The beach was empty.

Liza planted her hands on her hips and stared, frustrated, at the gently rolling waves. Then she had the sudden, frightening thought that everyone had been rescued and that she somehow had been left behind.

"PATRICK!" Liza suddenly burst out in terror, running down the beach and looking up and down for a sign. She drew her hand up to her chest in relief when she spotted Patrick about a hundred yards away. Then she squinted and felt her heart leap up to her throat with excitement. A boat! Patrick was walking out to greet a rescue boat!

"YAAAYY!" Liza cried, leaping and whooping down the soft sand of the beach. They'd been found! Soon they'd be back in a civilized place. She'd have a bath. She'd ditch her grubby rags. She'd do her nails and buy all new clothes. Maybe she could even get Courtney's parents to pay for it all. They were safe at last. Just the way she'd dreamed it.

"PATRICK!" she shrieked, watching as he helped the rescue party's boat up onto the beach. There was a woman wearing a wet suit, and a heavy-set man in a hat. "Patrick!" She ran toward him. "We're saved. Isn't it wonderful?"

Liza suddenly stopped jumping up and down. Patrick was slowly looking over his shoulder at her. And he wasn't smiling.

"Hi," she said, lowering her voice a little and slowing down. She glanced at the man and woman in the boat, then back at Patrick's glare. His eyes were hard and his lips were tight.

"Go back to the tent, Liza," he barked.

"What?"

"Go back to the *tent*," he shouted.

Liza was confused. "It's okay, hon. I'm happy to help." She started to slip her hand around his neck, then she felt him swing around abruptly and punch her in the jaw.

Liza felt a blast of pain in her face and staggered back, collapsing in the sand. She didn't understand. Slowly she opened her eyes. Farther down the beach, she saw two other fuzzy figures racing toward them. Gradually they came into focus.

"What the hell do you think you're doing, Patrick?" Jack was yelling, hurtling himself down the beach. He crashed into Patrick, then saw the small radio hooked onto Patrick's belt.

"Liza!" Winnie yelled, running toward her at top speed. "Are you okay?"

Liza ignored Winnie, watching in horror as Jack lunged for Patrick, trying to wrench the radio out of his belt. "He's got a radio, Winnie," Jack shouted. "See if you can get it."

Patrick fought back, but Jack managed to punch him in the stomach with his powerful fist. Winnie followed, jumping onto his back and pounding him as hard as she could.

"Winnie?" Liza murmured, rubbing her jaw.

"Give us that radio, you jerk," Winnie was yelling as if her life depended on it, grabbing for Patrick's wrist in the shallow waters while Jack held both of Patrick's arms sharply behind his back.

"It's okay," Liza called out. "Patrick didn't mean it."

"We trusted you, Patrick," Winnie shouted over the crash of the waves. "How could you risk our lives like that?"

Liza tried to hold her head up. "He was upset about the paintings," she cried out. "He couldn't face his life."

"Shut up, Liza," Winnie screamed. "Can't you see? He's running drugs with these creeps."

"No he's *not*," Liza insisted, standing up and wading out into the water toward Patrick, who was still struggling with Winnie and Jack.

Finally the radio slipped out of Patrick's hand. At first Liza thought it had fallen into the water, but then she saw that Jack had caught it. In a flash, he'd slipped it into his back pocket.

"Hold it right there," Liza heard a deep voice from the boat. She looked up and stared at the strangely familiar, middle-aged man. Crouching on the stern of the boat, his pudgy legs were braced and his burly arms held an automatic weapon, which was pointed directly at her.

Liza gasped.

She glanced at the blond woman in the wet suit, who also brandished a weapon at Winnie and Jack. "Make one move and you're dead," she snarled at Jack.

Liza's eyes fell back on the older man. "Hey," she said slowly. "You're the guy from the yacht-charter place."

"Shut up, Liza," Patrick said with a casual laugh, wading through the water and hopping on the boat. With a graceful sweep of his hand, he scooped his arm around the young woman and kissed her on the lips. "I've missed you, Nina." Then he turned and gave Liza a look of complete indifference.

Liza drew her hand up to her mouth in horror. "You lied. You lied about *everything.*" She staggered in the water, splashing and forgetting where she was. Patrick didn't care about her at all. He'd used her like he'd used everyone else. He was a lousy fake, and she'd fallen for it harder than anyone.

"Take the boat back about a hundred yards, so we're just to the south of the reef and over that patch of red sea grass," Patrick ordered Nina. "The shipment's somewhere between here and that reef to the north."

"Shrink-wrapped in those works of art for our protection," Nina said with a wry smile, her glossy blond hair spilling over her shoulder. She turned the key to the boat's powerful engine.

"You two dive for the stuff," Thomas barked, "then we'll get the hell out of here as fast as we can." He pointed his weapon at Winnie and Jack, then at Liza. "You three make any kind of a move and I'll blow your heads off."

"You son of a bitch," Jack exploded, rushing for the boat. "You point that weapon at these women one more time and I'll . . ." Liza watched in horror as Jack lunged for the boat, followed by Winnie. She turned to wade hurriedly for shore, but was so confused and upset that she was clumsy. Stepping on a sharp bit of coral, she jumped and then lost her balance in the shallow water.

"Aggghhh!" She struggled to stand up again, managing only to get closer to the boat, which Winnie and Jack were trying to tip over. Suddenly she felt a hairy arm around her neck, and her eyes widened in terror. Thomas Curio had hopped out of the boat into the shallow water. Now he had her in a tight grip, with his gun pointed directly at her head.

"Now," Curio panted, heaving her into the boat with one powerful arm. He looked at Winnie and Jack, who stood frozen. "You two make another move and we're blowing her head off."

"Oh God," Liza whimpered, lying on the bottom of the sleek vessel, shivering with fear. She watched as Curio clambered back on board, his thick, hairy legs dripping with seawater.

"Here's your wet suit, honey," Nina said to Patrick casually, as if she were perfectly accustomed to seeing women held hostage. She glanced coldly down at Liza. "Why don't we keep her? Then we can take her around to that spot on the reef the sharks like so much. She seems like a real pain in the ass."

Liza's heart was pounding in her ears. Her eyes strained up toward Patrick, who was zipping up his wet suit, his eyes like two green stones. "That's why I wanted to leave her on the beach, Nina."

Liza felt her heart split in two.

"No," Curio snapped back, jamming a cigarette into his mouth, then drawing out a gold lighter from his shirt pocket. "Let's keep her for now. We might need her later." He jabbed the gun into her head harder. "Just in case some of her friends need a little *convincing* to stay out of our damn business here."

Twenty-two

"**C**ome on, Tony," KC shouted, throwing her mouthpiece aside as soon as she and Mookie finally broke through the water's surface, still dragging Tony. "Come on, Tony. Breathe."

"His lips are blue," Mookie cried. Quickly he flipped Tony on his back, then pressed a valve on Tony's BC vest, inflating it. Together, he and KC pulled him to shore. "What happened to our air tanks?"

KC slapped the side of Tony's face a little as she kicked powerfully ahead with her fins. "Tony. Come on. Take some deep breaths. We're okay now." Tony's chest heaved, and KC could see that he was beginning to take in air. She strained to look over at Mookie while the water splashed and lapped around her neck. "He's going to be okay."

Mookie's lips were trembling. "What happened back there, man? I've never run out of air like that before. It scared the hell out of me."

KC nodded as her fin touched ground about twenty yards off the beach. Her head bobbed up and down with the waves. To the right, about two hundred yards away, she could see their camp. "I don't know for sure, Mookie. But I think someone tampered with the tanks."

Mookie helped Tony struggle to his feet and wrapped one lanky arm around his partner's waist, while KC held him up on the other side. "Why the heck would anyone want to do that?"

"I don't know," KC panted, suddenly desperate to breathe in the clean, fresh air. She'd never felt so relieved to see blue sky and feel the ground beneath her feet. "But something strange is going on. The air tanks, Patrick, the canvases."

"What canvases?" Mookie said between breaths, pulling Tony up onto the sand and laying him down.

KC crawled up next to them both, then pulled the mask off Tony's pale face while Mookie began taking off his fins and BC vest. Tony's eyes were closed and he was breathing, but he still looked pale and sick. "He needs to get to a hospital, Mookie. I think he went without air for too long."

Mookie was nodding, shading his eyes and pointing down the beach in the opposite direction of their camp. "Look. That must be the boat we saw above us when we were diving."

KC whirled around in the sand just in time to see a low-slung, narrow boat knife through the water close to shore. From a distance, she could barely make out three figures in it. But it definitely didn't look like a rescue boat. There were no identification numbers or symbols, no lights. In fact, KC thought it looked like the kind of boat that was meant to avoid people, not seek them out.

Something pulled at KC's mind. It was farfetched, she knew. But she was confused and angry enough about the air tanks to want to check it out. When she had looked between the canvases underwater, she was sure they hadn't been paintings. It had looked more like a package containing something. And now she knew she had to find out what it was.

"I'll be right back," KC said firmly, standing up and tightening the cinch on her vest. She checked her air-tank gauge and pulled her mask over her eyes.

"What?" Mookie burst out, his narrow face wide with alarm. "You're going back? Are you crazy?"

KC stood up and threw a glance down the beach. "I've got fifteen minutes of air left. You stay with Tony. I'll be back in a flash."

"KC," Mookie called after her. "Be careful out there."

"You bet I will," KC said to herself as she sank back into the water and swam swiftly out along the side of the reef until she knew she'd found the right spot. Then she descended into the shadowy depths, determined to find the paintings and discover what they held.

KC sank slowly and carefully through the eerie waters. Electric-blue fish darted anxiously about her hands. Huge, scarlet sea anemones beckoned with their waving tentacles. And below her, a jungle of red corals covered the ocean bottom. She kicked steadily ahead, her eyes fixed to the southern slope of the reef, hearing only the whispery sound of her own breathing.

Then, up ahead, she finally spotted the white drift of sand. She slowed, trying to control her breathing and save precious air. She spotted the partly opened package containing the canvases, then swam ahead, grabbing a corner. She thought about the day she had first met Patrick back in Thomas Curio's shop. He'd seemed so sincere about his painting. He'd seemed so terribly sensitive and honest. And she had very nearly fallen in love with him.

Carefully KC ran her fingers down the edge of the slippery package until she held the tattered section where the plastic wrap was unraveled and waving aimlessly in the water. Then, with trembling hands, she gently pried it open several inches and pointed her diving light inside. Her heart pounding in her ears, she peered between the canvases. She felt inside, groping for signs of the oil paintings, perhaps hidden deeper inside. But a moment later a clump of plastic packets began rising slowly up from the inside of the package.

KC's eyes widened. Stunned, she reached for one of the packets and felt it between her fingers. It was filled with white powder. She stared at it numbly. Patrick hadn't been carrying his precious art on the *Bluebeard* to Gregory Cays. He'd been carrying *drugs*.

Instinctively swimming backward, KC felt her eyes grow hot. Patrick had completely deceived her and everyone else. They'd put their lives in his hands, and he was nothing more than a drug smuggler, a ruthless liar with a handsome face and a first-rate talent for acting. She shook her head, watching the white bags floating up to the surface.

But when she turned around to swim back to shore, she realized that she wasn't alone in the water. Over her left shoulder she could see two swiftly moving divers in black wet suits, one carrying a knife and the other carrying a drawstring bag. KC kicked frantically away, her pulse throbbing in her throat. They had to be the people from the boat, and they had to be after the drugs.

KC felt sick when she felt a hand grab her arm. She whirled around and stared, horrified at the eyes behind the mask. It was Patrick, brandishing a six-inch-long knife. Behind him, another diver was rapidly collecting the packets of drugs and stuffing them in her drawstring bag. KC's heart stopped. Patrick's green eyes were looking at her, but they were the cold and lifeless eyes of a killer now. She could almost see the heartless smile in them as he brought the knife to her air hose and cold-bloodedly sliced it through.

There was a burst of spraying bubbles and a sudden deadly clutch in her throat. KC knew that her life was hanging by a thread, but she still grappled with him as he dragged her toward the jagged reef. She grasped for her weight belt, managing to unhook it. Then she grabbed Patrick's mouthpiece, hoping to get another breath before he let go. But before she could turn toward him, she felt his steely arms pushing her away.

There was a dull thud as her head hit a sharp edge on the reef. She saw clouds of bubbles, then felt her head spinning away from her, as if it were disconnected. Her body floated up, her limbs like lead. She couldn't move, she couldn't breathe, she couldn't think. And then she saw only blackness.

Winnie backed slowly up the beach, her body shaking and water streaming down her legs. Her eyes were fixed numbly on the knifelike powerboat in the distance. She could still see Liza's flame-red hair, and the glint from the gun that Thomas Curio held to her head.

"Bastard!" Jack spit out, dragging his fingers through his hair and staring. "That smooth-talking, lowlife *bastard*."

"I can't believe it," Winnie whispered, trembling. "Patrick had a radio? He was running *drugs*? We actually trusted that guy?"

Jack narrowed his eyes. "There was something about him that I never liked."

"Were you suspicious?"

Jack shook his head, clenching his jaw and watching the boat blazing across the blue water. "Not really. It was more that he didn't seem much like a sailor to me. He just wasn't on top of it," Jack said tersely, digging his heels into the sand. "And he always seemed glad to let me take the helm."

Winnie bit her lip. A single tear slipped down her cheek as she threw herself down on the sand. "Now we're really stuck. They're probably going to kill Liza. Then they'll come back and kill us, too."

Slowly Jack crouched down, and Winnie could see his St. Christopher medal swinging from his neck. "Don't be too sure," he said, drawing something out of his pocket. "He let me get away with his radio." Jack held it up for her to see. Then he pulled out the antenna and thoughtfully raised it.

Winnie's mouth fell open in shock. *"The radio,"* she gasped, bending over with sheer relief. "I thought it dropped into the water."

"Yeah, so did Patrick," Jack whispered, staring at it as if it held the secret to life.

Winnie's eyes widened. She sat up and put her hands on his shoulders, looking into his eyes. Behind her, she could hear the slow rise and fall of the waves. For a minute, everything was quiet, as if nothing had happened. Overhead, a sea gull screamed. "You're going to use that radio, aren't you?" she asked.

Jack sighed. "A part of me wants to throw it in the sea, Winnie."

Winnie lunged for the radio, but Jack held it up in the air just in time. "Please don't do this again, Jack," she cried. "I want to go home."

Jack put the radio down and grabbed Winnie around the shoulders, kissing her. "Look. We're going to get home. It's just a matter of whether the Coast Guard rescues us, or someone else, Winnie. If I call the Coast Guard, Patrick and his friends could be gone by the time they arrive. Then the only one who gets found is *me*."

Standing on her knees in the warm sand, Winnie let her shoulders drop. It was his decision, not hers. He was the one who'd saved the radio, and now he should be the one to decide whether they should use it. She let her eyes drift over his high forehead, dark eyebrows, and the clean line of his jaw. Then she lifted her hand up and stroked him gently on the cheek. She took a deep breath, closed her eyes, and lay back in the sand, exhausted.

Only a few seconds passed before she heard the click of the radio being turned on. She made a fist and let a small smile of victory spread across her face as she heard Jack's words.

"MAYDAY. MAYDAY. MAYDAY. THIS IS THE CREW OF THE *BLUEBEARD*. THIS IS THE CREW OF THE *BLUEBEARD*. THE BOAT HIT A REEF ABOUT THIRTY MILES SOUTHEAST OF SUCIA ISLAND THREE DAYS AGO. IN EMERGENCY SITUATION NOW. I REPEAT. EMERGENCY SITUATION. THREE ARMED AND DANGEROUS INDIVIDUALS ARE HOLDING ONE CREW MEMBER HOSTAGE. POSSIBLE ILLEGAL DRUG TRAFFICKING INVOLVED. OVER AND OUT."

"Huxley," Courtney was shouting over the wind, "if these people are running drugs, they're probably armed."

Huxley nodded, steering his small wooden skiff out of a hidden cove located at the bottom of the cliff path. "I just want to get a look at them, Courtney,"

Huxley yelled back as he straightened the outboard motor. "I want to see how they operate and report them to the authorities."

"But we could be killed," Courtney cried, grabbing on to the side of the boat as Huxley jammed the throttle and sped out into the open water. They were just slightly to the north of the camp, but they could see the reef ahead, and the drug runners' boat beyond it.

"If I don't do this, who will?" Huxley said with grim determination, his eyes fixed on the narrow boat idling in the water.

Courtney clenched her teeth, trying not to panic. She wasn't ready to get involved with a bunch of drug-running thugs. But then, they were near their camp on the beach, and she'd been away from the group for a day and a half. Were KC, Winnie, and the rest of her friends in danger? She had to find out.

"I'm going to slow down as we approach," Huxley said, bracing his legs as they bounced against a series of swells. "We're just a couple of kids on vacation, Courtney, okay? Just wanted to say hello. We don't know anything about drug boats. Nice and easy."

"Okay," Courtney said over her shoulder. "Then at least we can get a look at their faces."

Huxley's mouth tensed, and Courtney could see the muscles in his arms tightening. As they approached the highest part of the reef that jutted toward the beach, Huxley slowed and made his way carefully through the toothy coral.

"Stick your head over the bow and let me know if I'm about to slice this boat open on the reef," Huxley asked her. Courtney had been trying to keep an eye on the narrow boat ahead of them, but now she climbed up to the bow and leaned over the water.

"So far, so good," Courtney said. "No—look out. Veer to your right. Yeah. Okay, sharp right." Courtney's eyes scanned the clear water, brilliant with coral and sea life. But then something caught her eye in the reef about ten feet ahead of the bow.

"Wait, Huxley," Courtney breathed, staring at a tiny line of bubbles rising steadily to the surface. She squinted ahead. It was hard to see in the glare of the shimmering water. But there was something black and yellow moving slowly up against the reef.

Huxley moved ahead carefully, the motor putt-putting quietly through the coral. Courtney looked again. The yellow vest. The waving dark hair. She gasped out loud. "KC! Oh, my God. Stop. *It's KC!*"

"What?" Huxley asked.

Courtney's whole body was shaking with terror. The boat drew near. She could see KC's limp body struggling feebly in the shallow water, her dark hair swirling around her inflated yellow BC vest. "KC!" Courtney screamed, throwing herself over the edge of the boat and pulling KC's head above water.

"Get her in!" Huxley shouted, leaning over and taking one of KC's lifeless arms.

They lifted her body into the boat, then looked in horror at the sliced air hose that flopped around KC's neck.

"Quick," Courtney ordered, her eyes running over KC's bluish face. She pulled off her mask and pushed away the useless mouthpiece. "Help me get her on her back, Huxley."

A moment later Courtney had propped KC's neck and chin up and was placing her lips on her friend's, blowing air into her lungs as steadily and as expertly as she could. "Check her pulse," she cried. "Is she alive?"

Huxley loosened KC's vest and put his head against her chest. He kept his ear to her heart for a moment, then rose. "She's alive."

"Come on, KC," Courtney urged her between breaths, her voice quavering with fear. "Come on."

KC's legs began to stir languidly at the bottom of the boat. Then Courtney heard her cough. Water began to spill out of the corner of her mouth, and her hands stiffened and trembled. Courtney felt a surge of relief. "KC! KC, you're okay. You're going to be okay."

Twenty-three

*L*iza felt sick. She was crouched at the bottom of the narrow boat's stern, her head dropped onto her knees. Her muscles ached, and her hair felt like a mop of salty ropes. But she didn't care anymore. She just wanted her ordeal to be over, no matter how it turned out.

She clamped her eyelids shut, trying not to think about how stupid she'd been. Winnie and Jack had managed to get away from these thugs, but she'd been too stuck on wanting to believe Patrick. And now, because of that, she was probably going to end up like one of Thomas Curio's beer cans—crushed and forgotten off the shore of an island no one ever heard of.

Just then she felt a rocking motion. An elbow

hooked over the edge of the boat and Liza cringed inwardly as Patrick's dripping head emerged. A moment later Nina popped up on the other side of the boat, holding her drawstring bag of white packets victoriously in the air.

"Fine, fine," Thomas gloated, taking the bag from Nina. "Run into any trouble?"

Patrick climbed the small ladder that hooked over the boat's edge and pulled himself in. "Ran into an old friend down there, actually," he said coolly, sitting down on one of the boat's cushioned seats while Nina slipped in next to him. Together, they pulled off their masks and fins and began stowing their air tanks and regulators.

"One of the kids from the yacht," Nina said with an offhanded nod, shaking out her silky blond hair. "Snooping around our valuable package."

Liza's eyes darted up. "Who?" she said in a tiny voice. "Who are you talking about?"

Patrick looked down briefly at her. "KC," he said with an icy shrug. "Miss Spring Break Scuba-Diving Champion. A determined but ultimately stupid girl. She found the package with the canvases containing our little shipment here."

Liza was confused. "She found your paintings?"

Nina burst out laughing, then reached for a tube of suntan lotion in a compartment next to her seat. Patrick chuckled too, shaking his head and giving Liza a hopeless look. "Uh, right, the paintings, Liza. I hate to break it to you. I mean, I know we're both soul mates in *art*." Patrick paused, trying to control his laughter. "But they were just blank canvases. Our shipment was hidden inside."

"You don't . . . You aren't . . ." Liza whimpered, finally burying her face in her hands and sobbing.

Thomas leaned toward Patrick and narrowed his eyes. "I hope you didn't let KC get away."

Nina threw her head back and laughed. "Are you kidding? Patrick and I have been around long enough not to leave any witnesses."

Liza gasped, covering her face with her hands. KC? What had they done with KC?

"Yeah," Patrick said lightly, standing up and looking out toward the reef. He drew out his diving knife and plucked it lightly with the pad of his thumb. "The beautiful KC Angeletti ran into a little trouble with her air hose down there."

"Good," Thomas said, relieved. He turned on the ignition. "Time to cruise on out of here. Too many people. It's making me nervous."

Liza was shaking with horror and fear. She couldn't believe it. Patrick had actually murdered KC in the water? It was too horrible to think of.

"No, wait," Patrick called out. "There's something I want to check out."

"Yeah," Nina said eagerly, turning around to face Thomas. She stretched out a tanned arm and casually rubbed in her lotion. "These college kids were onto some kind of sunken galleon site just off the reef here. It hasn't been investigated before. Patrick's pretty sure we could run into some gold. Come on, Thomas."

"We don't have time," Curio protested.

"Take this boat out about three hundred yards," Patrick said sharply. "Do it, Thomas. Just point the damn boat and *move*. We're gonna look for a patch of rust-colored sea grass. I want that treasure."

Liza wanted to curl up under a seat and die. Patrick was a monster and so were his friends. Everything was a horrible nightmare. She hadn't fallen in love with a gorgeous artist. She had fallen in love with a brutal killer. What kind of person was she? She felt tears running warm and fast down her face, sensing that everything would soon be over for her. They'd killed KC, and soon they'd kill her, too. Lifting her face, Liza leaned back against the boat's stern and let the warm Caribbean air flood over her. She stared at Patrick's rugged face against the blue sky, suddenly wanting to know the truth. He was going to kill her anyway, so why shouldn't he tell her what she so badly wanted to know?

"Patrick," she shouted over the roaring engine. She watched his cold green eyes move slowly toward her as the boat bumped out toward the reef.

"What?"

Liza drew in her breath and crossed her arms over her chest. "Why did you do it? Why did you lead me on?"

A slow, disgusted smile spread over Patrick's face. Nina let out an amused laugh as she shook out her hair and looped an arm around his neck. "This was a business trip, Liza," Patrick told her. "Got it? You got too close on the boat, so I had to distract you by pretending there was something between us. You made a lot of noise when those helicopters showed up on this damn island." Patrick winked at Nina. "All I had to do was make a move for your body and you shut right up, didn't you?"

Liza felt hot new tears building up behind her eyes. "But—but what about KC? Weren't you interested in *her*?"

Patrick looked over at the reef. "Well, as you can see, Liza, I wasn't really interested in a long-term thing with anyone."

Liza shuddered.

"But KC was beautiful and interesting and fun to flirt with," Patrick said offhandedly, ignoring Nina's irritated look. "Who wouldn't flirt with a babe like her?"

"Shut up, Patrick," Nina snapped.

Patrick grabbed Nina's arm and shook her. "Look. What do you want from me?" he snarled. Then he looked down at Liza with steely eyes. "Like I said. This was a business arrangement involving a lot of money, and I did everything I could not to screw it up, okay? Now, Thomas set this deal up, and so far, everything's working out just fine."

"If you cared about your lousy drugs so much, why did you let them go overboard during the storm?" Liza burst out, sobbing. "Why didn't you just let me die back then?"

"Because the damn wrapping was coming loose!" Patrick shouted back at her. "If you'd managed to pull them back on board, you would have seen that they were just blank canvases. You'd ask a lot of questions that I didn't want to answer. Besides, I knew the packets were watertight. I could always dive for them later."

Liza dug her nails into her sticky hair, sobbing. "I should have known," she cried. "You were always running away from me. And at night . . ."

Patrick laughed. "At night," he cried with glee, nudging Nina in the ribs. "Man, it was tough getting away from you then. But I had to have some time to myself, Liza, didn't I?" he said with a sarcastic smile. "I had to radio my progress to Thomas and Nina. I had to take a look at that handy little treasure map KC, Mookie, and Tony provided. And one night, it was rather important for me to put our treasure hunters' air tanks out of commission so they didn't find the treasure before I did—or stumble upon my very important little shipment stowed between the canvases. Of course, KC must not have used her regular tank. If she had, she'd be up there on the beach catching her breath with those two clowns from California, instead of lying down there with a sliced-up air hose."

Liza looked at him in disgust. "You're an animal!"

"Is he ever." Nina snuggled up to him, giving Liza a sly look.

"Okay," Patrick called over his shoulder to Thomas. "Now veer to the right a little. Do you see that sea grass up there? The rust-colored stuff?"

"Got it," Thomas growled back.

Patrick zipped the top of his wet suit over his chest, then slipped on his fins and air tank again, while Nina did the same.

"Wait," Liza sobbed. "You've got to tell me. The

shipwreck, the reef. Did you actually plan it all?"

Patrick stood up and scanned the clear water for the sea grass. Then he laughed out loud. "Right, Liza. Hey, I can control the weather." He gave her a mocking look. "No way. I was planning to meet Thomas and Nina on another island. But the storm came up and the boat got away from me."

"I thought you were an experienced sailor," Liza accused. Patrick, Nina, and Thomas all laughed as the boat slowed. Thomas cut the engine, then picked up his gun again and turned around to point it at Liza.

"I may be a pretty good actor, Liza," Patrick said, lightly kissing Nina's lips as they headed for the ladder, "but I'm a lousy sailor. Especially in bad weather."

"Look!" Winnie screamed, running out to the beach and waving her tattered T-shirt frantically in the air. "The Coast Guard's here!"

She dropped down on her knees, almost crying with relief. Help had arrived at last. But what good was it now? Liza was being dragged out to sea with a gun pointed at her head, Courtney was lost, Tony was deathly ill. And worst of all, her best friend, KC, hadn't returned from her dive.

After radioing for help, they had found Mookie and Tony on the beach, panicked because KC had been gone for the last half hour, even though her tank had had only fifteen minutes of air left. Mookie had run back to the storage tent for a spare tank, then returned to the water to look for KC. But he still hadn't returned.

"Hey!" Winnie screamed at the top of her lungs, as a large white cruising boat with a high deck roared through the water toward them. Winnie took in the fluttering U.S. flag and the crew standing along the railing. In the sky, she could see the outline of a blue and white seaplane coming in for a landing to the north of the reef. "Over here. We're over here." She covered her face with her hands, sobbing. "What's left of us."

Jack ran out from the tent compound and the two of them greeted a dinghy buzzing toward them from the anchored Coast Guard vessel. A uniformed man and woman jumped out into the shallow water.

Winnie ran up to them, hysterical with worry. "My friend, KC . . . she's lost . . . Mookie hasn't come back. We need some divers . . . please . . ."

She felt the woman's hand on her shoulder and looked up into her sympathetic face. Winnie shook her head, unable to speak.

Jack stepped forward. "I'm afraid we're in a lot of trouble here. Down the beach about a quarter of a mile there are three people in a lightweight boat picking up a drug shipment and holding a young woman from our party hostage. They're armed and dangerous."

"Do you know their names?" the woman asked quickly, glancing down the beach.

"Yeah," Winnie finally said. "Patrick Hanson and Thomas Curio from St. Ramos. And another woman. Young. With blond hair."

The Coast Guard officers exchanged meaningful glances.

"The woman they're holding is Liza Ruff," Winnie continued. "Look, we also have a sick friend up in the tent. He needs to get to a hospital fast. And we're going to need a search-and-rescue for the island. Another woman from our party, Courtney Conner, is missing."

Winnie watched desperately as the two officers nodded at each other. The man pulled out a small radio and began barking orders to the boat and the plane. Meanwhile, the woman jumped back into the skiff and raced back to the Coast Guard vessel. A few minutes later, a whirling red light began to blaze on its deck as it zoomed out to the reef where Thomas and Patrick's boat was anchored.

"Okay." The officer pushed his hat back a little. "Let's get your friend in the tent. The plane can get him over to the Gregory Cays Hospital in about twenty minutes."

Winnie and Jack turned to go up the beach with the officer.

"How long you kids been out here?" he asked, glancing at the ragged group of tents. He drew a notebook out of his uniform.

"Three and a half days," Jack replied, stuffing his hands in his pockets. "Our boat ran into that reef out there in a storm. The *Bluebeard*, out of St. Ramos."

"Uh-huh," the officer replied, turning to wave at the seaplane that had landed in front of the beach and was now cutting its engine. "Bad storm. Now I'll need your names, and the names of the others."

There was a moment of silence as the officer stared

at Jack, then at Winnie, waiting for their reply. Winnie slowly took Jack's hand. He lifted his face to hers. His eyes darkened for a moment. Then he squeezed her hand and looked up at the officer.

"My name is Jack Frederick Cruz," Jack said calmly. "And this is my friend, Winnie Gottlieb."

Winnie watched as the officer started to write their names. She saw the pencil pause on the paper, then his lips part slightly, as if he were remembering something important. He looked up at Jack, then pushed his hat back on his head and let out a long sigh. "You've been keeping us busy, Mr. Cruz."

Winnie bit her lip and squeezed Jack's hand as two men in the plane hopped out with a stretcher for Tony. The officer stared at Jack for a moment longer, then pulled his radio out of his belt. Switching on the power, he spoke into it.

"This is Captain March. This is Captain March speaking. Radio in this message to headquarters ASAP. We have found the missing son of Charles Frederick Cruz. I repeat. We have found the missing son of Charles Frederick Cruz. Over and out."

Liza bit the inside of her lip, watching Thomas grab another beer out of the cooler. For the last twenty minutes, they'd been waiting for Patrick and Nina to return from their search for the Spanish galleon. The sun blazed down on their heads, sending a steady trickle of perspiration down Thomas's cheeks.

Liza tapped her broken fingernails nervously on her knees, staring absently at the miserable straw hat on his scraggly head. She wondered if his arm was stiff from pointing the gun at her for over an hour. She tried calculating how many beers he'd consumed. Finally she decided to try talking to him. Sure, Thomas was an armed bully who would think nothing of putting a bullet into her head. But after all, he was a man, wasn't he?

"Hey," Liza said, crossing her bare legs casually.

"What do you want?" Thomas snapped, wiping his dripping forehead and staring irritably at the glaring surface of the water.

"A beer," Liza heard herself say.

Slowly Thomas turned his paunchy face in her direction. "A *beer*?"

"Yeah. I'm thirsty," Liza said lightly, bending over and pretending to adjust her shoelace. She knew full well the angle showed her skimpy bathing-suit top to its best advantage. Slowly she lifted her eyes and met his stare. "Well? Are you a gentleman or what?"

Thomas dug into the cooler. He started to hand the bottle to her. Instead, Liza gathered her courage and stood up. "That's okay," she breathed, moving toward him. "I'll get it. You don't mind, do you?"

Thomas tiredly pointed the gun at her, then relaxed when she sat down on the cushioned seat behind his. "I guess you're not going anywhere," he mumbled as Liza took the beer delicately from his hand and twisted off the top.

"No," Liza said wistfully, taking a polite sip. "Not until Patrick and his girlfriend come back, anyway. What's taking them so long?"

Thomas gave a disgusted shrug.

Liza leaned toward him a little. "Those two. I don't like the way they talk to you, Thomas. I mean, it sounds like this is sort of your operation. But they're treating you like dirt."

"Tell me about it," Thomas said, turning to look at her over his left shoulder, his gun hanging limply from his hand. "I'd beat the crap out of them both. But we're in this thing too deep together."

Liza took another swig from the beer bottle. As she did, she could see the white outline of a Coast Guard boat zooming around the reef. So far, Thomas was turned slightly her way, so he couldn't see it. All she needed to do now was distract him from looking around. Maybe she could even reach for his gun.

"Thomas, look at me," Liza said suddenly.

His eyes widened, and from the droop of his head, Liza could tell that he'd had one too many. "What?"

"You may be in a racket that I don't exactly agree with," Liza said forcefully. "And you may not have the best of intentions as far as I'm concerned." Liza leaned toward him a little, revealing more cleavage. "But you're a human being, Thomas," she pointed out, desperate to hold his attention. "And you deserve more respect."

"Yeah, yeah, yeah," Thomas grumbled, looking away for a split second, just time enough for Liza to snatch the gun from his hand and throw it into the water.

"I feel a lot better now!" Liza shouted, scrambling away from him as he lunged for her. "Well, well, well, look who's coming," she yelled victoriously. "Don't try anything, Curio, or they'll haul you in for assault and attempted murder as well as drug trafficking."

"Why, you little bitch," Thomas sneered, grabbing for her.

"HOLD IT RIGHT THERE," Liza heard an official-sounding voice booming over a megaphone. For a moment, Thomas froze. Liza watched as the huge white Coast Guard cruiser drew near. "THIS IS THE COAST GUARD. I REPEAT. THIS IS THE COAST GUARD. YOU ARE UNDER ARREST, THOMAS CURIO."

Liza's heart began to slow, and she felt her shoulders begin to collapse with relief. But just then the boat rocked and she saw Patrick's and Nina's heads popping over the side of the boat. Patrick looked around quickly, then slipped his hand swiftly into a compartment near the ladder.

Liza gasped as Thomas grabbed her arms from behind, and watched in horror as Patrick and Nina both toppled into the boat, then grabbed their hidden weapons, pointing them at her head.

"THIS IS THE COAST GUARD. PUT YOUR WEAPONS DOWN. YOU ARE ALL UNDER ARREST. I REPEAT. YOU ARE ALL UNDER ARREST."

Liza was sobbing in pain. Thomas had her arms pulled back so tightly, she thought they were going to pop out of their sockets. "Please, no. Please."

"Let us go," she heard Patrick shout viciously up to the Coast Guard boat. "Let us go, or we'll blow her head off."

Twenty-four

KC was doubled over in Huxley's boat, grasping Courtney's shoulder with one hand and Mookie's with the other. Her lungs felt like lead, her stomach was churning, and she couldn't shake the terror from her heart.

Minutes ago, she'd been under thirty feet of water, looking into Patrick's eyes as he slit her air hose and left her for dead. It was impossible. Patrick Hanson. The gentle artist with the slender hands who had taught her to sail and dive and feel sure of herself again. It had all been a lie. He was a drug runner and a cold-blooded killer. The shock had run through her body like a freight train. She pinched herself, just to be sure she was really alive. But all she could feel was the numbness of her skin.

"I—I really should be dead," KC said shakily, gripping Courtney's hand. "It was a one-in-a-million chance that you came by when you did."

"But we *did* come, thanks to Huxley," Courtney said with relief. "And you *are* okay."

KC nodded, patting Mookie's shoulder and looking at Courtney's strangely peaceful face. She stared past her at the strange guy with the blond beard and the string of shells who was sitting quietly by the outboard. "Thanks," she said seriously to Huxley. Then she turned to Mookie. "Thanks for coming after me, Mook. Even if these guys did get to me first."

"I would have been too late," Mookie pointed out, rubbing his face and looking out over the reef. Suddenly he straightened up. "Hey, it's a Coast Guard boat!"

KC turned and watched as a small white cruiser with a high bridge and a fluttering U.S. flag churned toward them at high speed, its bow lifted into the air. After carefully skirting the dangerous coral, it zoomed toward them. KC grasped the edge of Huxley's tiny boat as its wake rocked them. The white bow loomed slowly in front of them, and on the deck she could see a line of scuba divers, suited up and ready to go.

A man in a white uniform leaned over the railing and stared at the four of them. "We got a call about a diver in trouble," he shouted down. "KC Angeletti?"

"She's okay," Courtney yelled back, hugging KC. "We found her just in time."

The Coast Guard officer scratched his head, and

motioned for the scuba divers to stop their preparations.

"She was attacked by a guy named Patrick Hanson," Mookie called. "It looks like he's hooked up with some drug runners out of St. Ramos."

The man nodded. "We're onto it. In fact, we've got another boat headed over there right now, looking for them. They're holding someone from your party. A Liza Ruff. Pretty dangerous stuff, I'm afraid."

KC steeled herself. Patrick had enough ice water running through his veins to kill Liza, too. She lifted her head and looked into the officer's eyes. "I know exactly where they are. Take me on board. I'll show you where."

Courtney clutched her hand. "KC, you're not well. We need to get you back to camp."

"No," KC burst out, fueled by her anger and outrage. "Mookie can come with me. It's not far. Just up the beach a little. Please. Let me go."

"Fine with us, miss," the officer said, lowering a small ladder over the side of the boat. "Come on, you two."

"Be careful, KC," Courtney called. "We've made it this far, and we're going home together. We're going home, and don't you forget it."

KC and Mookie climbed on board and took their seats just as the boat lurched ahead, speeding down the coastline. KC stared across the smooth blue water to the white line of the beach and the softly nodding palm trees. As they moved along the coast, she scanned the cliffs for the flat boulder she, Mookie, and Tony had used to mark the rust-colored sea grass. If Patrick was out there, she knew he had to be after the treasure. It was obvious by now he'd discovered their secret.

As the boat roared through the water, KC stood up on her knees and looked ahead. "It's not far away. It's around this bend here in the beach," she shouted over the engine. "It's . . . oh, my God."

KC's heart stopped. As they rounded the curve, she could see a narrow powerboat rocking gently in the water about fifty yards off the beach. Even from this distance, KC could see Liza standing on the bow of the boat, holding a life preserver. Patrick was holding a gun to her head while an older man and a blond woman stood behind him, aiming at the officers on a huge Coast Guard vessel.

"They're letting Patrick and his goons get away!" KC shouted.

"With a threat like that, the captain's got to," the Coast Guard officer replied tersely. "They're not going to risk the girl's life. These drug-running types aren't afraid to use their guns on innocent people. It happens every day."

The officer grabbed his radio and clicked it on. "I don't think Hanson and Curio have seen us. They're too intent on making the hostage exchange. Now I want you to get down."

KC, Mookie, and the Coast Guard divers dropped to the bottom of the boat. Then they watched the officer make a quick call on the radio.

"Hold on to your hats, everyone," the officer said

grimly, pulling a heavy gun from a compartment near his wheel. "We're going to storm the boat."

KC felt a lurch as the officer pulled back on the throttle, sending the boat into warp speed. Smashed up against the stern with Mookie, she looked at the officer ducked down behind the wheel as he roared forward, his gun aimed at Patrick and the two others. The next moment, she heard a loud blast from his gun, and another in the distance. KC brought her hands up to her ears, clamping them down tightly as the wind blew her hair and the salt water sprayed into her face. She could hear dozens of shots banging and whistling over their heads. The boat heeled over as it hurtled through the war zone. She waited for one of the bullets to pierce the thin fiberglass side, wondering if they'd ever leave the island alive.

"All right!" the officer called out. "The girl's okay. She's in the water and a little upset. But okay."

"Thank God," KC whispered to herself, grasping the seat in front of her and lifting her head up into the wind. "What about the others?"

"Thomas Curio, Patrick Hanson, and Nina Waller-stein," he shouted over his shoulder. "We've been trying to catch these guys in the act for two years."

KC and Mookie stood up as the boat roared toward the scene of the shoot-out. Several armed officers were jumping onto the drug-running boat, quickly handcuffing Thomas. Meanwhile, KC could see Patrick collapsed inside of the boat, gripping his bloody arm. Nina lay wounded on the boat's wide stern, attended by a team of medics from the Coast Guard boat.

"Sonavabitch!" Mookie screamed at Patrick as their boat swept around Thomas's boat.

Tears sprang to KC's eyes as she grabbed Mookie's shoulder. But her eyes were glued to Patrick as they drew near. She stared at his white, drained face, and as he looked up briefly, she bravely lifted her chin and narrowed her eyes as if she were staring into the face of death itself.

"Okay, we're going to pick up the girl," the officer called back. "Let's give her a hand. Ladder."

"HELP! HELP!" KC could hear Liza's scream in the distance over the squabbling sea gulls. "They're gonna kill me. Get me out of here. I can't swim. Can't you see that? I can't swim."

KC crawled toward the ladder as the boat neared Liza, who was clinging to a doughnut-shaped life preserver, flailing one bare arm in the air. "KC!" Liza wailed over the whine of the idling engine. "Patrick. Patrick was gonna kill me. He's a killer. Oh, my God, he's a killer."

With tears in her eyes, KC reached down over the side of the rocking boat and clasped Liza's outstretched hand. Water poured off Liza's shaking body and her red hair was plastered to her cheeks as she hauled herself up. With the help of the two others, they finally pulled Liza into the boat.

"They were going to kill me," Liza sobbed, falling into KC's arms. "Patrick and—and his *girlfriend*. I thought he cared about me, KC. I thought he cared."

KC put her arm gently around Liza's trembling shoulders while one of the officers draped them with a thick blanket. "I know, Liza," KC whispered softly as the boat roared back to the camp. "I know."

"Twenty minutes in a hot shower."

"Thirty."

"A double bacon cheeseburger, extra pickles, hold the onions."

"Twinkies."

"A lounge chair next to a large, empty swimming pool."

"A manicure."

"A steak, man. A big steak with A-1 sauce all over it."

"What about you, Huxley?" Courtney nudged him, poking a stick into the campfire. "What's the first thing you're going to want when you get off this island?"

Huxley shrugged and let his blue eyes twinkle back at her. "I haven't thought about it much. Everything's here, really. Everything you could want in life."

"Agghhh," Liza gasped, falling backward.

Winnie threw a chunk of coconut across the fire at him. "Give me a break, Huxley. Come on, let's torture him until he tells the truth."

"You're warped, Winnie." Jack laughed. "Huxley here is the sanest guy I've met in my life. He's telling the absolute truth."

Courtney stretched out on her side in the sand next to the fire. Too much had happened that day for everyone to really absorb. For now, at least, everyone seemed to feel more like forgetting the nightmares than remembering them. There would be plenty of time for that. She watched as Liza and Mookie broke into a corny song, then scrambled into one of the tents, looking for a limbo stick. This would be their last night on the island. Tomorrow at noon, the Coast Guard would be back to take them to Gregory Cays. The morning would be spent packing.

Putting her hand on Huxley's shoulder, Courtney pointed her head in the direction of the moonlit beach. Together, they walked out to where the warm, lapping waves could run over their toes. Behind them the campfire was a tiny orange flicker. In front of them was a full, yellow moon and a sky full of stars. She wanted to kiss Huxley right then. But something made her hold back.

"Hi," Courtney said shyly, clasping her hands behind her back.

"Hello there," Huxley said, stroking his beard and giving her a mischievous smile.

"Think my friends are crazy?"

"Oh, yes. Terribly crazy. Demented. Must be awful for you," he teased.

Courtney took a deep breath and felt the warm breeze swing her hair across her shoulders. "Come with us to Gregory Cays."

"What?"

"Just for a day or two," Courtney asked, trying to steady her voice. "Until we fly out?"

"I see," Huxley murmured.

Courtney sneaked a look at his face in the moonlight. His hair was swept back off his tanned forehead, and his blue eyes were narrowed in concentration. "You've been here for so long, Huxley," Courtney said quietly.

"Wouldn't it be good for you to break away and get your bearings?"

"It might," Huxley said. Courtney bit her lip hopefully, watching his eyebrows lift, then fall. He shook his head, slowly at first, then with conviction. "No. No, Courtney. As much as I'd like to, it wouldn't be good."

Courtney dropped her head and stared down at the luminous white sea foam swirling around her feet. She felt Huxley turn toward her. His hand slipped down her cheek, then he lifted her chin toward him. "I've made a promise to myself," Huxley said, his eyes looking intently into hers. "People break promises so quickly, so easily, for so many little reasons."

"It's not little to me," Courtney replied, looking bravely into his eyes.

"I didn't mean that," Huxley burst out, slipping an arm around her waist and pulling her close. "You're important to me, Courtney. You're probably the best thing that's happened to me since I came here."

Courtney fell against his chest and put her arms around Huxley's neck. "But you're sticking with the orchids, the solitude, your thoughts."

"Yes, Courtney," Huxley said gently.

"But you'll visit me when your time is up here," Courtney asked, her throat tight with sadness.

"I promise," Huxley whispered, taking his shell necklace and slipping it over her head. "You can keep this for me until we meet again. And we will, Courtney. Believe me, I'm a man who keeps his promises."

Twenty-five

"To the blue of the Caribbean sea," KC called, lifting her glass in a toast. "May it stay that way forever."

"And wait for our return," Courtney added, clinking glasses with KC.

"I'm going hiking or something, next vacation." Liza leaned forward conspiratorially, adjusting the blazing yellow scarf wound through her hair. "No water. No swimming or seasickness pills required."

Winnie, Jack, Mookie, KC, and Courtney all laughed in the candlelight, their glasses hovered over the extravagant restaurant dinner. KC breathed the smell of distant frangipani and roses in the Gregory Cays Hotel garden. Their table was on a huge outdoor balcony on the second floor, lit with tiny sparkling lights and filled with flowers on every table. Below, she could see the terraced gardens that led down to a wide lawn, then the sandy beach and shimmering bay.

KC looked around the table with satisfaction. She wanted to remember every detail, every smell and every sound, every face and every word. It was strange how a brush with death could change a person. But KC knew she'd never be the same. From now on, she was going to relish every bit of her life.

"Here's to Tony," Mookie said with a shy grin, lifting his glass. His blond hair was combed back neatly for once, and he wore a faded tropical-print shirt tucked into his jeans. "Sounds like they're going to let him out of the hospital tomorrow."

"Hip-hip," Liza called out.

"Hooray!" everyone shouted over their raised glasses, attracting the attention of the restaurant's elegantly dressed customers.

"And here's to our reward, too," Mookie finished, grinning at KC.

KC smiled back. On their way to Gregory Cays yesterday, the Coast Guard had informed her that there had been a five-thousand-dollar reward posted for information leading to the arrest of the ringleaders of a major U.S./South American cocaine connection. Patrick, Thomas, and Nina had apparently been an important Caribbean link—Thomas using his yacht-charter business to arrange shipments through his handpicked network of skippers like Patrick, who usually worked charter boats and private yachts. According to the Coast Guard, the *Bluebeard* was an ideal situation because Courtney had needed a skipper quickly, and didn't have time to fully check his references.

"The reward is Tony's too, Mookie," KC reminded him. "You and I may have led the Coast Guard to Patrick, but Tony's our partner. Right?"

"Gee," Liza mused, scribbling on a cocktail napkin. "One thousand six hundred and sixty-six dollars apiece. That'll buy you some fun."

"It will pay for next year's tuition at the U of S," KC said, happily digging into her salad. "And a few extras. And it will get Mookie and Tony home."

"You deserve it," Courtney said quietly, taking a sip from a crystal glass. "How's your arm, by the way, Mookie?"

"He showed me the actual shark-tooth marks," Liza giggled. "But that beast never really did sink his teeth into you, did he, Mook? What's the problem? Not juicy enough?"

Mookie flexed his skinny arm and tried to look fierce. "Guess not. The hospital checked it. But it's just a surface wound."

Winnie slipped her hand around Jack's waist and snuggled closer to him. "I can't believe your story about the sunken treasure, KC. How did you keep it a secret?"

KC shrugged. "Who knows if there's treasure? Patrick told the Coast Guard he looked at the shipwreck, but said it had been carrying spices."

Jack leaned back and laughed, tickling Winnie's ear. "The guy's a pathological liar. For all we know, he saw a thousand gold bricks. He'd never tell us, that's for sure."

"Hey, Tony and I are coming back in the summer," Mookie said. "We talked about it in the hospital. We'll save part of the reward money, work part of the summer break, then come back here with our earnings. And if KC still wants in, she can join us."

KC felt a thrill. "Reward money, a candlelit dinner, a treasure in my future? I'm feeling very rich. Very rich indeed."

"I'm glad everything worked out for you," Courtney said with a quiet, peaceful smile. "For all of us. I mean, it didn't quite work out the way we'd planned. But I guess nothing ever does, exactly."

"But for once you're not picking up the dinner tab," KC interrupted, laughing as she bit into a perfect slice of passion-fruit mousse. "Because for once in my life, Courtney Conner, I am."

"Do you believe in destiny?" Winnie murmured, her head resting on Jack's shoulder as they walked slowly through the hotel gardens toward the water.

Jack put his arm around Winnie's waist. His white shirt felt clean and stiff against her bare skin. His brown hair was brushed back, and his tiny gold earring glinted in the dim light. "What do you mean, Winnie? Are you asking if our meeting here was somehow planned?"

"Yeah," Winnie said softly. "I'm asking."

"It *is* strange," Jack agreed. He reached over and ran his knuckle thoughtfully up and down her bare neck. "We literally ran into each other at the right moment."

"In a dark alley." Winnie giggled for a moment as they headed down the stone steps that led to the beach. It was past midnight now, but the moon was shining brightly.

"It changed everything for me, Winnie," Jack said abruptly, stopping at the bottom of the stairs. He turned to look at her, then reached his hands around her waist, lifting her onto the stone bulkhead at the top of the beach. He crossed his arms on her legs and gazed up at her. "It's hard to explain. But the problem with running away is that you always run away alone. And you sort of—"

"Go into your own world," Winnie finished, nodding and biting her lip.

"And the loneliness gets worse," Jack said. "And it turns into me against them."

Winnie looked past Jack's shoulder into the sparkling sea. "Yeah. Me against them. And you think you'll always be alone, or different."

Jack bent Winnie's head up and kissed her tenderly on the mouth. "You're not alone anymore."

"I know."

Jack hugged Winnie's legs, then lifted her back down to the sand and took her hand. "I love you, Winnie."

Winnie squeezed his hand and shivered. Together, they walked down to the water.

"I called my dad today," Jack said.

Winnie whirled around. "You did?"

Jack shrugged and ran his fingers through his hair. "He wasn't as mad as I thought he would be. He was just sort of relieved that I was okay and everything. Even checked in with the registrar at Harvard. I guess they're going to give me incompletes, so I can make the courses up this summer."

Winnie stared at the water swirling around her toes. "Calculus."

"Yeah, you can thank calculus for all this," Jack laughed. "If I'd taken some other four-credit class, I wouldn't have met you." He pulled her around and looked into her eyes. "And you, Winnie. Are you going to be okay?"

Winnie shrugged, kicking the water out and splashing her skirt. "Yeah. I think I am. I guess I never realized how much I'd been running away. I mean, not just running away to the Caribbean, or running away from Josh. It was more like not being very honest with myself."

"I know."

"When Josh and I were married I always thought everything was so great because we talked and argued all the time," Winnie tried to explain. "But I didn't know how to listen to him, Jack. If he said something I didn't want to hear, I just shut him out."

Winnie turned and buried her face in Jack's soft shirt, feeling the tears run down her face.

"I guess we're both going to have to start all over again," Jack said, stroking her hair and holding her close. "And someday soon, Winnie, you're going to see me again. I may have to go back and face my life right now, but I'm never going to forget you."

"Caribbean Airways Flight 342 departing Gregory Cays for Miami will be boarding in ten minutes at Gate 12."

Courtney, KC, Liza, and Winnie hurried through the crowded airport. Gift shops stuffed with colored shells, orchids under plastic, and postcards rushed by in a blur. Gaily dressed senior citizens stood in large tour groups, having their pictures taken. "This is the first time I've actually been happy about losing a suitcase full of clothes," Liza called over her shoulder, striding ahead in sneakers and a practical shorts and T-shirt outfit. When they'd unloaded the *Bluebeard* before it sunk, they'd pulled out food and survival gear. The rest of the cargo, including their clothes, was now lying at the bottom of the reef. Courtney had bought everyone one set of clothes in Gregory Cays, and insurance was expected to cover the rest. "Why do we burden ourselves with all the material stuff of life? I feel so free and light now."

"That kind of attitude is going to last for another four minutes," KC whispered into Winnie's ear.

"Three." Winnie giggled back. "Wait until she gets the insurance settlement from Courtney's parents. She'll have a whole new set of spiked heels and plunging necklines."

Courtney linked elbows with Liza. "You're a sport, you know that?"

"Yeah," Liza cracked, "even when I'm about to get my head blown off. Even when I'm sliding into the sea at night during the worst hurricane of the century. God, I can't believe it all happened."

"I don't think it's really sunk in yet," Courtney said wistfully. "It's strange, but this week should have been the worst of my life."

Winnie slowed and smiled back at Courtney. "I know. But when I think about it, it was really the best week. I'm sorry I was such a witch, Courtney. It was really hard for me at first. But if I hadn't come . . ."

Courtney gave her an understanding look. "You wouldn't have met Jack. And you wouldn't be smiling right now, Win."

"No." Winnie drew in her breath. "No, I wouldn't."

"Hey, KC." Liza grabbed her by the arm as they turned toward their gate. "How about that Patrick? Mr. Dreamboat, huh? What did we ever see in that guy?"

KC shook her head and smiled at Liza, hugging her around the waist. "We saw what we wanted to see."

"Ha. And that was a lot, wasn't it?" Liza laughed back. "I still can't believe I actually risked my life for that guy. Not even for him—for his nonexistent *paintings*. Then he turned around and stuck a gun to my head."

"We'll be telling our grandchildren about this one," Courtney said, her voice suddenly tight with emotion. Huxley's face kept rising up in front of her. She wanted to remember it all: the little house on the hill, the smell of the orchids, the quiet of her thoughts.

"You bet we will," Liza agreed, spotting the gate

and starting to skip. "And when I do, I'm not going to remember the sharks and the treasure and the shipwreck. The story's going to be all about four friends from college."

"Four completely different friends," KC added.

"Who found they had a lot more in common than they thought," Winnie said, shaking her head in disbelief.

"We're survivors," Courtney confirmed, engulfing her friends in a huge hug.

"And whatever happens back at school," Winnie said intently, "we're not going to forget this. We're going to back each other up, no matter what. Starting right now."

☎

1 (800) I LUV BKS!

If you'd like to hear more about your
favorite young adult novels and writers . . .
OR
If you'd like to tell us what you thought
of this book or other books
you've recently read . . .

CALL US at 1(800) I LUV BKS
[1(800) 458-8257]

You'll hear a new message about books and
other interesting subjects each month.

**The call is free to you, but please get
your parents' permission first.**